SMALL TOWN EMP

Survive the Chaos

Survive the Aftermath

Survive the Conflict

RELAY PUBLISHING EDITION, JULY 2019

Copyright © 2019 Relay Publishing Ltd.

Grace Hamilton is a pen name created by Relay Publishing for co-authored Post-Apocalyptic projects. Relay Publishing works with incredible teams of writers and editors to collaboratively create the very best stories for our readers.

Cover Design by LJ Mayhem Covers
www.relaypub.com

SMALL TOWN EMP BOOK ONE

SURVIVE
THE CHAOS

GRACE HAMILTON

BLURB

When the lights go out, anarchy reigns supreme.

After journalist Austin Merryman's wife died, he and his four-teen-year-old daughter left home to travel the country in an old RV. But the comfort and renewal they sought soon descends into chaos.

After a message from an old college buddy leads Austin to a bridge in the middle of nowhere, he finds his friend—now an NSA agent—waiting to give him a USB drive. Before the contents can be explained, machine gun fire strafes the bridge, killing Austin's friend and forcing Austin into the raging river.

Rescued downstream by a beautiful veterinarian, Austin learns that EMP attacks have thrust the world into eternal darkness—and separated him from the only person he has left. Now, he'll move heaven and earth to locate his daughter and make it to his brother's prepper hideaway in Utah.

But the post-apocalyptic world is no longer a friendly place. Resources are growing scarce. Factions break out along ethnic and religious lines. Everyone is willing to do whatever it takes to survive in an increasingly hostile environment. And Austin's daughter is caught right in the middle of this splintering society.

But an even deadlier foe stalks them as they struggle across the landscape. Someone who hasn't forgotten about the USB drive Austin possesses.

And they'll do anything to get it back.

A ustin Merryman stored the last of the dinner dishes in the small cupboard of his thirty-two-foot fifth wheel. The RV wasn't an ideal living space for a man and his four-teen-year-old daughter, but they'd been managing to make it work. As he and Savannah constantly reminded each other, it was both easy and difficult to keep the small living space clean. It only took a stray pair of shoes or a few dishes on the tiny kitchen counter to make things look untidy, and both of them were guilty of forgetting the fact on a too-regular basis.

Waiting for Savannah to emerge from the little upper bedroom, he folded a blanket, tossed it on the couch, and put the TV remote back in the little caddy mounted on the wall. Austin liked things neat, though he knew Savannah had to clean up after him just as he was cleaning up after her now.

"Savannah!" he called out, checking his watch again.

She popped her head out from around the upstairs corner of the fifth-wheel, a hair dryer still in her hand. "What?"

"I have to get going."

She shrugged as she wrapped the cord around her dryer. "I told you, I don't need a ride. Leave already."

"I'll be back within an hour or so. Where are you going exactly?" he asked. She'd told him she was going to the creamery for ice cream with the girl who lived on a nearby farm; somehow, he couldn't believe it was that simple. He wanted to, but he'd seen the way she'd ogled that boy they'd run into in town —and the way they'd leaned in to each other to talk. He remembered being young and carefree. Yeah, it had been a long time ago, before life and the world had given him a much more jaded view of things, but he remembered. And Savannah was too pretty for him to forget what he'd been like as a teenage boy.

"Dad, I already told you. We're going to get ice cream," she groaned, adjusting her hair in a hand mirror. "Me and Cassie."

Out with it, Austin. "Are you going to see that boy?" he asked.

She glanced over to meet his eyes and then gave him that maddening teenage shrug again. "He might be there," she replied.

Right. He might be there. Austin kept eyeing her, trying to decide whether or not to trust her—not that he had much choice, but still. She looked so much like his late wife that it hurt sometimes. Her long, light brown hair had been brushed to a high shine and left loose around her shoulders. She'd only asked him to buy her lip gloss and mascara thus far. He dreaded the day she wanted to go full face-paint. He preferred the clean, youthful look that befitted her fourteen years over the girls her age who he'd seen with more makeup than a supermodel wore.

And he had to admit, she didn't give him as much stress as he knew many fourteen-year-olds dealt their parents. Even with tonight being a warm early summer night, she wore something he couldn't quite object to. For tonight's ice cream trip, she'd donned the black flowy shirt with the shoulder cut-outs that she'd begged him to buy her on their last mall visit. And it wasn't truly revealing, so he couldn't complain. It just made her look far more mature than he liked, reminding him that he had to accept that she was growing up.

"I want you home by ten," he reminded her. "Not at the farmer's house with your friend down the street, either. Home."

Finally starting to move down toward the door where he stood, she quirked her lips in a frown. "Dad, it doesn't even get dark until like nine-thirty," she argued.

"Ten, or don't go at all. You don't need to be walking around after dark. There are wild animals out here," he lectured her.

"I have my phone," she said, brandishing it as if the expensive gadget were a gun. He wished it were, the way she looked.

"And the service out here sucks," he told her, "as you remind me all the time. Animals aren't going to wait for you to call for help, either."

The look she gave him told him she was mentally slapping her hand to her forehead, even if she was smart enough not to actually do it in front of him. "My phone has a flashlight and Cassie knows this area. We'll be fine, Dad."

"Don't take rides from strangers, and remember what I told you if anyone tries to grab you."

She got to within a foot of him and leaned back on the couch in obedient daughter mode. "I remember: palm to the nose, fingers in the eyes, and knee to the crotch," she recited robotically.

"Upward palm," he corrected her.

She rolled her eyes. "Fine. I got it. Maybe you should just have me carry mace or something," she suggested.

Austin grinned, gesturing her toward the door to get her moving. "That's a good idea. I'll pick up some bear spray tomorrow when we go into town for groceries," he commented, only half joking. He had to hide a grin when she gasped in a breath like they were in a horror movie.

"Dad! *No!* I can't be the only girl carrying bear spray around!"

"Sure, you can. If you want to wander around by yourself, Savannah, you'll do exactly that."

She looked in the mirror on the wall, doing one last primp of her hair as Austin forced himself to remain patient. "You are so overreacting. We're in the middle of the country," she grumbled. "The nearest town has a population of like two hundred people," she finished, exaggerating the low population by a few thousand.

He shrugged back at her, now holding the door open as a heavy hint that he wanted them both out if she was going. "Small towns have bad guys, too. And plenty of teen boys who don't always know when to keep their hands to themselves," he added.

She shook her head in disgust. "I'm old enough to date, Dad, and Malachi isn't like other teen boys."

So, she was planning on seeing him. Damn. He just curbed himself from telling her she had to stay home, knowing he couldn't watch her all the time. But he wouldn't consent to dating. Not yet. He caught her eyes with his before he emphasized, "No, Savannah. Not yet."

"Da-a-a-d." She dragged out the word.

This wasn't a conversation he was going to have again tonight. She was growing up too fast. His wife had made him promise to take care of her, and that's what he would do, even if it meant dragging her around the country and keeping her out of the reach of boys.

"Savannah, be glad I'm letting you go at all. I could insist on driving you to the creamery and meeting the boy who may or may not be there," he warned her.

He heard her mumble something under her breath but didn't bother asking what she'd said as he stepped into the doorway, hoping she'd get the hint that he really had to go. It had probably been one of those snappy comments that would only irritate him further. Austin grabbed his cellphone from the table beside the door and slid it into his back pocket as he stepped outside. It didn't do a lot of good to carry the thing out in the mountains of west Kentucky where he and Savannah were currently staying, but he might as well. Despite it being inconvenient when it came to keeping track of Savannah, he liked the idea of being somewhat off the grid. So what if cell service was spotty? It gave them more time to focus on the moment, the here and now—wherever they happened to be on any given day.

When Karen had died a little over a year ago, he'd used part of the life insurance money to buy the fifth wheel. He'd waited until Savannah had finished the eighth grade and then they'd hit the road. He just couldn't stand being in the house with all the reminders. He'd planned on traveling through the summer, and then it had turned into a year. He still couldn't go back and face her clothes, the pictures of them on their wedding day, and all those little things in the house that were reminders of her.

So, now, he traveled the country with his daughter, doing stories about things national reporters were too busy to worry about. She could homeschool easily enough, and he liked the salt of the earth people and discovering little secrets in small towns and out of the way places; writing about them felt worthwhile. It was a way for him to fulfill his need to travel and make a living while still being a good dad to his daughter.

Finally, Savannah stepped down the two steps of the trailer and looked at him, daring him to say something about the mascara she had piled on. She was pushing it and she knew it.

"You look nice," he said with a smile, completely throwing her off. "Thanks," she mumbled, slipping her own cellphone into the back pocket of her jeans.

"Be careful, please," Austin reminded her. "Be aware of your surroundings, and call me if you need anything," he said, giving her a quick hug.

"I will, Dad. Stop worrying, okay?" she said, squeezing him back. "We're just getting some ice cream. It isn't that big of a deal."

After she checked for her key, he locked the trailer door, though even he admitted it was a little silly considering they were out in the middle of farmland. Still, it was an old habit, and one really never knew when someone could stop by and rifle through their things.

Turning away from the door, Austin watched as his daughter cut across the pasture, dodging horse manure as she headed towards the dirt road that led into town. He shielded his eyes with his hand and saw Cassie standing under a tree by the roadside, gesturing for his daughter to hurry. He waved back when Cassie spotted him and sent him a big wave, happy to know Savannah had made a friend—especially one who lived just a few farms down the road. In another moment, Savannah picked up her pace, almost jogging as she rushed to meet her friend. He watched for another minute as they met and bumped shoulders before starting the mile or so's walk into town.

Austin would have driven them, but Savannah had wanted to walk, and he was going in the opposite direction anyway. He climbed into his black F-350 and started the diesel engine, taking only a quick glance at the GPS before bouncing down the bumpy driveway and heading for the highway. Callum Barker had called him a few days ago, completely out of the blue, and asked to meet. Austin had thought it strange, but Callum insisted it was important and that the story would be worth his time. He'd also promised the meeting would take less than five minutes, which meant Austin would be home in plenty of time to make sure Savannah met her curfew—and to go looking for her if she lingered in town with that boy.

By the time he hit the highway, the meeting had taken over the fore of his thoughts. Austin remembered Callum as being a little off when they'd been in college, one of those conspiracy-type guys, but he'd sounded desperate on the phone. And they'd spent enough nights drinking together that Austin figured he at least owed him the gas it would take to hear him out. He figured he'd meet him, give the guy the proverbial pat on the head, and promise to look into the evidence he presented and be on his way. Maybe it would even be an interesting diversion from his usual stories and offer a brief change of pace. That couldn't hurt, right?

The meeting place was a twenty-minute drive from the farm, set in some corner of nowhere. When Austin had punched it into his GPS, the dot had looked like it was in the middle of a forest, on the bank of a river with nothing else around it.

"Where am I going?" he muttered after driving about ten miles up the highway. The GPS was telling him to take a right turn on a muddy road that was barely wide enough for his truck to squeeze through the trees.

He heard the first branch scrape alongside his truck's side after driving only fifty meters or so, right around the moment his GPS alerted him to a lost signal. He was on his own. In another minute, he grunted with annoyance and brought the truck to a stop. A fallen tree blocked the so-called road ahead —if he wanted to meet Callum, he'd have to go the rest of the way on foot.

"This better be worth it," he grumbled. Before long, he could hear the rushing river and knew he was close. Callum had said there'd be an old covered bridge that was out of commission, so that's what he kept an eye out for. Looking around, though, he could see why it'd be out of use. The old road was near completely overgrown with trees and brush; it didn't appear to have been driven on by anything more than an ATV in a long time.

With it being the end of June, the spring melt had left the river high and loud, lapping at the banks and splashing an angry path as it cut through the area. Deeper in, the road started running parallel to the river, and Austin could barely hear himself think for the noise it made once he came to see the covered bridge ahead. Picking up his pace, he remained careful not to slip and fall on the muddy terrain of the road as he headed up the side of the river toward the bridge. It looked rickety at best, perched about fifteen feet over the rushing water below.

"Hey!" he called out, noticing Callum standing in the shadows of the covered bridge, close to the other side of the river.

The man's bearded face and shaggy hair made him look much older than the forty-something years Austin knew him to be. Austin himself was forty-four, and Callum had been a year behind him in college.

"Hi, thanks for meeting me," Callum said, his eyes darting

around the area as he reached out to shake hands, glancing back to look over his shoulder now and again.

"Sure. What's all this about?" Austin asked, gripping the other man's hand tighter to bring his attention back to the meeting.

Callum nodded and leaned back on the side of the bridge, gesturing for Austin to come right in beside him. Austin stepped in to stand closer, their elbows nearly touching, and waited. He'd come this far, so he might as well play along. The clandestine encounter had his senses heightened, too, even if he figured his old friend was overreacting. It was hard to not let the man's nervousness rub off on him.

"I've been working as a contractor with the NSA," he started, his words nearly lost under the sound of the river below.

So, this might be something after all.

Anytime any government acronym came up, Austin listened. A journalist's instinct made that common sense. There was always some shady cover-up that went unnoticed until a whistleblower came forward. And despite the fact that Austin liked the quieter stories he'd been pursuing, he wouldn't mind a big story being dropped in his lap. It'd been a long time since he'd written a juicy piece about some government agency trying to pull one over on the country.

Callum held up a USB stick stored in a plastic case. "I trust you, Austin. It's been a long time, but we know each other, and that means something, me knowing the type of guy you are. That's why I called. This has everything you need. I need you to get this to the folks in DC."

Austin raised an eyebrow, not touching the drive. Was this a story or not? "Who exactly do you suppose I give that to?"

Callum shook his head, looking a little crazed as his eyes darted back and forth—apparently, he hadn't expected any questions and now just wanted to get going. "You have contacts! I know you do! You wrote a lot of political stuff a long time ago." The USB stick bobbed in Callum's hand, emphasizing each word.

Austin nodded, but still didn't reach out. "That was a long time ago, Callum. I've been freelancing for a while. Maybe you can tell me—"

"You have to get this to the right people," Callum cut him off. "You have to. This has to be made public," Callum said, but in a voice so low that Austin had to lean closer to hear him over the raging water below.

So, it *was* a story, then—he wasn't some errand boy, after all. Curiosity getting the better of him now, Austin reached out to take the stick. It was warm in his hand from being clutched so tightly by his old friend. He stuffed it in the front pocket of his cargo pants and pulled the zipper closed for safekeeping. "I'll do what I can. What's all this about?"

"It's big. You'll see."

"Big?" Austin asked, starting to get a little annoyed about the mysterious tone his friend was keeping up. Why couldn't Callum just spit out what this was about?

But before Austin could press him, the sound of an ATV cut through the trees on the other side of the raging river. Austin looked along the bridge to the road, trying to find the source of the sound. In a flash, the ATV and rider came into view all at once, an AR-15's barrel pointed directly at them to shut off whatever he might have planned to say next. It took his brain another moment to process what he was seeing in the shadows of the woods, and by then the driver had pulled to a stop and was dismounting the vehicle—only some ten yards up the road, where it was blocked by an old chain running across posts to block the bridge. Callum stood still beside Austin, apparently just as frozen.

Austin shoved at Callum's shoulder to get his attention, and then turned to head back the way he'd come. They had to get to his truck and do it fast. "Run!" he shouted.

The sound of gunfire echoed over the covered bridge, old wood splintering as the .223 bullets slammed into the wood around them and sent Austin diving to the ground. Austin looked up, towards the road he had walked in on, then back to the ATV driver moving towards them, his gun still aimed in their direction. The gunman was wearing all black leather with a helmet shielding his face.

If he stood, he'd be shot; he couldn't outrun a bullet. More shots rang out as Callum began to rise up and lunge into a sprint, and Austin saw Callum drop before he made it a full step, blood blooming over his chest, his beard already covered in the red liquid—he'd been shot in the head first. He was dead, no question, and now the driver would be free to focus on Austin. Without thinking for a moment more, Austin rolled sideways under the old bridge's railing, bracing himself for the frigid waters below even as his body hit water and rocks at the same time, shots ringing out from above.

He gasped as his shoulder went numb and his head went under the icy-cold water. His skin felt like he'd been hit with a million pinpricks. The current swept him under the bridge some fifteen feet above his head, and there was nothing to do but let it. A hail of bullets had begun pelting the water a foot from his head when he'd resurfaced, but he was helpless to try and swim away from the gunfire—the current was too strong, and he'd gone numb with cold and pain anyway. A second later, Austin's head slammed into a rock as the water carried him away, bullets following him before fading away into nothing.

2

Savannah waved goodbye to Cassie as she headed down the paved road pitted with potholes, anxious to meet up with Malachi Loveridge. Small shops lined the town's main road facing the post office and a fire department on the other side, and she was reminded that Malachi seemed to be the one exciting thing about this tiny town. Her father would never have agreed to her meeting a boy, let alone him, which was why she hadn't told him the full extent of her plans. Technically, though, she hadn't lied. She had gone to the creamery with Cassie, and she had eaten ice cream. And now she was going to the revivalists' campground to meet Malachi.

Besides, her dad had nothing to worry about. It was church. How dangerous could it be? Her dad should be happy she was going to church instead of going out and doing the things that other kids her age were doing. It wasn't like she was sneaking off to a party, after all.

Halfway there, she was glad she'd forced herself to remain at a walk instead of allowing herself to skip along like a schoolgirl. Malachi was sitting on the single bench outside one of the town's two gas stations, just waiting for her.

"Hey," she said, butterflies circling her stomach as she walked towards him. His lips lifted in a big smile, and Savannah had to bite her lip to keep from grinning like a fool, forcing a casual smile onto her face instead.

"Hi, Savannah," he said, having risen from the bench to greet her.

She felt her heart kick up a beat as she stared into his dark brown eyes, his long black hair falling into his face before he quickly pushed it back. He wasn't a lot taller than her, and was a good six inches shorter than her dad, but nobody was as tall as him. Her dad was six-foot-four inches tall, and his height alone made him intimidating, which had been effective in scaring off almost every boy she had met—so far. Something told her that Malachi might not scare so easily.

"Hey," she said again, feeling like an idiot but not knowing what else to say.

His eyes twinkled like he sensed her nerves and appreciated them, and then he grinned, his perfectly straight white teeth on full display. "Are you ready to go?" he asked.

"I am. Am I dressed okay? I've never been to church in a tent," she commented nervously, hoping her skinny jeans weren't too casual. At least they didn't have holes, she thought as she fell into step beside him.

"You look beautiful, and my dad welcomes people no matter what they are wearing. It's come as you are," he assured her.

"What is a revivalist gathering exactly?" she asked. It had occurred to her earlier to ask her dad, because she was curious, but then she'd realized it would only make him suspicious of her coming out that night. She could have looked it up but hadn't bothered. Why not just ask the super-cute boy who'd asked her to come along?

"We travel the country, spreading God's word. We set up a tent in the middle of nature because it seems more natural, and we feel closer to the Holy Spirit when we're in nature. Plus, it's much more relaxed than a normal church. I think you'll like it. People from all walks of life can come in, sit down, and listen to the music or one of the sermons. Plus, we offer a community potluck dinner in our dining hall, which is really just another tent, for those who want to stay for a while. It's all very laid back," he said, his hand brushing hers as they walked.

Savannah did think it sounded better than the average church she'd come in contact with, few as they'd been in her life. Her family had never been the church-going type. The very idea of people doing nothing but church for a living was foreign. "Are you Baptist or Catholic?" she asked.

Malachi chuckled beside her before reaching out and taking her hand in his. Their fingers laced together as they reached the town limits and continued on to where the tents had been set up. He seemed to be thinking about what to say to her, and the butterflies in her stomach felt like they were caught up in a full-blown tornado. She prayed her hand wasn't sweaty.

"No, nothing like that," he finally answered. "We aren't really an organized religion. We don't like to label ourselves. My family loves the Bible, and has devoted their lives to spreading the Word," he explained. "It's kind of that simple."

Savannah nodded, pretending to understand. His hand holding hers was all she could think about. It was the first time a boy had ever held her hand, and she wanted to remember every second of it.

"Do you live in the tents?" she asked next, wanting to move away from religion before Malachi realized how little she really knew about it.

"No, we have a few motorhomes that we live in. Probably not much different from you and your dad. It's not so bad. It's like camping, but with the luxury of hot showers and beds."

So, they're just like us, but his parents' work is religion while Dad's is journalism. Okay. That doesn't sound too strange, put like that. "Will I meet your family?" she asked aloud.

"Sure. We can stay and have refreshments with them after the service if you'd like."

"I would like that," she said, getting up the nerve to squeeze his hand for emphasis. "I have to be home by ten, though."

"The service is usually over by nine, if not earlier. I'll make sure you're home on time," he assured her.

"Do *you* preach?" she asked him.

He shrugged his shoulder beside her, their arms brushing. "Sometimes. We offer a service geared towards young people and I sometimes talk then. I don't think of it as preaching. We're talking and sharing, not lecturing or anything like that."

"That sounds nice," she murmured. "I wouldn't mind listening to you, too," she added more bravely, looking up just in time to see a flush rise in his cheeks.

"Thanks, Savannah. Oh, hey—hear that? Those are our tents up ahead."

The sound of singing could be heard in the distance now. Malachi picked up the pace as they headed for the larger of two white tents set up in a field. Several picnic tables were lined up in a row between the tents, red-checked tablecloths covering each one and held down by covered baskets and platters. To the left, there were several cars in the pseudo-parking lot, and behind the tent, Savannah saw two motorhomes, and a small cargo trailer parked to the side.

"What's that?" she asked, pointing to the white trailer.

"We pull that behind the motorhome. It holds the tents, chairs, speakers, and generators and stuff we need for the service," he explained.

"Oh," she muttered. This was a bigger operation than she'd imagined, though she wasn't quite sure what she'd had in mind.

Malachi said hello to a few people as they walked towards the open doors of the large tent. Savannah couldn't help being surprised to see close to thirty people already seated inside and singing a hymn together. She'd hoped to blend in, at least at first, but Malachi strolled down the aisle of folding chairs, her hand in his as he walked to the front row and gestured for her to take a seat. The butterflies in her stomach escalated as she noticed a woman with black hair identical to Malachi's staring at her. Savannah smiled, knowing that had to be his mother. His mother smiled back before her eyes moved to her son.

Malachi squeezed her hand a little tighter before releasing it. Beside him, Savannah folded her hands together and placed them in her lap, doing her best to appear interested as the hymn ended and an older man stepped up to a podium, welcomed those who'd gathered, and began giving what was most definitely a sermon.

"That's my grandpa," Malachi whispered into her ear.

"He seems nice," she replied, feeling a little silly, but what else could she possibly say?

And then, Malachi remained silent beside her, and the sermon droned on. Growing bored, she found her mind wandering as she looked around the tent—or, at least, she looked around what she could without turning around and being obvious about it. She at least needed to *look* like she was listening, after all. What she saw felt calming, though, in an odd way— old-fashioned. There were lights hung from some of the poles above, and the feel of a breeze running from between panels of the tent. She could hear the sound of what she guessed to be several generators humming in the background, and figured they were being used to power the speakers and microphone Malachi's grandfather was using.

Every once in a while, someone would call out "Amen" or "Praise Jesus," snapping Savannah's attention back to the man at the mic. And, each time, she was reminded that Malachi's mother was watching her. Savannah had a feeling her boredom was written all over her face, too, judging by the way Malachi's mother was looking at her. So much for first impressions.

When everyone stood up and began to sing again, Savannah stood, as well, but she didn't know the words. She tried to move her mouth, pretending she did, but imagined she looked ridiculous. Once again, she felt Malachi's mother watching her. Thankfully, it was only the one song she had to get through, and then there was a prayer, a round of amens, and people turned and started talking to one another.

"Would you like to stay for cookies and cider?" Malachi asked.

Savannah looked around, half afraid the sermon would begin again if she didn't drag Malachi away now. "Is it over?"

He caught her hand with his again and laughed. "Yes, it is. I'm sorry you were bored."

"No, no! Not at all!" she lied.

"Come on. I want to introduce you to my family," he said, leading her towards the back of the tent where other people were already filing out, chatting amongst themselves.

Nerves made her palms sweaty as he led her towards the campers in back. Savannah could see several people talking, including Malachi's mother, and guessed she was about to meet the whole family.

"Mom, Dad?" Malachi called out, gaining their attention.

"Malachi," his grandfather greeted him first, nodding at Savannah with a friendly smile.

"Hi, Grandpa. Great talk tonight," Malachi said.

"Thank you, Malachi. Who do we have here?" he asked, turning his warm brown eyes back to Savannah.

"This is Savannah. Savannah, this is my mom, dad, and grand-pa." He introduced her around the circle.

Savannah shook each of their hands, hoping her palms weren't as wet as they felt.

"It's nice to meet you, Savannah," his mother said with what looked like a forced smile. "I'm Tonya, and this is Jim," she added, gesturing towards Malachi's father. "And this is my father, Eli."

"It's nice to meet you all," Savannah answered. "Malachi's told me so much about you. I'm glad I could make it tonight."

"We are also, Savannah," Jim Loveridge answered. "Are you staying for refreshments?"

"We're going to grab some cookies, and then I need to walk her home before it gets dark," Malachi answered.

His mother smiled, her eyes already moving toward a couple who were trying to get her attention.

For her part, Savannah just felt grateful to have introductions out of the way, and gladly followed Malachi back towards the smaller tent.

"I don't think your mom likes me," she whispered.

Malachi laughed. "Just like your dad won't like me."

Savannah giggled, instantly feeling a little better about the awkward introduction. "Good point," she acknowledged.

Malachi grabbed several cookies, placing them on a paper plate before walking around the back of the tent. The generator humming along behind the tent was too loud for them to actually have a conversation, and he gestured past it, toward the woods beyond their campground. He kept moving into the trees until the sounds of the generators and crowd had grown into a blur—until they had a little privacy, too, Savannah thought to herself.

"We can sit back here," he said, settling on a fallen log.

Savannah sat down beside him, looking around and taking in the peacefulness of the little clearing he'd brought her to. "This is nice."

"I like to come back here in the morning. It's so peaceful. The generators are off then, and sometimes deer will come in really close," he said quietly.

"I would love that," she said on a sigh, smiling a moment later when she heard choir music being pumped through the speakers set up around the area. From here, it didn't matter that she didn't know the melodies or understand religion like Malachi did—it was just a nice melody to serve as background.

"It would be a good place for you to write the poetry you talked about the other day," Malachi replied after a few seconds.

She couldn't stop a smile from spreading across her face.

"Maybe one day I can meet you here and see those deer for myself."

"*I'd* like that," he whispered.

And just like that, there was a notable change in the atmosphere. Savannah could see him looking at her, his gaze dropping to her mouth. She tried to regulate her breathing. *He's going to kiss me!* Tonight would be her first kiss ever, just like she'd been hoping all evening, and lucky for her, it was going to come from a handsome boy who was kind and sweet. Who appreciated a peacefulness like this just like she did…

She closed her eyes, waiting for the moment, holding her breath and feeling his face getting closer to hers.

Suddenly, the air went even more still, unnaturally so.

Everything had gone silent. The generators had stopped humming along, and there was no choir music pumping through the speakers. The immediate, abrupt silence was deafening.

Savannah's eyes popped open. No longer focused on her, Malachi looked around the area. Neither of them made a move as they waited for something to happen, for some sound to fill the air. The silence was eerie, after everything had been so vibrant and full of life a few seconds earlier. It was as if a switch had been flipped.

"What happened?" Savannah asked in a whisper.

He shook his head, looking toward the campground now as if he was torn between staying with her and returning to his family. "I have no idea."

And then, they heard a woman scream—*"Dad!"*

Malachi jumped up. "That's my mom!" he yelled over his shoulder to Savannah, already rushing from the little spot in the trees by the time Savannah rose to follow.

"Jim, call nine-one-one—it's his heart!" Savannah heard Malachi's mother scream.

Savannah raced around the tent's corner to see Malachi's grandfather lying on the ground, gasping for air and clutching at his chest. Malachi's mother was kneeling beside him, tears streaming down her face as she continued looking back and forth between him and the small crowd around her, begging for help.

Jim Loveridge stood nearby, repeatedly pushing buttons on his phone. "I can't get a signal. My phone's dead!"

Even as Malachi knelt by his mom and grandfather, Savannah reached into her back pocket and handed his dad her phone. "Here!"

He grabbed it and began furiously pushing at the screen, sliding his fingers back and forth. Then he looked back at her. "Turn it on!"

She snatched it back, noticing the black screen and pushing

the power button. She waited, and then pressed the button again. *Nothing.* "It's dead," she muttered, staring between it and Mr. Loveridge. "The battery was full when I left," she told him helplessly.

Malachi looked from them to his mom again and grabbed her shoulder for attention. "Mom, we have to do CPR," he ordered her.

"I don't know how!" she wailed.

"I do," Savannah said, getting to her knees across from Malachi and thanking her lucky stars that her father had insisted she take that class. She could do this, and let Mr. Loveridge and the others find a working phone.

Malachi checked his grandfather's pulse, then looked at Savannah and shook his head. The training came rushing back to her. "ABC," she said, swallowing down her nerves.

Immediately, she went about lifting the old man's chin and opening his airway before leaning her ear down to check for breathing. Nothing. She used her fingers to trace the line up his chest, between his rib cage, before clasping her hands together as taught, straightening her elbows as she leaned over him, and then beginning chest compressions.

Between sobs, Malachi's mother kept wailing, "Save him!" until another woman finally pulled her into an embrace and let her cry into her shoulder as Savannah and Malachi focused on the elder man lying prone before them.

Savannah worked hard, exhausting herself until Malachi took over. Then, she leaned back on her haunches, watching people run around the area. Everyone was panicking. Jim was grabbing phones, trying to call for help. Several people offered to drive them to the hospital, only then discovering that none of the cars would start.

When Malachi grew tired, Savannah took over again, giving compressions in a steady rhythm while silently praying the man would cough and open his eyes like she'd seen in the movies so many times. How long had they been doing this, though? Her arms ached. Finally, Malachi took over again. It had to have been at least five minutes, she guessed, maybe longer. Probably longer, considering the adrenaline and how she ached anyway.

Her eyes drifted back to the man lying lifeless on the ground. His color was gray, and his lips were blue. He was gone. Her phone was her only way to tell time, but it felt like they had been on the ground forever; she just couldn't know for sure.

She could see Malachi struggling again, and put her hands over his even though she'd barely caught her breath from her last turn. "I'll take over."

He nodded, leaning back, wiping the sweat from his brow as she compressed Eli Loveridge's chest again, just like she'd done on the dummy in the CPR class. She pushed away the pain in her arms and shoulders, and focused on the rhythm. She wasn't sure how long she'd been working over the man when another man kneeled beside her. "I'll take over," he said in a low voice.

Savannah looked at the newcomer, then Eli. She knew it in her heart that there was no saving him. He'd been down too long, and the nearest hospital was at least thirty miles away.

She didn't want to admit it, though. Her own heart hurt, knowing what Malachi and his poor family were going through. She wouldn't be the one to tell them that Eli was gone. She couldn't.

What seemed like an eternity later, the man stopped compressions and checked for a pulse. "I'm sorry, but he's gone," he said in a low voice.

Malachi jarred upward and shook his head. "No! You can't stop!"

His long hair bounced and waved over his face as he pushed the other man out of the way and began compressions again, crying out as he did so.

"I'm so sorry," Savannah whispered, her own heart breaking as she heard his mother wailing behind them.

3

Amanda Patterson pulled the stick up on the Ag Cat crop duster she was flying low over the rows of corn she'd planted that season. It had been a long winter, setting her behind schedule by at least two weeks. She glanced down below as she made a tight circle and pushed the button to spray pesticide over her fields. She was near on being done now, and looking forward to a leisurely ride on one of her horses to end the evening.

This Ag Cat was nothing like the fighter jet she had always dreamed of flying, but it was as close as she would ever get. Her life had not gone according to plan. Her career in the Air Force had ended abruptly, and now she was back in Kentucky, owner and operator of her own farm as a part-time farmer and part-time vet. Definitely not what she'd envisioned doing for the rest of her life.

She made another low pass before circling back, climbing higher for the pure joy of it before lowering her altitude for precision spraying. She'd begun lining up for another spray when the engine cut out and her gauges fell flat.

"What the hell?" she asked aloud, a feeling of pure terror shooting through her before she tamped it down and focused on the problem.

She tried to restart the engine first, but got no response.

"Okay, relax. I'm not too high, I can land in the field," she told herself, clutching the stick and surveying her options.

Unfortunately, the barn was between her and the open pasture beyond it. Her altitude was too low for her to clear the barn, too, and veering in either direction now could put her in the trees or crashing into her own house. The only way to the best landing place was directly through the roof of her ancient barn — its brand-new roof.

"Crap," she muttered, the nose of the plane already dropping lower as she literally began to fall out of the sky. At least her horses were out in the far pasture and wouldn't be terrorized by whatever happened next.

She set her jaw and stared through the tinted shield attached to the helmet she wore. She didn't want to die and only hoped that the helmet would be enough to save her life. If she hit the gas tank against the edge of the barn's metal roofing, a helmet wasn't going to do her a lot of good. If only she'd waited one more season to replace the roof, or stuck with traditional shingles…

"Come on, please, please, please," she chanted, holding onto the stick and doing her best to will the nose of the plane over the top edge of the old building her father had built some thirty years before. If she could skate over, or only really hit the landing gear, she might be able to just glide in.

And then the nose of the plane hit the top of the barn, the jolt causing her to bite her tongue. Metal screeched so loudly that Amanda was near deafened. She sent up a silent prayer as the plane's force crumpled wood and metal beneath and around her. Then the roof was behind her, her sturdy plane still surrounding her as she began to fall the remaining twenty feet to the ground. With a bone-jarring thud, the plane slammed into the grassy pasture and slid across the ground for a good forty feet before coming to an abrupt stop, just missing the old oak she'd always loved.

Amanda blinked several times before pulling the helmet over her head. The plexiglass above her head had popped open on impact, making it easy for her to escape the cockpit of her crashed plane. She cut her hand climbing out but didn't have time to worry about it. Her old red barn was on fire. Sparks from the metal on metal contact must have ignited the old wood supporting the roof once she'd sheared off metal paneling, and it would be just a matter of time before she lost the old structure now.

She rushed to the well pump to turn on the water. There wouldn't be enough water or pressure to save her barn, maybe, but if she could wet the ground surrounding it, she'd at least ensure that the fire wouldn't spread to the nearby trees or fencing, let alone her house. She pulled up the pump handle and aimed the hose toward the barn, expecting a stream of water and getting nothing. There was no power. Why, she didn't know, and she didn't have time to wonder what had killed it. She had the old pump that pulled water from the stream running alongside her land, and it would be full this time of year with mountain run-off. If she wanted to wet her land and safeguard the rest of her property, she had to hurry. Already, fire was eating up the sides of the barn.

She raced across her driveway and towards the stream running some twenty feet beyond her property line, already mentally going over the steps needed to hook up the pump that would hopefully provide enough water to run the hose. The gas-powered pump was her back-up for when storms knocked out the power. Thankfully, the stream turned into a roaring river during the spring melt, which was always another problem in and of itself, what with the threat of its water flooding the area. Every year, her driveway became a pond, but it had yet to flood her basement this year.

But, if there had to be a fire, this was good timing. The horses were down in the far pasture, and she'd checked the stream level early that morning—it was running high.

The pump was stored in a small shed near the stream, at the very edge of her property. She'd already yanked open the door and started to drag it out when she heard a cry for help. Spinning around, she only had to take a few steps toward the water before she saw a man clinging to a large tree branch hung up on a boulder. He was at the center of what was normally a tranquil stream, but after the rains and warm weather, it had become a violent, raging river cutting through vegetation and swallowing up the usual banks, running even higher than it had that morning. Typically, the stream was about ten feet wide; now, it was bulging and pushing twenty feet.

"What are you doing?" she yelled, momentarily forgetting about the fire behind her. She knew the question was ridiculous, but it was all she could think of. Who in their right mind would go in the water when it was running like this? What on earth could he have been doing?

He said something, but she couldn't hear him over the water. With one last glance toward the shed, she instead moved to the edge of the water. From here, she could see the man looked like he was struggling not just to hold onto the branch, but to stay above water.

"Help, please," he moaned, his lips bluish in the fading light. One of his legs bobbed in front of him on the water, and his arms remained wrapped around the thick tree branch that looked like it might give at any time, though it had clearly become stuck fast where it was after being pulled along by the current this far. The man had to have been crazy to venture into that water, she thought.

"Stand up!" she ordered him.

"I can't. My leg," he groaned.

Amanda turned to look behind her. Smoke was rising in the air, tinged by orange. Her barn was going up in flames, and there was no telling whether or not the fire would spread. The ground might be wet from the rain the night before, but it might not. Yet, she didn't have time to save the man and also safeguard her land and home. She could only do one. And the man in the river would die if she didn't help him—that much was becoming clearer and clearer, every second she stood there.

"Dangit!" she muttered, leaving the pump and stepping close to the bank of the fast-moving water.

"Help," he moaned again, his voice disappearing as his head slipped underwater for a brief second before he came back up sputtering.

Amanda looked left and right, trying to find a way to reach him without getting pulled into the strong current herself. This water wasn't all that deep, but the jagged rocks and the debris pulled into the water as it made its way down the mountain always made it treacherous. And that current would make it extremely difficult to remain standing even a foot from the bank.

Plus, she was dressed in jeans and a t-shirt with her old pair of Nikes—not exactly the best outfit for jumping into water that was probably around fifty degrees. She stared at the man, noting how pale he'd gone. He'd soon be suffering from hypothermia, assuming he didn't drown first.

"Can you try to stand?" she called out, already knowing the answer.

"My leg. I think it's broken," he said, his teeth clenching as he spoke.

Of course, it is. Damn. "Okay, hold tight," she told him, trying to keep her own voice calm. "I'm going to have to come in to get you." Not waiting for a response, she went back to the small shed and began digging around for anything she could use to help the rescue mission.

She had no rope stored there, so the garden hose she used to connect to the hose near the house was her only option. She grabbed it and ran back to the bank, grateful to see he was still holding on and that the branch hadn't yet been dislodged.

"I'm going to throw out the hose. I need you to grab on and I'll pull you in," she instructed him.

He made a grunting noise she took as a yes and she quickly threw the end of the fifty-foot hose towards him. He reached out, but the stream carried the end away from him before his hand got close. He slid under the surface of the water again.

"Hold on!" she cried out as she reeled the hose back in, realizing he was too weak to hold on much longer. Her eyes scanned the bank again. They locked onto a sturdy tree near the stream's edge, some ten feet upstream. Focused on getting to the drowning stranger now, she didn't think twice about what she was about to do as she tied the hose around the large tree trunk that sat rooted half in the swollen stream, yanking on it until she was satisfied it would hold her weight. And, hopefully, the man's, as well.

"I'm coming," she called out.

"Hurry!" he yelled.

Amanda pulled on the hose again, testing her knot before sliding down the incline to the water's edge and taking her first steps into the stream. And then, there was nothing to do but try it. She gasped out loud when the icy water closed over her feet, splashing around her legs as she took another step in. The water was threatening to knock her off balance already, and she was less than three feet from the bank. She wrapped the end of the hose around her wrist several times and then waded farther in.

"I'm here," she said, her voice stilted as the water rushed around her waist, chilling her to the bone. She kept her grip tight on the hose and couldn't help glancing back to the bank —if the hose or her knot broke, or she let go, the current would have her; there was no way the tree branch this man was relying on would hold both of them.

"My leg," he groaned again.

Her grip tightened on the wet hose. It would have to hold both of them now. "I need you to wrap your arms around my waist. I'm going to walk at an angle towards the bank, okay? Let your body float out behind you with the current. I'll never be able to carry you, so that's the only way. You look like a pretty solid guy," she pointed out, hoping he was still thinking straight through the freezing cold and pain he had to be feeling. He was going to have to reach out to her—she was still two feet away, and the hose wasn't stretching any further.

He nodded jerkily but didn't shift his grip or his hands. "I'm so cold," he whispered. "I don't know…"

"I do know, and I'm going to get you out of here, but I need you to hold on a little longer. I can't get any closer, so you have to help me here."

"I'm weak," he mumbled. "More help…"

"It's just me, mister. And the cold water. That's sapping your strength faster than you can blink," she told him. She swallowed down lecturing him further even as she wondered what kind of idiot went into icy water without wearing proper protective equipment, but there wasn't time for that. Her legs were starting to go numb with cold also, just like her hands. This man had to be dead tired, and it was probably a miracle he'd held on as long as he had. The human body in fifty-degree water could only survive a few hours, but exhaustion could set in within an hour or two. She braced herself as much as she could where she stood, knowing they both had to get out of this water as soon as possible.

When he remained as he'd been when she reached him, clenching the tree branch, she gripped the hose with only one hand, anchored by her wrapped wrist, and reached out with her other to grab his hand.

He shifted his grip, and finally one cold, shriveled hand clasped hers. She yanked hard, pulling him towards her before she lost her chance.

"Let go of the branch!" she screamed as the man nearly pulled her under.

He immediately released the death grip he'd had on the branch and swung his arm up and over to grab her forearm. She pulled him towards her until his arms could wrap around her waist in a strong vise. With him holding onto her now, she renewed her grip on the hose and began using all of her strength to drag his body at an angle, not going directly against the current. It was easier to move at an angle. Her only other option was to let the current sweep them downstream until she could catch something to hold onto, and she didn't like those odds.

"Hold on," she said, gritting her teeth together as she took another step, using the hose to pull her body through the water. If anything, it felt like the current was strengthening, determined to pull her away from the bank, though she knew that was just the cold talking.

Still, the man's heavy weight behind her made it difficult to move, every step requiring every ounce of strength she could muster. The soggy bank looked so far away, but the hose held and they made slow progress sideways toward safety.

"We're almost there; don't let go," she grunted, propelling her body another step closer to the bank. She felt him use his one good leg to push off the rocky bottom, propelling her forward.

The second she got close enough to brace herself against a tree rising out of the flooding water and lean into the bank, she turned to grab one of his arms. "I need you to pull yourself onto the bank," she told him, struggling to catch her breath. Without the water to lighten his body weight, Amanda doubted she could lift him.

"I'll try," he grunted.

He let go of her waist and weakly gripped at the damp earth along the newly-formed bank, which was nothing more than grass and mud. It was at the height of her chest, though, and he couldn't stand upright. He wasn't going to make it, she realized. He didn't have the strength to pull himself out of the water and onto the steep edge of the bank, let alone without anything sturdy to grab hold of and use for leverage.

"Okay, okay. Hold the hose." She helped him get a grip on the hose alongside her hand, and then pulled herself up the hose a few feet until she could safely clamber up the bank, her fingers digging into the grass and mud. Back on the bank, she scuttled sideways until she was just above the man, then shifted so that her leg dangled beside him as she held a branch of the nearby tree to steady herself. "Grab my leg!" she shouted, bracing herself for the extra weight.

He did as he was told, and she didn't have to tell him what to do next. In seconds, he'd managed to pull himself up to her waist, and she released one hand from the tree in order to reach down and grip his arm, helping him struggle up until his butt was on the bank. Then, finally, she released her grip on the tree that had thankfully stood its ground and rose to hook her arms under his armpits and pull him further onto the bank, safely away from the raging stream.

He groaned out a curse as she stopped to try and catch her breath, his head back on the ground and his hands clenched into fists. She stared down at him, noting the wild look in his blue eyes. They looked unnaturally blue against the pasty white color of his nearly frozen flesh.

"Thank you," he muttered, and then it looked like he attempted to sit up, but agony passed through his expression as he fell back, unconscious.

"Great," Amanda muttered.

She turned to look back at the house. Her barn was almost completely engulfed, but it appeared that the fire was staying confined to the structure itself; even the nearby fencing hadn't caught—there must have been enough rain to keep it and the surrounding land just damp enough for safety's sake. Good enough. It was too late to do anything about her barn or her plane. The priority was getting this man back to her place to assess his injuries and call for help. The boonies were no place for a life-threatening illness or injury.

Amanda plopped down beside him, checking him over for any serious, obvious injuries. He'd said his leg was broken, but she was worried about a head injury or internal injuries. Possible hypothermia was also a problem, but it hadn't set in yet—it would probably become the priority if it did, but she thought they were out of the woods now that he was on dry land.

Taking stock of him, her eyes roamed over the tattoos covering both his arms. She knew better than to judge a book by its cover, and ignored newly uncovered tats as she lifted his soaked t-shirt, looking for any wounds or bruising that would indicate internal bleeding. She couldn't help but notice he was in good shape. She guessed him to be late thirties, maybe his early forties, and athletic. There was a deep gash over his rib cage that would need to be cleaned and stitched, she guessed, along with what was the start of some bruising that could indicate a broken rib or two, but no signs of internal injuries. And yes, she agreed that his leg was broken when she took another look at the angle it had come to rest at. Or, rather, angles.

There was no way to tell how he'd come to be in the stream,

and she had no idea if his injuries were the result of an accident or being tossed around in the churning water, but it didn't matter at the moment. Her fingers moved into his thick black hair, gently checking his scalp for lacerations and finding none. She did feel a large bump on the side of his head—a concussion, then.

She looked between him and the house, and then glanced at her crumbling barn again before looking back to the stranger. "Well, crap," she murmured, the full weight of the last ten minutes of her life slamming into her.

4

Austin blinked several times, staring up at the orange-streaked sky. His head was pounding, and he was cold —really cold. And wet. His left leg throbbed distractingly, and he felt as if he'd just been through the rinse cycle in a washing machine. His hand reached up to touch his forehead, feeling out a prominent bump beneath his hair.

"You're awake," a woman's voice said, startling him.

He rolled his head to the side and saw a woman walking towards him. "You..." He swallowed the dry word that would have come next, thinking he'd sounded like a frog just then, and tried again. "You're the one who pulled me out of the water."

She smiled. "It's generally a nice tranquil stream, but you

happened to go for a swim when it's swollen and violent. It only feels like a river right now because of the spring run-off."

"Oh," he muttered, trying to orientate himself. "But I… I fell into a river."

She grimaced above him, and then crouched down to meet his eyes. "You're lucky to be alive, then—this stream branches off from the river more than a mile from here, and if it looks like this, I can only imagine what the river's like right now."

"It's cold, too," he grunted. She half-smiled at the joke, and he looked back to the sky. It was still light out, but barely. He was guessing it was around nine. He needed to get back to the trailer and let Savannah know he was okay. First, though, he needed a hospital. He was convinced his leg was broken.

"I brought a pair of crutches," she said, brandishing a pair of metal ones.

He stared at them for a moment, wondering if she was serious. "For me?"

"I can't carry you," she told him. "I thought about making a stretcher out of a blanket if I couldn't get you up, but that was my last resort," she muttered.

He sat up, jarring his leg and wincing with pain when he moved it. "I think it's broken."

"You said that already," she replied dryly. She squatted in front of him again. She was pretty, was his first thought. She had shoulder-length black hair, soaked and sticking to her olive skin around her face and neck. Her wet t-shirt clung to her body, showing off her trim figure. And he knew he shouldn't look, but she was an attractive woman and he wasn't blind. A little broken, but definitely not blind.

"I'm sorry, my head is a little foggy. Can you take me to the hospital?" he asked.

"I tried calling for help, but my cell is dead and the power is out. That's why I brought the crutches. I think they're about our only option, though I'm going to go get my truck now that you're awake" she added.

"We'll make it work, then," he acknowledged, still wondering how he'd stand on the crutches. "Sorry to be a bother," he muttered.

"It's fine. The hospital's about twenty minutes away. Sit tight and I'll bring my truck closer," she said, standing and jogging away, leaving the crutches beside him.

He bent his good leg and tried to get to a standing position, but it wasn't going to happen. He'd just have to wait for his savior to come back. The sky seemed to be getting darker by the minute, but he kept his eyes on the rushing water a few yards in front of him and shook his head. The woman was right that he was lucky to have escaped that water with his life. Someone had tried to kill him. Callum was dead. It felt surreal. He was a boring fluff journalist. Stuff like this didn't happen to him.

Her footsteps behind him were what grabbed his attention. Her truck had to have the quietest engine he'd ever heard—he hadn't heard a thing.

"I'm going to need some help up," he confessed without looking at her, a little embarrassed to be so helpless. It wasn't something he was used to.

"Uh, well, bad news—my truck won't start," she said, halting beside him with a bewildered look on her face.

"Your truck won't start?" he echoed. First the power and her phone, and now her truck? Who was this lady?

"Nope. Dead. Nothing turns on. I drove it a couple hours ago and it was fine," she added, apparently reading the judgement on his face. "I don't know what's wrong with it."

"Is the battery dead?"

"I don't see how. It's a new truck. The battery should be fairly new."

He closed his eyes. "Okay, so, no power, no phone, and no truck. How far are we from town?"

"It's about twenty miles to Irvine. That's the closest hospital."

"What?" he asked, his head jerking back to look up at her.

She shrugged a shoulder. "That's the closest real town. They have a small hospital."

"Holy crap. I fell into the river north of Stanton," he said, shaking his head.

She let out a low whistle. "That's forty miles away."

"Forty miles!" he practically shouted. "Look, you have to help me get back there. My daughter…"

She frowned deeper now. "I'm sorry. I don't know *how* to get you there right now, but first things first, okay? We need to get you back to the house so we can start warming you up."

Austin swallowed down the panic in his gut, and then her words struck home. He didn't feel cold anymore, and that was a dangerous sign. He closed his eyes and took a deep breath, trying to pull his wits about him.

"I'm Austin, Austin Merryman. Thank you for saving me. Please don't think I'm ungrateful. I am. It's just… I really need to get home."

She squatted in front of him. "Austin, I'm Amanda Patterson. I'm a veterinarian and can take care of your leg until we figure out a hospital trip. I have some painkillers back at the house, but first we need to check you out and make sure you don't have any other injuries. Let's take care of the most pressing matters first. I need to get out of these wet clothes I'm wearing, as well."

"I hit my head," he said, the throbbing reminding him of the rock he'd slammed into seconds after he'd hit the water.

"Austin, I'm going to help you stand up, and then you'll need to use the crutches to support the majority of your weight. Can you do that?" she asked, her voice calm—clinical.

It grounded him, as he imagined she'd meant it to, and he nodded. "Yes."

"Okay, put the crutch under your right arm. I'm going to lift you from behind," she instructed, moving behind him.

"You're not going to be able to lift me," he grumbled.

"I got you out of the stream," she shot back.

She made a good point. With her help, he managed to get to his feet—foot. He swayed a little, blinking several times to try and right the suddenly spinning world.

"I need a second," he muttered, his hands gripping the crutches.

He inhaled through his nose, breathing through the pain rocketing through his body. The wave of dizziness made him sway on his one good leg so that he appreciated her hand catching his elbow for support.

"Take a minute, breathe slow and deep, and we'll move when you're ready," she said, her hand on his back, its warmth coming through the soaked shirt. Beside him, she was even shorter than he'd realized—maybe a few inches past five feet; she was right that he'd have to get to her house mostly on his own foot and the crutches.

"I'm ready," he said, taking a first shaky step forward.

By the time he managed to make it up the three steps onto the covered front porch of her home, he was exhausted. He had zero strength left. Ahead of him, she opened the screen door and gestured for him to go inside.

"Have a seat on the couch," she ordered him, lighting some candles near the door so that he could see.

He hobbled over on the crutches before he collapsed onto her couch, grimacing in pain as the action jerked his leg once again.

"I'll be right back," she promised, heading out of the living room.

He let the crutches fall against the couch beside him and squeezed his eyes closed, pain threatening to pull him under. When he'd managed to swallow it down and get past it, he opened his eyes and looked around the farmhouse. It looked cozy, with a plaid throw tossed over the back of a recliner and a small flat-screen TV on a plain stand. It was simple, very much like other farmhouses he'd seen and been in. When Amanda returned with more candles, she wore dry clothes herself and didn't waste any time before ordering him to take off his shirt. He leaned forward, struggling to pull his soaked t-shirt off. It was only with her help that he managed. She immediately covered him with a warm blanket, tucking it in around his neck.

"Pants," she told him flatly.

He grimaced. "Really?"

"Your leg is broken, right?"

He nodded.

"Your pants are wet, right?"

He nodded again.

"Then strip, Austin. You're covered with a blanket and I promise not to peek," she added, a cheeky grin flaring up on her face.

"Thank you," he told her, struggling to get his frozen fingers to work to undo his belt buckle. There was no way he was asking her for help with this. He managed to get the pants halfway down his thighs before she had to take over, working at the soaked shoelaces of his boots before gently pulling the pants down over his injured leg. It still hurt like hell.

"I need to clean the cut on your side before we deal with this leg," she said next, ignoring the fact that he was essentially naked under the blanket.

Austin nodded yet again—what else could he do? "Okay."

"I might need to stitch it closed… since I'm really not sure how to get you to the hospital," she said, the last words coming more hesitantly.

His eyes popped open. "What? That bad?"

"I mean, I would have preferred we wait, but we can't wait too long," she advised him.

"Why?" he asked.

She shrugged, her eyes squinted in thought. Even in the candlelight, he could tell she was concerned. "It isn't bleeding," she answered, "which is a good sign, but I don't want to risk an infection. The sooner we close it, the lower the risk of an infection. You have about twelve hours after an injury to stitch it," she explained.

Twelve hours wasn't much time when they didn't have an immediate plan. "That does it, then. Stitch it."

"Are you sure?" she pressed.

He stared up at her. "You said you were a vet, right? You know what you're doing?" he asked.

"I do. I'm guessing you might need eight to ten stitches. I have a numbing agent that will help," she said, holding up a bottle.

"Do whatever. I need to get home. My daughter, she'll be there alone, wondering what happened to me."

Amanda gently sat down on the couch beside him, clearly

trying not to shift the cushion below his injured leg as he maneuvered the blanket away from his side.

"What did happen to you?" she asked, dumping a clear liquid on a gauze pad before she pressed it against the injury that he'd barely even realized was there. He blamed the frigid temperatures for numbing his body, which was a small blessing. He imagined he'd be very stiff and sore tomorrow, not to mention covered in bruises.

"I fell off a bridge," he lied.

She raised an eyebrow. "You should learn to be more careful."

"I'll keep that in mind."

She smiled tightly and held the gauze to his side as she pulled a candle positioned on the table behind the couch closer. "Ready?" she asked. He nodded and expected real pain when she put a needle to his skin, but there was only a pinch before he felt tugging and some stinging as she continued. Maybe along with the cold, the numbing agent had truly helped dull the sharp pain he knew he should be feeling. If anything, the stitching hurt just less than getting a tattoo. As he watched her tediously pull the black thread through his skin, he remembered the pain he'd felt in his side when the bullets had started to fly. That was it. He'd been grazed by a bullet and hadn't even realized it in the moment. He wasn't about to tell this woman he'd been shot at, though.

Finished with his side, she pronounced his break a simple one and used a horse splint to brace his broken leg before using some hot pink vet wrap to keep it in place. The support of the brace provided almost immediate relief. He could already feel the muscles in his leg relaxing a bit.

"Sorry about the pink—it's all I had on hand," she said with a grin. "We'll do a real cast tomorrow if we can't figure out how to get you to the hospital. I took care of a dog's broken leg just last week," she said, as if to make him feel better. "So if you can handle the color, we'll be okay."

He shrugged, thinking he was at least beyond lucky that he'd landed in a vet's hands rather than the average farmer's. "My masculinity can handle a pink cast if it comes to it."

"Good. Now, I have a camp stove. I'm going to fire it up and make us some hot soup," she said, taking off the latex gloves she'd been wearing. "I'll light some more candles, as well."

"I really need to get home," he reminded her tiredly.

"Austin, I understand you need to get back to your daughter, but I honestly don't know how to get you there. Not tonight. Tomorrow, I can get to a neighbor and see about help—the closest farm's a few miles down the road."

He took a deep breath. "That's right. No phones or power."

"Even my plane died," she muttered under her breath.

For a moment, he thought he'd imagined her words, but then

she nodded when he repeated, "Your plane died?" and the hairs on the back of his neck stood up.

She ran a hand through her thick black hair. "Yeah, one second I'm up in the sky, doing my thing, and the next, my gauges fell flat."

"You were in the air?" he asked, searching for obvious signs that she'd survived a plane crash and finding none.

"I was for about two minutes before I slammed into the barn and basically fell to the ground," she said on a small laugh.

"Are you okay?"

"Yep. Little cut on my hand. Can't say the same for my barn, though."

He leaned his head back against the couch as she walked away, trying to put all the pieces together. In his head, he was creating a timeline like he would have if he'd been writing a story. The timeline and the facts that he knew for sure. His brain kept coming back to one thing. It couldn't be that, however. That was... not possible. He wouldn't let himself suspect it.

"Here," she said, coming back into the living room. "Take these."

"What are they?" he asked, taking the small white pills from her palm.

"They're antibiotics. With that gash on your side and the crap that was in that stream, you need to get started on antibiotics right away."

He popped them into his mouth and swallowed them down with the bottle of water she handed him. "You said you're a vet. These were meant for animals?"

She grinned. "People, dogs, horses, all the same."

He'd have to take her word for it. "Tell me something. Do you have a computer?"

"I live in the country, not the dark ages."

"Does it turn on?" he asked, ignoring her joke.

"I'll check."

With that, she disappeared for a few seconds, and then came back with a newish-looking laptop in her hand.

"Does it turn on?" he asked when she seemed to be struggling with it.

Amanda looked up at him, meeting his eyes now. "No. How did you know?"

He ran a hand down his face, feeling the scruff on his jaw. "It's just a suspicion. Your phone, is it completely dead?"

She nodded. "Black screen."

He bit back a curse. "Radio? Do you have a radio?" he asked, looking around her living room.

She disappeared and returned with an old-school, battery-powered radio. "It's dead. I thought the batteries were good, but maybe not."

"Great," he mumbled, his mind whirring as he put together the pieces of the puzzle in front of him. His brain was a little jumbled after being slammed into a rock and then frozen, and he wanted to think he was wrong anyway.

"What is your suspicion?" she asked, settling into the nearby armchair.

He felt a little ridiculous saying it, but maybe he needed to say it aloud and then process it. "I don't know. I'm trying to put all the pieces together. This seems a little too science fiction to believe."

"What's too sci-fi?"

He looked away from her. "I don't know. Like… it's like something knocked out the power grid."

She stared at him. "A downed power grid wouldn't kill the electronics in my house or my truck," she whispered.

He looked her in the eye then, finally ready to sound like a nutjob. "Have you ever heard of something called an EMP? That's what I'm starting to wonder about."

Her eyebrows shot up. "EMP. An electromagnetic pulse?"

"You know about them?"

She nodded as she leaned back, still staring at him. "I do. I was in the Air Force for a few years, in the cybersecurity department. I know a lot about them."

"What do you think? Is it a possibility?" he asked, wanting to know he wasn't crazy. Or, really, maybe hoping he was.

She looked thoughtful. "You know, I think it is. Wow. How crazy is that?" she asked softly.

"If it was an EMP, this whole area's going to be in a blackout," he said, fear for his daughter mounting.

She covered her mouth with one of her small hands. "Oh my God. I didn't think it would actually happen. Maybe it wasn't that. It could be—"

She stopped talking. He waited, hoping she'd offer a better suggestion. Austin was only vaguely familiar with what an EMP was, and remembered it being explained as frying the computers and electrical components in just about everything in the vicinity of such a pulse. He'd been treated to that expla- nation and a lot of hypotheses about how far-reaching damage might be by the preppers he'd met about six months before. They'd gone to great lengths to prepare for an EMP, and had not only stockpiled food and water, but put radios and other electrical equipment in Faraday cages. He hadn't thought they were crazy, but he had thought they were preparing for a one-in-a-million disaster and would have been better off putting their money elsewhere.

Now, it seemed they'd been the smart ones.

"I have a feeling you aren't the only one who didn't think it would happen," he muttered. "I have to get out of here. I've got to get to my daughter. Forget the hospital—if this is an EMP, there's no point. I can't leave Savannah alone. I have to go," he said, sitting up again and reaching for a crutch.

"Austin, you can't, not right now." Amanda leaned forward, putting her hand on his arm to freeze him. "How old is your daughter?"

"Fourteen."

"Okay, so she's not a little kid. She'll go home and wait for you. We'll find a way in the morning. It's going to be pitch black out there," she said in that familiar, calm voice.

He looked out the living room windows. Night had fallen, and without the benefit of headlights or a flashlight, navigating the dark terrain would be dangerous. He couldn't risk another injury.

A lump formed in his throat. "You're right."

"Good, settle back down and I'll get us some soup. You need to rest. I'll check on my horses and then I'll keep an eye on you throughout the night. You might have a mild concussion."

"Thank you."

She shrugged, her expression serious. "I think we're in this together now. So, soup, then I'll take care of my horses and you'll rest. I need to make sure that fire's out, too, but it was supposed to rain tonight and it seemed to be dying earlier, so that shouldn't take long."

"I'm sorry. I wish I could help," he said, feeling a little useless.

"Rest, Austin. That's what you need," she said, sounding confident everything would by okay. "And if you're sure you want to find your daughter and forego a hospital—though, honestly, I'm not sure how we'd get you there or what they could do that I couldn't, if our guess is right—then I'll put a cast on that leg of yours first thing in the morning."

"Yeah," he acknowledged. "That might be best."

He watched her force a smile before she left the room.

He nodded to himself, trying to accept the way things had changed in just a few hours, and the state he was in on this couch. "Okay then. I'll be right here," he said belatedly.

5

Savannah sat at one of the picnic tables, watching the Loveridge family as they hugged one another, cried, and did their best to come to terms with the death of the family patriarch. One of the members of their revival group had covered Eli with a white sheet, but he was still lying in the same spot.

Everyone had held hands around the body while Jim Loveridge had said a prayer. Savannah had held Malachi's hand, but the close contact had been nothing like earlier. After the prayers and a song, everyone had drifted away from the body and the Loveridge family, and Savannah had found herself retreating to sit nearby and observe; she didn't want to drag Malachi away from his family sooner than she had to, and she knew he wouldn't let her walk home alone. Some of the people who'd traveled a long way to come to the revival were still hanging around, and she knew exactly how they felt. She also felt kind of stuck. Her home on wheels was probably only a couple of miles away, but it was dark and quiet, and the night had unnerved her. She'd told herself that Malachi wouldn't let her walk home alone, and she thought that was the case... but she also didn't want him to.

Her eyes scanned the area again. She felt like an outsider, an interloper. She needed to leave and let them be alone. The other people left were lingering on the other side of the clearing, huddled in small groups and talking in harsh whispers, gesturing wildly. Savannah didn't know them at all. She wasn't a Loveridge, but she wasn't one of them, either, panicking over cars or cellphones.

After Eli's death, it had become clear that none of the vehicles would work. A few families had gathered purses and other belongings from their vehicles and set out walking. They were long gone now, and Savannah was left thinking about her dad and wondering where he was. Was he back at the trailer, or had he been stranded somewhere, as well? Would he come looking for her? He would if he could, she knew, and a new pang of regret shot through her over the fact that she'd lied to him about where she'd really planned on coming that night. He wouldn't know where to look for her if he tried.

Feeling invisible, she eavesdropped on the many conversations happening around her. One of the people who'd been at the revival mentioned something about a government shut-down. Someone else claimed it was an enemy attack and World War Three had just been started. Savannah didn't know about all that, but something big and something very terrible had happened for everything to have shut down like this.

Her gaze moved back to the Loveridge family silhouetted in the glow of candles and lanterns that had been gathered. If the situation hadn't been so awful, it would have been beautiful out here in the country with no light pollution. She was glad this family had each other, at least. When her mom had died, it had just been her and her father in the hospital room. She would never forget how it had felt to leave the hospital without her mother. Now, it was only her and her dad—no one else. Malachi still had a full family to care for him, regardless of the tragedy they'd just suffered.

Just then, he looked over at her and smiled. She smiled back, giving him a small wave. He said something to his mom before giving her a quick kiss on the cheek and making his way towards the table where Savannah sat. He perched on the bench beside her, his eyes on the ground in front of him and his hands resting in his lap. She could feel the grief rolling off of him and almost moved away to give him more space. Her own grief over her mother was still raw; feeling his made it hard to keep her own in check. As the night had gotten calmer, her own emotions had been bubbling over with memories.

"Sorry to have left you alone," he told her.

"No, don't be sorry. I'm fine. Your family needs you."

"My mom is pretty upset," he said quietly. "He was so healthy, so happy."

"I'm so sorry about your grandpa, Malachi. Really."

"Thanks. It's terrible, and I'm... I'm really going to miss him," he said, choking on a sob before regaining his composure. "He was a friend."

She gave him another minute, and then made her decision. "I should get going. Your family needs time alone."

His face shot up, and he focused on her for the first time since coming to the table. "It's dark, Savannah—you can't walk home alone," he replied, his voice strained.

"I'll be okay. Stay here. Help your mom. Did anyone get ahold of emergency services?" she asked.

"No. I have no idea what's happened, but no phones work. None of the cars will start, and Dad can't get any of the generators to run again. I think that's what killed my grandpa."

She stared at him, trying to catch up with the change in topic. "What killed him?" she asked.

"He had a pacemaker. It's like everything electrical just stopped working, including his pacemaker. He was so healthy, that has to be it."

"Oh. Wow. I'm so sorry, Malachi. That's just awful," she said, putting her hand over his.

"Did you hear that one guy talking? He thinks the power grids were all shut down," Malachi added, looking at her.

"I did hear him say that," she replied, not wanting to add any more stress. She'd been hoping the people talking about war were overreacting and that everything would be back to normal in a few hours. By the time she got back to the RV, even.

"I'll ask my mom if it's okay for me to walk you back," Malachi said as he rose from the bench, and though Savannah felt like she should protest again, she didn't.

He returned a minute later with permission to walk her home, and they slowly headed out of the revival area and back towards town. The moonlight and brilliant stars on the clear night were so pretty, and she felt freer now, leaving the campground behind and listening to the crickets beginning their night songs. With Malachi beside her, his hand occasionally brushing hers, she could almost forget how horribly things had gone wrong. If this was the beginning of a war, she knew she would never forget the exact moment it had happened and who she'd been with. Malachi had more than earned a strong place in her life story. She only hoped it was a long life story, and that it wouldn't be cut short by whatever it was that was happening.

They'd been walking in silence, both lost to their own thoughts, when a gun shot rang out. Malachi and Savannah froze, looking at one another. "What was that?" she whispered.

"Maybe someone is hunting in the forest," Malachi offered doubtfully.

"At night?"

He shrugged. "I don't know. Stay close."

Malachi took her hand now, and they walked a little farther, neither of them talking as they moved. Her eyes darted left and right, trying to see through the trees lining the right side of the road. Everything looked shadowy—even in the field on the opposite side of the road from the trees. It was eerie, and she couldn't wait to get home, but she tried to tell herself that the creepiness of the night was all in her head.

Talking would help break up the extreme quiet, but unfortunately, Savannah had no idea what to say to the boy next to her. She knew he was hurting, but this wasn't something that a hug would help with. Her own personal experience told her clearly that no amount of hugs would make the pain go away. This was something he would have to deal with on his own, working through all the painful emotions that were sure to plague him over the next several days and coming weeks.

They were on the very outskirts of the town, which was itself totally dark, when her thoughts were broken into again.

"Watch out!" Malachi shouted suddenly, grabbing her arm and

yanking her to the left as a man on a bike turned the corner of a building and nearly ran them over as he raced past.

"Oh my God! What was that about?" she shrieked.

Her answer appeared in the form of another man racing around the corner, a gun in his hand as he waved it around, shouting at the man on the bike.

"Stop! Stop! I'll shoot!" he screamed out as he shoved past them.

"We should go back," Malachi whispered, looking after the two men.

"I've got to get home. My dad will be worried sick," she insisted. "Just walk me through town, please?"

Malachi nodded and they kept going, stopping only when they reached the gas station where she'd met him earlier.

"Whoa," Malachi gasped, staring at the broken windows of the storefront. The gas pumps' hoses were lying limp on the ground with a car parked nearby. The whole place looked deserted.

"What happened?" Savannah asked, walking towards the store.

"Savannah, wait, don't get too close," Malachi warned her, grabbing her arm to hold her back.

Instead, she pulled him along with her, drawn to the chaos.

There was glass everywhere, with the door of the store partially ajar, hung up on a package of diapers on the ground. Something was horribly wrong, and Savannah kept moving inside the store.

A scream tore from her throat when she saw the shop owner lying in the glass inside the store, dark liquid pooling under his head. There were broken beer bottles scattered around him, one just beside his open hand as if he'd tried to use it as a weapon and then dropped it upon falling.

"Let's get out of here!" Malachi ordered her, grabbing her hand and pulling her away, dragging her down the road back towards the campground his family had set up. Savannah didn't argue, knowing that they were closer to his home than hers.

More gun shots sounded out as they raced out of the store, these coming from farther down the road, in town somewhere. A scream followed by more gunshots echoed around them as they raced back toward the trees.

"I need to go home!" she cried, sliding to a halt.

Malachi held her hand tighter and tugged her into the trees. "Tomorrow, Savannah. Listen to what's happening in town. We can't go back through there. Not tonight."

Another gunshot put the exclamation point on his words, and she nodded even though she could feel herself crying now. Without more needing to be said, Malachi began running again, her hand still in his as he pulled her along at a break-neck pace.

By the time they burst into the open area where Malachi's family was carrying the body into the main tent, Savannah was completely out of breath and had a stitch in her side. She bent down to catch her breath as Malachi went to his parents, yelling to get their attention.

Everyone stopped and turned to look at him. "What's wrong?" Malachi's mother demanded.

He shook his head, his eyes wide as he looked back and forth between Savannah and his family, shock suddenly getting to him. "Shooting, in town. Mom, someone shot the store owner —we found him, and the store was deserted!" Malachi stared between his parents, apparently waiting for some reaction, but everyone had gone statue-still.

"We ran back here," Savannah explained, stepping in beside Malachi. "We kept hearing gunshots as we ran."

"I think the town is under attack, Dad. There was screaming, and so much gunfire…"

Malachi's father rushed forward at that, wrapping his arms around his son. "It's okay. God will protect us."

"Dad, something really bad is happening," Malachi said, his voice raspy.

Savannah hugged herself, wishing her dad was there with

them. Now that the adrenaline was wearing off, she felt terrified. What was happening?

"The world's gone mad!" Jim Loveridge said, as if answering her question. But it was the same question she saw on everyone's faces—everyone's but his, really. "This is what we've been preaching about. This is what we've been trying to warn people about," he continued, stepping back with his hands on Malachi's shoulders as he looked into his son's eyes.

One of the men who traveled with the family dropped to his knees and began to pray outside the tent. Another one followed suit. Jim turned to look at them, praising them for turning to God in their time of need, and Savannah took advantage of the moment to step up beside Malachi.

"What is he talking about?" Savannah asked in a hushed voice.

"It's the end times," he said, his eyes going wide with what almost looked like excitement.

"What?" she asked.

This can't be happening. This is a nightmare, not real life. Before she could give voice to her thoughts, however, Jim Loveridge walked towards her, took her hands in his, and smiled.

"This was predicted in the Bible. Society will fall," he told her calmly. "Chaos will ensue. It's time for us to go home."

"What do you mean, society will fall?" Savannah asked, looking beyond him to Malachi. He'd seemed so normal, but this... this wasn't normal.

"Famine, food shortages, lawlessness, it's all raining down upon us," Jim Loveridge said, looking up at the sky.

Savannah felt a sudden rush of doubt and fear. It was time for her to go. She didn't know these people all that well, and they seemed a little too excited about impending doom. If it was what they were predicting, she wanted to be with her dad. The last thing she wanted was to be with a group of strangers who seemed excited about the idea of the Bible predicting chaos.

"I need to go home," she whispered.

"No! You can't! It isn't safe," Jim said, a little too loudly. He looked at his wife, and Savannah saw the woman was nodding, her mouth set in a firm line.

"But, my dad—" Savannah began.

"We'll take you home in the morning, when it's daylight," Malachi's mother said firmly.

Her husband agreed. "Tonight, we pack up. We'll set out on foot tomorrow."

Savannah looked between them and Malachi, who seemed stunned. "Where will you go?" she asked.

"Home," Jim replied simply.

"Where's home?"

"Salt Lake City," Malachi answered. "That's where I was born."

"You're going to walk to Salt Lake City?" she asked incredulously.

Jim smiled. "It's the only way. We'll escort you back to your father in the morning."

She shook her head, unable to process the thought of walking that far. "Thank you," she muttered, not happy to be stuck overnight, but not exactly looking forward to walking through the town where it did appear that people had lost their minds. Hopefully, her father would understand her being out overnight—maybe he wouldn't even be back till morning himself, she reminded herself, if he'd also gotten stuck somewhere because of that meeting he'd headed off to.

"Thank you for trying to help out earlier," Jim said, motioning toward where Eli lay.

Savannah nodded, trying not to look at the covered body. "I'm so sorry for your family's loss."

"God has a plan. We can't know that plan, but we can accept it," he said, his tone weirdly serene.

Savannah nodded again. She couldn't have been so calm about it, but knew some people felt that way. Everyone had to deal with the loss of loved ones in their own way. "Thank you for letting me stay," Savannah said with a smile she didn't feel.

"Of course. Malachi, take her over to the trailer and talk with Gretchen. She'll get her set up with a cot in the kitchen tent," Jim said.

Immediately, Malachi took Savannah's hand and turned to face her. "I'm sorry I couldn't get you home. I know you must be worried about your dad."

"It's okay," she said, her voice going tight. "Your family is probably right. It isn't safe out there right now."

He ushered her away from his family, back toward the smaller tent. "We set up cots in the kitchen tent area after everyone goes home. We keep extra on hand in case anyone needs a place to stay for the night," he explained.

"Does that happen often?" she asked.

He let out a long sigh. "It does. My family has fed and sheltered many homeless people during our travels. We tend to collect people, as my mother would say. Gretchen is one of them, like her boyfriend Tim. They might as well be family in a lot of ways."

"That's amazing. Your family is so generous," she told him, some of her doubt from earlier draining away with a reminder of how kind-hearted this family seemed to be.

"Thank you. We like to do it."

"Malachi, the farm we're staying at..." Savannah began, thinking of it only now, "they have a lot of horses and even a few donkeys. Maybe the owner would be willing to let your family have a couple. You have so far to go. Wouldn't it be nice to have a couple horses?"

Malachi stopped walking. She could barely see his face in the dark shadows of the trees they were now standing in, but she sensed his excitement when he squeezed her hand. "That would be amazing. Maybe we can find a cart or a wagon like they used in the old days. I know I saw one in someone's yard on the other side of town," he said.

Savannah smiled, happy enough just to have brought him some joy on such a horrible night.

6

Savannah couldn't help feeling anxious as she walked with Malachi a few feet in front of his parents in the bright morning light. She'd wanted to run home to see her father as soon as the sun had come up, and did even now, but the revivalists had taken their sweet time packing things they wanted to take with them. Eli had been buried the night before, while she'd slept, and so the morning had been dedicated to planning. They'd talked about taking down the tents, but Jim had decided to leave them up for anyone seeking shelter. The tents were far too big and cumbersome to carry home, he'd pointed out. After what had felt like forever, once they had packed up as much as they could carry, the group of ten or so people had finally set out for the farm where Savannah had been staying with her father.

"Are you sure you're going to walk all that way?" Savannah

whispered.

"We have to. We can't stay here and live in a tent," he replied.

"But you've been living in tents," she pointed out—reasonably, she thought.

Malachi laughed. "No, we've had our motorhomes, with water and electricity and beds. We haven't actually been *living* in the tents."

"What if it isn't what your dad said? What if this is some kind of freak accident and things will be back to normal in a day or two?" she questioned, still not ready to believe the world was ending. "Then you'll have to walk back here to retrieve everything."

And, truly, even the way Malachi's family was acting didn't seem all that real. She'd certainly seen her fair share of wacko religious groups, as well as all the crazy Facebook posts about an apocalypse just around the corner. They were always disproven, though. It seemed like there was always someone claiming the end of the world was going to happen on a specific day, and then the day would come and go with the world completely unchanged. Granted, this did feel different and unlike all those doomsday warnings, but there'd been nothing to indicate things were about to get turned upside down last night. It had just happened. The fact that Malachi's family was embracing it almost felt stranger than the event itself.

Malachi simply looked at her, however, his eyes not nearly as bright and full of life as they'd been the day before when he'd come to meet her. "I believe my father," he said firmly.

"Okay," she murmured.

They continued walking in relative silence until they found themselves near the gas station where the man had been killed last night. Savannah couldn't help but stare at the scene, suddenly afraid to even pass it by.

"We need to keep going," Jim said in a soft voice, he and the rest of the group having overtaken the two teens on the road.

Malachi took her hand. "I'll be with you."

She nodded, walking behind two of the men that were a part of the group. Soon enough, the band of revivalists were past the dreaded gas station that looked unchanged from the night before, heading on down the middle of the road through town and passing the creamery as they walked around a few cars stalled in the road. It felt like she was walking through a ghost town. Everything had gone completely still and quiet. If there were people around, they were staying hidden.

When they were able to leave the town behind, she let out her breath and gripped Malachi's hand tighter in a quick 'thank you'—soon, they were at the head of the group again, her RV feeling within reach.

"Up there!" she called out as soon as she saw the fifth-wheel in the distance.

"Be careful," Jim advised her.

She had to fight the urge to run towards her home on wheels. "We can cut through the pasture!" she hollered, easily sliding between the two strings of barbed-wire that were stretched along the roadway to keep the horses in.

Malachi kept her hand in his and the group walked through the pasture behind them. Savannah's eyes scanned the area, her heart sinking. She should have known it when he hadn't come running to greet her, but she'd put off accepting it.

"He's not here," she whispered, slowing her walk as she reached the RV and looked around for her father's truck.

"How do you know?" Malachi asked.

"His truck isn't here," she said, willing herself not to cry. Where was he?

"It could have stalled like the others," Malachi offered.

The small group approached the trailer with Savannah in the lead. She tried to open the door, only to find it locked. Trying to tell herself that that meant he was still sleeping inside, she reached into her pocket and pulled out her key, fumbling with the lock before finally flinging the door open.

"Dad?" she called out, knowing he wasn't going to answer.

"Maybe he's looking for you?" Malachi suggested when it became apparent he wasn't there.

"Oh, he's going to be so mad," she groaned, going inside the trailer to make absolutely sure he wasn't inside.

Malachi and his family waited outside while she searched the small space, looking for a note or any signs he'd been there at all since they'd stepped outside together the night before.

"Could he be at the house?" Malachi offered when she stood in the doorway of the trailer, her spirit crushed.

"Yes! Let's go find him!"

The group started toward the sprawling farmhouse that had been built at the turn of the century and added onto over the decades. Savannah scanned the area as they approached, noticing the barn doors were wide open. That wasn't normal.

"Hold up!" Jim called out.

Savannah stopped walking, turning to look at Malachi's father. He was staring towards the carport... where she could see a body lying on the ground. Her first thought was that it was her father lying there, and she couldn't move. Her voice got lost somewhere in the giant lump lodged in her throat.

"Stay here and let my dad check," Malachi said, moving to stand in front of her, blocking her view of the body lying next to a tractor.

She blinked, and she thought she nodded, but she couldn't be positive. Ignoring Malachi's impulse to protect her, she stepped to the side, watching Malachi's father. It felt like an eternity as Jim walked up to the man, squatted beside him, and reached out to check for a pulse. Jim took a few more seconds before standing and coming towards where she and his son stood.

She knew she was holding her breath, but couldn't seem to force her lungs to expand. Jim's face told her it was bad. His lips were pressed into a thin line, his eyes sad and overly gentle.

"How old is your father?" Jim asked her.

What? She hadn't expected that. "Forty-four?" she said, a question mark on the end of her word.

A sigh left the man's throat, and a look of relief crossed his face. "It's not your father," Jim said confidently.

"It's not?" she squeaked.

"No. The man over there is much older—I'd say in his late sixties."

"Oh," she said weakly. The fact that it wasn't her father was a relief, but to think…

"Who is it?" Malachi asked.

"The farmer. Bob Little," she said quietly.

Malachi's mother moved to hug Jim. "What happened?" she asked.

"I'm afraid he was shot," he replied.

Savannah wilted, leaning against Malachi for support. Then she turned around to look at the barn, realization dawning as she started moving towards the building.

"Where are you going?" Malachi asked.

"The horses!" she cried out, picking up her speed.

She burst into the barn, her heart sinking as she realized her fear had been correct. Staring at the empty stalls, the doors all left open, she could only shake her head.

"Where are they?" Malachi asked from behind her.

"Gone. They're all gone."

There was a silence in the barn as they all processed what had happened. The lingering scent of horses and manure hung thick in the air. Straw lay scattered about the floor in front of each of the empty stalls.

"Someone stole the horses," Jim said, stating the obvious. "In these times, they're going to be valuable enough that people will kill for them."

"I'm sorry," Savannah said, looking back at Tonya and then Jim.

Jim reached out to grab her hand, holding it between his hands and looking her in the eye. "It isn't your fault. This is all God's plan. We have to accept it. We can't know what our future holds, but God does. We'll walk. Moses walked. Jesus walked. His followers walked for hundreds of miles. We can walk."

Savannah had no idea how the man could be so calm, so easy, but was glad he wasn't as devastated as she was. He almost sounded excited about his long journey. The man could be so normal one second, and then, the next, he said or did something that triggered her defenses.

"I'm so sorry. I had hoped to talk Mr. Little into giving you a couple horses."

Jim smiled. "We're in good health. God will provide. We should get going while the weather holds."

"Right now?" Savannah gasped.

"There is nothing holding us here. The sooner we get home, the better."

Before she could think what to say, Malachi grabbed her hand. "Come with us!" he suggested.

"I can't! My dad... I can't leave!" Savannah had near shouted in desperation, panicked at the very idea of leaving him behind. But they couldn't leave her here alone, could they?

Jim and Tonya Loveridge exchanged a look. "Sweetie, it isn't safe for you here. We can't leave you here in good faith. We'll take care of you."

She shook her head, staring among the three Loveridges. "I'm not leaving. I can't leave. My father is out there. He's probably looking for me right now," she protested.

"We can't leave you," Malachi said softly.

"I'm not leaving," she said, holding her chin up and putting her hands on her hips.

She couldn't understand why they thought they were suddenly in charge of her. She wasn't an orphan. Her father was out there somewhere. He was probably furious with her for worrying him. She wouldn't worry him more by walking away now.

Malachi looked at his parents. "Can we stay here a day or two until her father returns?"

His question took her by surprise—she'd hoped they'd stay, but thought it would be the adults who insisted, not him. He cared about her! He *really* cared, and didn't want to leave her alone. And, what a relief that she hadn't had to ask; she didn't think she could have gotten up the courage. Savannah looked at Malachi's parents, hoping they would agree. She wasn't going to go with them. She couldn't.

"You could stay in the house," she suggested. "Bob didn't have any family around. This might all be better in a day or two, too. Then, you could take your tents and your campers. You won't have to leave anything behind and come back for it," she pointed out.

She could see their hesitation and looked to Malachi, silently pleading with him to convince his parents it was a good plan.

"Let us talk about this," Jim answered them, a slight scowl on his face. "Your mother and I need a minute."

Malachi grabbed her hand and led her out of the barn, giving his parents some privacy. She looked around the farm, wondering if whoever had stolen the horses would still be nearby. They would have left the area, right? The worry was one more reason to hope the Loveridges would stay, at least until her dad returned.

She and Malachi walked around the area in front of the barn before passing by the other adults, who'd set to burying the farmer, and heading for the house. "We should wait for my parents," Malachi whispered.

"We're only going in the house," Savannah promised. "I need to see if Dad's inside, or maybe he left a note."

Malachi shook his head nervously, but followed her to the front door that was partially open. She knocked, feeling a little ridiculous considering that the man who lived in the house was lying dead outside.

"There could be someone in here! The someone who killed him," Malachi hissed.

"Then the horses would be here," she pointed out, pushing the door further open. "Hello!" she called out, stepping inside.

The living room with the worn couch and the old recliner looked just as it had every time she'd come over to visit or to give the man the rent for the week. It looked completely normal. They kept moving, turning left to go through an archway that led into the old kitchen.

"Wow," Malachi said, the single word summing up what they found.

The cupboards were all hanging open. There was a bag of rice spilled on the floor, various spices canisters and boxes tossed about, and the refrigerator door left wide open, as well. A funky smell was already starting to develop. The kitchen had been ransacked.

"I guess whoever killed him wanted his food," Savannah said, shaking her head.

"And carried it off on his horses." Malachi walked to the refrigerator and closed the door as if that would make it all better. Savannah turned around, taking in the sight of the mess and wondering what would have made someone act so horribly.

"Mal?" they heard Jim call out.

"In here!" he replied.

His parents appeared in the kitchen a minute later, their faces revealing their own shock at the scene before them. Tonya's mouth opened to form words, but then she closed it without speaking, her eyes wide as she surveyed the damage, as if it wasn't real.

"No way. We can't, Jim!" Tonya exclaimed.

Jim reached out and put an arm around his wife's shoulders. "Shh, it's okay. We'll be fine. It's the right thing to do."

"What's going on?" Malachi asked.

"We've talked about it, and we'll stick around for a day or two and wait for Savannah's father to get back. If he doesn't show up, we'll have to leave. We can't stay here, especially after seeing this," he said, waving an arm to encompass the kitchen.

Happy for the short reprieve, Savannah smiled in thanks. She just knew her father would be back sometime that day, even if he had to walk from wherever it was he'd gone to. He couldn't be all that far, and she knew her dad was tough. He would fight back if anyone tried to hurt him. She refused to believe anyone would shoot her father like they had the farmer. No way. There was no way this world would leave her without any parents. Plus, nobody would have reason to hurt him—all he had on him worth stealing would be his truck, and that was no good at the moment if things around town were any sign to judge by.

"Thank you," she said sincerely, focusing on Malachi's mother since she knew Tonya was against the decision.

The woman nodded, but it was her husband who answered. "Savannah, I'm willing to put my faith in God to keep us safe. I know how important it is to stay with family, especially in times of crisis. We'll offer you our company for two days," he said firmly.

"Okay. I'm sure he'll be back today, any minute now."

Jim looked her directly in the eye. "This is a dangerous place. My family is in no position to hang around here. We aren't violent people. We don't know how to defend ourselves and, honestly, I don't believe I would ever be able to raise my hand against another human. I need to do what's best for my family. We'll stay for two days, max. If your father doesn't return, you can come with us," he said, as if that were her only option.

Savannah nodded—not agreeing with him, but not openly arguing with him. "I understand. I appreciate you staying." She would smile and pretend to go along with whatever Malachi's parents said for now.

"Why don't we clean this up?" Tonya suggested, clapping her hands together.

"Clean it up?" Savannah repeated.

"Well, I can't function in a messy kitchen. Jim, you and Mal go help take care of the farmer. He deserves a proper burial. We'll have a small service for him later."

There was a new note of matriarchal determination in the woman's voice now, and Savannah was a little surprised by her take-charge attitude. In the brief time she had known Tonya Loveridge, she'd been meek, leaving all the decisions to her husband. Even five minutes ago, she had appeared to be shaken to her very core. This was a complete change in her personality. Savannah could actually admire this new woman standing in front of her and doling out orders like a drill sergeant.

Jim looked proud, as well. "We'll do that," he said before giving his wife a quick kiss on the cheek.

Malachi waved before they walked out of the kitchen. Savannah watched them leave, wishing Malachi could have stayed to help; being alone with his mother felt awkward, at best.

She turned to look around the kitchen once again, watching as Tonya closed cupboard doors and then disappeared into the dining room. She returned a few minutes later with a broom and a dustpan, smiling as she came back into the kitchen. For her part, Savannah began picking up items that had been scattered on the floor, setting them on the counter to be washed or put away. Cleaning the kitchen seemed like the least important problem in her opinion, but she didn't want to do anything to irritate the Loveridges. She did *not* want to be left alone.

7

Austin's eyes felt like sandpaper had been rubbed over them. He blinked several times, trying to orientate himself to his surroundings. It was the throbbing in his leg that brought it all back in a painful flash.

"Savannah," he mumbled, moving a hand to his face, rubbing the beard stubble and then his eyes.

Finally, he opened his eyes, staring up at the ceiling of Amanda's living room. He was on the couch, his broken leg piled high on several pillows. He looked down his body, covered with a blanket, and could see his toes peeking out. He didn't dare try to wiggle them. He'd done that once and paid a hefty price. Simply enough, he was stuck. Helpless. He couldn't walk out of the house and get to his daughter. Not even if he tried.

"Hey."

Amanda's scratchy voice had come from behind him, and he shifted to look for her. "What time is it?" he asked.

She laughed, the emotion behind it genuine. "I have no idea. I would guess around eight or nine, maybe. How's the leg?"

"It's fine. I need to get out of here, Amanda. I didn't mean to sleep so late," he groaned.

"I'll get you another pain pill and some antibiotics. You'll need to take them with food. I'll see what I can throw together," she said, yawning.

He watched her fold a blanket and put it on the coffee table next to the couch. "Did you sleep out here?" he asked her.

"Yep. I slept in the recliner just in case you started running a fever or got some wild idea to try and walk out of here," she said, stretching her back.

"Thank you," he said, wishing again that he didn't need this kind woman's help.

"Of course. Sit tight and I'll be back in a second."

Austin closed his eyes, breathing through a fresh wave of pain. He knew from experience that it was the second day of an injury that was always the worst. But he'd broken enough bones to also know that the pain was temporary. He could get through it.

He heard a knock on the front door then, and his eyes popped open as he involuntary stiffened, pulling the tender bruised muscles in his broken leg. With his position on the couch, he was blind to seeing much of anything. He could see the top half of the front door over the back of the couch, but little else. He felt completely exposed under this blanket in only his underwear, unable to walk. He needed his clothes. Suddenly, he remembered the drive Callum had given him. He wondered if it was still in his pocket, and if so, if it had been ruined by his impromptu swim. The case had looked waterproof, but there was no way to tell for sure without testing the thing. How to do that was something else entirely.

Interrupting his thoughts, Amanda walked through to the door. "Who is it?" she called out without opening it.

That was smart, Austin thought, but if anyone on the other side wanted in, the door wasn't going to do much good stopping them.

"It's Daniel Carver! I've got a heifer trying to calve and it isn't going well! Can you come help?" he hollered through the door.

Austin waited to hear what Amanda would do. He sat up on his elbows, peering over the couch, and watched her open the door, propping a long .22 rifle behind it. He smiled. She was *very* smart.

"Daniel, hey there," she greeted the man she obviously knew.

"Do you have phone service?" She popped her head outside. "Did you drive over here?"

A tall, lanky man wearing Wranglers, a button-up plaid, and a white cowboy hat stepped through the door when Amanda stepped back inside. Austin didn't have to see his feet to know he'd be wearing boots. The guy was a legit cowboy. He pulled off his hat, revealing a full head of brown hair that was a little too long, a ring around his head from where the hat had been sitting.

"My truck is toast," he said, nodding to Austin now that he saw him. "I don't know what happened. I rode my horse over here. My phone doesn't work, either, or I would have called you. I'm real sorry to barge in here like this, but she's been laboring all night. I waited as long as I could, but I would really appreciate your help," he pleaded.

Amanda looked at Austin, then back at her friend. "Sure. Let me grab my things and change. You go ahead and I'll be right behind you."

"You gonna drive over?" he asked.

"The battery in my truck died and I haven't had a chance to do anything about it."

Daniel nodded at her, and then glanced over at Austin one last time before walking out the door. Austin had a feeling there was a little jealousy happening there. Daniel was probably in his forties, and Austin hadn't noticed a ring on his finger. He probably had the hots for the pretty vet and didn't appreciate finding a man on her couch.

Amanda closed the door behind him and then looked to Austin as if to judge what Daniel would have seen or guessed was going on. With a chuckle, she shrugged before disappearing back into the kitchen. She came back a minute later with a can of Sprite and a bowl.

"Are you sure it's safe for you to go?" he asked.

She raised an eyebrow at him. "I've known Daniel most of my life. He's a good guy, and I can take care of myself anyway. As for you? Here's a bowl of Raisin Bran minus the milk and a warm Sprite to wash down the meds. I know it isn't gourmet, but it will put something in your stomach."

He moved to sit up a little more even as Amanda sprang into action, piling pillows behind him to prop him up. "Thank you, seriously, I cannot tell you how glad I am it was you who pulled me out of that water."

She grinned. "You did need a vet, that's for sure. Now, eat and take your meds; I need to change and get over to Daniel's."

Austin used the spoon to take a bite of the dry cereal. He nearly choked on the dry bran flakes. The can of warm soda barely helped wash down the cereal, and then he popped the pills in his mouth and took another drink.

"Are my clothes nearby?" he called out, not sure where she was in the house.

"I'll grab them. I hung them out to dry last night—hopefully, they've had a chance," she called out in response, her voice muffled.

Amanda came into view a few minutes later. "I'm going to leave my rifle next to you, just in case. Here's your clothes. The jeans are still a little damp."

"Great," he mumbled, eyeing the rifle and knowing he could do little to fend off an attacker in his current condition.

"I'll be as fast as I can. Daniel is capable. Once I deliver the calf, I'll be back," she told him.

He looked at the brown duffel bag she was carrying, with *Amanda Patterson* displayed in gold lettering on the side. "Be safe," he said, hoping it wasn't the last time he saw her.

What else could he do but wait, though? He truly was at her mercy, something he didn't like in the least. He had never been helpless.

"Trust me, calving is icky, but it isn't dangerous," she said with a smile.

Austin finished the cereal only because he knew the pain meds required it, the roof of his mouth feeling a little abused by the crunchy flakes. Having set the bowl down, he then leaned back against the pillows and let his eyes roam around the room. The silence was mind-boggling. He'd been on the Little farm for a couple weeks with Savannah, but it had never been this quiet. Here, there was nothing to break up the monotony of silence. No train whistles or rumbles of a diesel engine in the distance. He couldn't hear planes or anything overhead. It was dead silent. It was as if the wildlife that was normally out and about didn't want to disturb the quiet. He strained his ears, listening for the sound of a bird call, and still heard nothing.

It was too weird, too strange, and being alone and unable to move stirred up a little panic deep in his gut. Out of nowhere, he heard the screech of a hawk. Relief washed over him. For a brief moment, he'd been worried they were dealing with something much more sinister than an EMP.

"Okay, everything is still normal, minus electricity," he assured himself.

He relaxed for a few moments, but then realized he was facing another problem that was far more pressing than the lack of bird calls outside.

"Seriously?" he groaned, reaching for the crutches that were lying on the ground next to the Remington .22.

He had to pee. Having been on the couch for a good twelve hours, of course, he needed the bathroom. He was actually a little glad Amanda wasn't around now. She would have insisted on helping him, and that was the last thing he wanted help with from a complete stranger. Let alone a pretty female stranger. He threw off the blanket, only then remembering he was essentially naked. He debated on struggling with the jeans or taking the chance that he was well and truly alone and going outside in only his boxers. It would certainly make what he needed to do a lot easier.

Boxers it was. He had to go, after all, and knew it would be a long process to get his jeans on, especially considering they were still damp. He gently moved his wrapped leg, wincing with pain as he lifted it, turning his body at the same time and carefully putting it down. He grabbed one crutch, standing it in front of him while using his right arm to push himself off the couch.

"Dammit," he growled as the pain washed over him.

He managed to get to a standing position, though his leg felt like a lead ball hanging from his thigh. There would be no water, so using the toilet would be pointless. He was going to have to go outside. He vaguely remembered the covered porch he'd had to climb to get into the house.

"Screw that," he mumbled. He was not going down those stairs. He'd pee off the end of the porch. Desperate times called for desperate measures and a shelving of proper etiquette. There was no way he could go in search of a tree.

Just getting out the door was painful enough, but he hobbled along to the end of the porch facing away from the driveway and the swollen stream beyond it. As he relieved himself, he scanned the area. The burnt out remains of Amanda's barn were on his left, pasture beyond it. Directly in front of him, he could see what looked like corn growing about a foot high, moving in the slight breeze washing over the farm.

The air was already warm, and he could smell the charcoal and hint of smoke lingering in the air as the breeze kicked up. He used the crutches to walk back to the opposite end of the covered porch and saw her Ford 250 sitting in the driveway. He smiled, thinking they were kindred spirits with matching rigs, his just a little newer and shinier.

He scanned the area before heading back inside. His body was stiff and sore. He knew that, without the pain meds she'd given him, he'd have been in far more pain. It was his good fortune that had brought her to his rescue. Now, he just needed a little more good luck to leave and find his daughter.

Seeing the barn's remains had given him an idea, though. They couldn't drive off, and he was in no shape to walk forty miles on crutches, but surely, he could ride a horse. When Amanda got back, he was going to ask her to borrow one. He'd find a way to pay her or return the horse once things returned to normal. Fumbling his way back inside, he tried not to think about the fact that 'normal' could be a long way away.

Austin sat on the couch as carefully as he could, propping his leg back up and relaxing against the pillows. He was sweating with the exertion it had taken to go pee. That didn't bode well for his grand plans to ride a horse forty miles back to his trailer. Maybe tomorrow, things would look brighter. For now, he'd have to trust Bob Little to look out for his daughter. With that depressing thought, Austin tossed the blanket over his thighs, leaving his bare chest and lower legs exposed before closing his eyes and trying to breathe through the pain that was racking his body. He could feel the drowsiness growing with every passing second now, and welcomed the idea of sleeping through the pain. Soon, he felt himself drifting off, and didn't fight the urge to close his eyes.

"What the hell?" he snapped, jerking awake at the sound of a loud crash.

He jerked up to a seated position, only remembering he wasn't in good shape after his leg fell off the pillow. He cursed out loud, nearly biting his tongue; it felt like he'd broken the bone all over again.

He didn't have time to worry about the pain, though. Someone was in the house, and he was only lucky he'd cursed quietly instead of screamed outright. He gingerly rolled off the couch with the help of one crutch, finding the rifle and quickly checking to see if it was loaded. One bullet was not going to do him a lot of good, he thought angrily. What good was a gun with a single bullet?

Whoever was in the house was in the back room. They must not have seen him lying on the couch, and he had been hopped up on painkillers and not heard a thing until they'd gotten careless and loud with whatever they were doing.

"It's in that cabinet," a male voice called out.

More than one person in the house, then, which meant he absolutely needed more than a single bullet. A gun cabinet with a glass door was against the wall nearby, and he could see a shotgun and what looked to be another long rifle in the rack. He hated gun cabinets with glass doors—they were completely ineffective for actually keeping the guns safe, but in this case, it was a godsend. Not wasting another second, he pulled himself over to the cabinet, hoping there were some cartridges stored there.

The gun cabinet was locked, of course. He looked around and saw a framed picture of an older couple sitting on an end table. He grabbed it and did his best to shatter the glass as quietly as possible, using a nearby afghan to muffle the sound. He could hear the men in the other room, knocking things over and talking to one another. He was praying they were too loud to hear him.

Using one hand to keep himself propped up via the crutch, he kept one eye on the hallway as he reached in and found several boxes of shells and bullets. Without hesitating, he pulled the long rifle off the rack, quickly loaded the gun, and waited, knowing the thieves would be tossing the rest of the house soon enough. Leaning against the cabinet, the crutch under his armpit, he could just stay steady enough to use the rifle if he needed to.

Waiting allowed the pain to come back to him, though, along

with the drowsiness the meds had brought on. Austin blinked, trying to focus his eyes. The pain was crippling, and ignoring it was getting harder. He had to focus on making sure his aim was true when those men appeared. It'd been a while since he'd shot a rifle, and he wasn't looking forward to taking a life, but he would do whatever was necessary to stay alive.

"Come on, let's see if there's any food," he heard one of the male voices say.

He held the gun barrel up, pressing the butt against his shoulder, his finger hovering over the trigger.

"Whoa!" the first man down the hall called out when he noticed Austin propped against the gun cabinet, and in nothing but a neon pink leg cast and his boxers.

"What?" his buddy asked, appearing with a small box.

"Put whatever it is you're trying to steal down and get out of here before I kill you," Austin growled, gesturing to the door with the rifle.

The two men, or maybe older teens, were scruffy and unshaven—they looked to be homeless, and Austin would have bet money they were drug addicts. Only drug use had a way of making young men look so aged and worn.

"Dude, you can't even walk," one of the guys shot back.

"I don't need to walk," Austin answered. "I only need to

shoot. Put the box down and leave," he repeated, his voice calm and steady.

The two addicts exchanged a look, and Austin saw the moment they decided to ignore his demands. He fired off a shot, aiming over their heads so that it slammed into the wall directly behind them. Then he cocked the rifle again, prepared to shoot one or both of them if necessary.

"Dude!" one of them screamed, though the other seemed frozen.

"That was a warning shot. Put the box down or I shoot you first," he said, aiming the barrel at the guy carrying the box. "Then you," he said, moving the barrel to the other man, lining it up with his face.

The men looked at one another again, then back to Austin. "You can't chase us. We could just run out of here," the guy holding the box reasoned.

Austin smirked. "Run. I don't mind shooting you in the back. Can you outrun a bullet?"

"Leave it—we'll find stuff somewhere else," the first guy said, looking anxious.

There was a moment of hesitation from the guy with the box before he dropped it on the ground, pill bottles rolling out. Austin looked at him evenly, one eyebrow raised as he realized they had been stealing Amanda's vet medicine.

"Get out now before I decide to shoot you anyway," he warned them a moment later, when it seemed they were still debating their next move.

With that, the guys raced for the front door, leaving it open behind them. Austin didn't move in response; he just held the gun up, aimed at the door in case the guys came back. Eventually, his arm grew tired and he slowly lowered the gun, putting the safety on before resting it beside his outstretched legs. That had been close, and the tweakers weren't going to be the last of it. He had a feeling that anyone in the area who knew Amanda was a vet was going to be trying to do the same thing. Medicine and painkillers were going to be a valuable commodity.

Meanwhile, Savannah was out there all alone in the chaos. The thought of her encountering guys like he just had made his heart hurt. He had to get to her, to protect her. His only prayer was that the farm they'd been staying on was far enough off the beaten path that no one would mess with her. And while Bob Little was an old man, he was feisty. He'd protect Savannah until Austin could get there. There was enough food in the trailer for her to survive the next few days, at least. The water tank was full, too, which meant she would have clean drinking water.

"The pump," he groaned then, realizing the pump would require electricity to run.

Okay, so she wouldn't have water in the RV, but Bob had to

have a water tank somewhere on the property. Savannah was smart enough to know she had to boil the water first. Thinking of that, Austin took some small comfort in knowing their time traveling the country in the trailer had given her some basic knowledge in camping off-grid, and knowing how to handle a situation like this, much as anyone could if they hadn't been expecting it.

His eyes drifted to his bright pink leg before he looked down at his chest, the large gauze bandage on his ribs standing out against his tanned skin. There was no denying he was in rough shape. He couldn't simply get off the couch and go to his kid. The feeling of being helpless was hard to cope with, but he'd have to accept it—no matter what his parental instincts were screaming at him. Normally, he was a strong, capable man—not the man sitting on the floor, unable to stand on his own—but that wasn't today. Today, he was just short of helpless.

The only way he could help Savannah was to give himself a day or two to heal. "I'm coming, Savannah, I'm coming. You hold on and stay safe," he whispered, fighting back the sudden tears that threatened to fall as he imagined her all alone, scared out of her mind.

8

Savannah lay in the bed where her father should have been sleeping. She couldn't sleep in the farmer's house with the rest of the group. She wanted to stay in the trailer in case her dad came back in the middle of the night. Night after night, she waited up, hoping she would hear his truck pull up outside. There had been so many times when she'd fallen asleep and dreamed she heard the sound and woke up, expecting to see him standing there, wondering why she was in his bed. Every time, she'd been left sad and disappointed to find it was only a dream.

She heard a knock on the door of the trailer and pulled the pillow over her head. She didn't want to face the day. Every day had been a fight to keep the Loveridge family there. They wanted to go. They reminded her of that fact all day long.

"Are you awake?" Malachi called out in a soft voice.

The thin doors of the fifth-wheel did little to block sound. She rolled out of the comfy, queen-size bed and got to her feet, opening the door that separated the bedroom from the living space of their trailer and moving to unlock the door. Malachi was standing outside, smiling and holding out a plate of scrambled eggs.

"Hi," she said, stepping down to meet him.

"My mom made you some eggs," he said, presenting her with the breakfast.

The Loveridge family was resourceful. Every morning, Jim built a small fire in a firepit in front of the house, and every morning for the past three days, Tonya had eggs collected from the hens that the rancher had kept. The thieves hadn't taken the chickens, most likely because catching chickens was a lot like herding cats. There'd been talk about butchering one of the hens to eat for dinner, but no one in the group had the first clue how to go about killing and plucking the bird.

Savannah smiled. "Thank you."

She stood back, letting Malachi into the trailer. She self-consciously smoothed her hair down, slightly embarrassed to be seeing him the moment she rolled out of bed. The power still hadn't been restored, which surprised Savannah. Jim Loveridge was only more convinced he was right, and that they were headed for the so-called end times.

"Are you going to eat?" she asked, a little put off by being the only one with a meal in front of her.

"I already ate," he said with an easy smile.

She took the plate and sat it on the table, gesturing for him to sit across from her. He took a seat, but awkwardly, and suddenly she could tell by the look on his face something was wrong. He was acting different, and now that he was inside the RV, he wouldn't look her in the eyes.

"What's wrong?" she asked quietly, pushing the plate to the side.

"Savannah, my parents… they want to leave," he said, apology coming through in his voice.

"What? Already?"

"It's been three whole days. My dad said he's already given you a day more than he agreed to."

"But Dad's not back yet!"

Malachi looked out the window instead of at her. "I know, but it isn't safe here. Those men yesterday who passed by on the road, they could have hurt us. My dad says he knows they'll come back with guns. Savannah, we don't have guns. We have nothing to defend ourselves with. The baseball bat, shovels, and pitchforks are no match for a gun."

She shook her head, thinking about the group Malachi was

talking about. "They were only looking for food. They left when they saw your dad's friend come out of the barn with that shovel," she insisted.

He sighed, still avoiding her gaze. She followed his gaze, watching his mother heading off into the trees with a small shovel. Their bathroom situation wasn't pleasant. "But what if it's someone else next time?" he asked. "What if the people who shot that poor farmer come back?" he pointed out.

"Don't you think the police or National Guard will be here soon?" she asked.

He shrugged. "Maybe."

"Then, we can wait a couple more days," she begged. She stared into his dark brown eyes, waiting for him to agree. His hair had been pulled back into a ponytail, giving her a clear view of his face, but he still wouldn't meet her eyes.

"It's not up to me, Savannah. I don't want you to be hurt. This is for the best."

She groaned, fighting the urge to throw the plate of eggs at the wall. "I can't go. You said we could look for him today."

"I'm sorry. I will ask my dad if we can go into town again, but I have a feeling he will say no. It's too dangerous," Malachi stated, not for the first time.

"Malachi, I can't leave my dad," she whispered, tears threatening.

"Savannah, he isn't here. We haven't found his truck. Don't you think he would have come back by now if he could? You have to think about whether or not something's… happened to him."

Her mouth fell open. "Don't say that!"

It was something they had all been tiptoeing around the last couple of days, but she wouldn't think of it. Not really. Savannah knew her dad wasn't supposed to have been going far when he'd left that night. He had told her he'd be gone an hour, or maybe two. It made sense he would have walked back to the trailer if he could, yeah, but that only meant something had delayed him. It didn't mean he'd been hurt, or worse.

"I want you to be safe. Come with us. Let us protect you. Let *me* protect you," Malachi begged her, his eyes suddenly catching hers.

"How is it going to be safer at your home? How can you protect me? You said a shovel wasn't enough," she snapped, using his own defense to prove her point.

"Our city might not be in the dark. This could be isolated to this region," he said, parroting the words she'd heard Jim say several times.

"And if it isn't? What if the city is dark? You think the craziness here is bad, imagine what it will be like in the city!"

"We don't live in the city, but on the outskirts," he corrected her.

She rolled her eyes. "We're out in the boonies here and it's dangerous."

"Savannah, we have to go back home," Malachi said simply. "It's where we belong," he said, reaching across the table and grabbing her hand.

"I have to try and find him," she insisted, though she didn't pull her hand away.

Malachi nodded, pulling his hand from hers before pushing the plate back towards her. "Eat. You need to keep up your strength."

She sighed, knowing that they were at an impasse, and he wouldn't leave her alone until she ate the eggs. The chickens had been laying regularly, providing the Loveridges and their small group of followers with food, but the whole group had been eating plentifully. They'd found a deep freeze in the basement filled with beef, too, and Savannah knew that the stockpiled meat had helped make it easier for Jim Loveridge to keep his group on the farm for longer than planned. They had feasted on steaks that first night and been eating well at every meal since. Everyone had agreed that it would make sense to ration what food they had, but since nobody knew how to turn the beef into jerky, and there weren't enough canned goods to expect them to last long anyway, they'd been eating what was available.

Jim refused to contemplate the idea that they'd eventually have to loot for more food, though, and insisted God would provide for them, just as Bob Little's farm had provided for them over these few days. Savannah was beginning to wonder what God's provisions would look like if things got worse before they got better. She realized she really was in the wrong group, but it wasn't like she had a lot of options.

She finished the eggs that had long grown cold, and Malachi left her alone to change clothes. He was supposed to try to convince his father to let them go back into town, but she had a feeling that he was anxious to leave, as well. There was nothing here for any of them. She was holding them all back.

And she'd never forgive herself if something happened to them because they'd chosen to stay and wait with her.

9

Malachi Loveridge sat down in one of the plastic lawn chairs, doing his best to relax. The big fifth-wheel wasn't too far away, parked under a few trees to keep it shielded from the hot sun. He felt as if he were being pulled in two as he looked from the fifth-wheel back to the house where his family and their friends were resting.

His heart wanted to stay with Savannah, but duty told him he had to stay with his family. He wasn't the type of kid to rebel against his parents, either. They'd worked hard to shelter him from the tragedies of the world. He didn't even feel the *need* to rebel against them. They'd always home-schooled him, choosing to educate him in the Bible instead of math books, and he loved traveling the country with them. People always asked him if he felt like he was missing out on things other kids his age did, but he didn't. Not really.

At least, not until now. Any question of what other kids did brought to mind dating, socializing, and lately, Malachi only thought about Savannah. She was different than the other girls he had met. Plenty of girls came to the revivals, but none of them were as pretty or as smart as Savannah. She was special. He'd known it the moment he'd first seen her. Since then, his parents had talked to him a little about his feelings for her and warned him to be careful. She wasn't a believer in the Bible and could lead him astray if he wasn't careful. And he knew that, but he was also sure she could one day be just as faithful as his family if he got the time to teach her.

"Son, you look so peaceful out here," his mother said, coming to sit beside him in another lawn chair.

"Mom, can we stay another day?" he asked.

"Oh, Mal, you know what your father said."

"I do, but isn't it our duty to comfort the hurt?" he asked, purposefully using her own words.

She smiled. "You're a good son. You know we will do all we can to help your friend, but we have to think of her safety as well as yours. We can't force her to come with us, but we can pray about it."

"What if she's the one chosen for me?"

She looked a little surprised. "Malachi," she breathed out. "Really? Do you feel that connection with this girl?"

He shrugged, uncomfortable with the way his mother was suddenly appraising him. "I don't know. I feel something for her."

His mother reached out to him, putting her hand on his knee. "You're a young man growing into manhood. Young, pretty girls are going to catch your eye. They are a temptation. You have to be strong."

"Mom," he groaned.

She shook her head, the very motion cutting off more of a complaint. "Malachi, you know what is right and wrong. If she comes with us and you believe she is the one chosen for you, she will need to accept our Lord and Savior. You cannot let a pretty girl lead you down the wrong road," she reminded him.

Following his gaze to the RV, she patted his leg and walked away. He'd had a feeling that's what she would say. His parents would never allow him to marry a woman who didn't believe the same as they did. But Savannah was young, and he felt sure he could teach her to be a faithful follower of the Bible. His parents had always told him he'd meet someone made just for him, who'd follow with him on this path. It had never felt possible until he'd met Savannah. That had to mean something.

As if she'd felt him thinking about her, Savannah exited her trailer and headed his way. Her long hair blew in front of her. He smiled, watching her push it away. He could see the stress and worry on her face, and hated to see her hurting. He wanted to make her smile again.

"Hi," she said, taking the seat his mother had vacated.

"You look nice today," he complimented her.

She groaned. "I need a shower."

"You're beautiful."

"Thank you," she murmured, a flush rising in her cheeks as she glanced away. "What'd your mom say? Did you ask her if you could stay another day?" she asked anxiously.

He nodded, looking away. "I did. They say we are leaving early in the morning."

She put her head back, looking at the sky and sighing. "He has to come back!"

"I'm sorry, Savannah. I really am. I can't imagine what you're going through. My family is here for you, though. They will take you in. You can live with us."

She turned to look at him, horror on her face. "My dad isn't dead!"

He sighed. "Okay, but until you find him, you should stay with us."

She was quiet for seconds, and then a full minute. Finally, he saw something shift in her face. "Okay," she said.

He sat up straighter, shocked she'd given in. "Really?"

"Yeah... yeah, I think so. I don't want to be here alone. I've been thinking about it a lot today, and I think it's what my dad would want me to do. He'd want me to stay safe. I'll leave him a note, letting him know where we're going so that he can come after me whenever he gets back."

Malachi couldn't stop smiling. "Great! Let's go tell my parents!"

He grabbed her hand and together they headed inside the house. His father was sitting at the dining room table, a map spread out in front of him. He and one of the revivalists were quietly talking, tracing their fingers over the map.

"Dad," Malachi called out.

His father turned to look at them, his eyes going to their joined hands before looking back at his son's face. "What is it, Mal?" he asked.

"Savannah will be going with us tomorrow," he announced, pride and excitement feeling like they'd burst his chest.

His father's eyes lit up. "Great!" His face turned to Savannah's, grinning in relief. "I look forward to having you along."

"What are you doing?" she asked, moving forward to look at the map.

"We're planning our route home," he replied.

She stared at the map, and then spoke slowly. "I know this place," she said, putting her finger on Colorado, near to where Jim Loveridge's finger had been left pointing.

"You do?" Malachi asked, moving forward.

Her eyes lit up as she turned to him. "Yes! My Uncle Ennis lives in the area, right outside of Denver. It's on the way to Salt Lake City. I can go there and wait for my dad!"

Malachi couldn't help feeling a little disappointed to hear she was still looking for a way not to go back to the city with them, but he swallowed down the emotion. "Great!" he said, faking the enthusiasm in his voice. At least she'd still be traveling with them.

Savannah looked happier than she had in days, too, which made him happy. "I should go pack!" she exclaimed, and with that she gripped his hand with a tight squeeze before hurrying away.

He watched her walk out of the house before turning back to his dad, trying to hide the disappointment he felt.

"She loves her family," his father said quietly.

Malachi nodded. "I know."

"If it's meant to be, it will happen. Don't push these things."

"Dad, we need to arm ourselves," he said, abruptly changing the subject.

His father stared back at him a moment, as if processing the jump, but then shook his head. "No. We will not raise arms against anyone. We are all God's children."

"It's dangerous, Dad. You've said it time and again. We have to be able to protect ourselves. We can't carry those shovels and pitchforks five hundred miles," Malachi argued.

"We will not hurt people!" his father said, standing up to face him.

"Jim, he's right," his friend Ken said.

All but holding his breath now that an adult had voiced agreement with him, Malachi waited for his dad to say it was wrong and went against the Ten Commandments. He turned back to look at him, a sadness in his eyes.

To his surprise, he confessed, "You're right. I saw a gun in the closet of the master bedroom."

"I'll get it," Malachi said, relieved at the idea that he would have a weapon to defend his family and Savannah. He would not ask his father to carry the gun or use it. It would kill his father if he had to take another man's life. Malachi would carry that burden.

Malachi walked to the back bedroom, opening the closet and rummaging around in the dark until he saw the small wooden box on the floor. He pulled it out and opened it, finding a revolver. It looked to be an old gun, like the kind the cowboys used in the old days. Malachi carefully took it out of the box, feeling the weight of it in his hands. He tried to turn the circular barrel, but had no real idea how to check to see if it was loaded. Carefully, he instead carried the gun out to the dining table, where Ken was still sitting with his father.

"Uh, Ken, do you know how to check and see if there are bullets in here?" he asked, holding the gun at his side, pointed at the ground.

His father looked at the gun, shaking his head before excusing himself. Ken rose and took the gun from Malachi's hand, holding it in his palm and smiling.

"This is an old gun, a Smith and Wesson Chief Special," he said with awe as he easily popped open the barrel and showed Malachi. "Empty. We'll need to see if we can find some rounds. It looks like it's in good shape, but I'd hate to have this thing misfire and hurt someone."

"How do we know what kind of bullets it needs?" Malachi asked, completely unfamiliar with firearms.

"This is a .38 special. She packs a punch—assuming we can find something to load her with," Ken replied, closing the barrel and placing the gun on the table.

Malachi stared at it, wondering if he could use the gun to actually hurt someone. It suddenly felt wrong, as his father had always said it was. Jim Loveridge wasn't a man who believed in an eye for an eye—he believed in the sacredness of life,

God's greatest gift, and felt that nobody had the right to steal such a life from another man. No matter what.

"Maybe we should leave it," Malachi said in a low voice. "Dad thinks—"

Ken put a hand on Malachi's shoulder, cutting him off. "I'll handle it. You and your dad don't need to worry about this," he assured him.

Malachi nodded, not without some relief, and headed out of the house. His earlier conviction to take on the burden for his father was waning. He wasn't sure he was ready to take on the responsibility that came with being the group's primary protector, as that gun would assuredly make him.

10

A ustin used the crutches to move across the soft earth of the pasture, making his way towards Amanda, who was chatting happily to her horses. The pain was still present in his leg, but it was more of a dull ache now, thanks to the pain meds. It was the cut on his side that had been bothering him more than anything that day. It made it difficult to move on the crutches, stretching and pulling the injured skin.

"What are you doing?" Amanda gasped when she saw him walking towards her.

"I got tired of sitting on that couch," he answered simply.

He also wanted to prove to her he wasn't a complete invalid. He needed to show her he could move around without a great deal of pain. It was the only way he was going to convince her he was ready to leave her farm.

"Austin, you can't overdo it," she lectured him, one hand still on her horse's nose.

He ignored her comment, looking at the mare she was petting. There were three other horses happily eating grass a short distance away.

"Can we ride them?" he asked.

"I can ride them fine," she returned.

He shook his head. "I can't stay here any longer. I need to get back. I understand you don't want to go. I'm not asking you to, but I am asking you to let me borrow a horse."

"I can't let you go alone, and you know it," she said, her lips tightening with frustration.

"I don't know that it's up to you, and I know for damn sure that you can't stop me if I want to leave," he growled.

They had been having the same argument for days. He'd been itching to go while she had been adamant he not leave until he'd healed—or, healed more, at least. The cut on his rib cage had been mildly infected. Making the situation worse, he'd ripped a stitch out yesterday while maneuvering on the crutches, earning him a stern lecture from his pseudo-doctor.

"Amanda, I appreciate all you have done for me, I really do, but I can't sit here knowing Savannah's out there on her own. I'm assuming you don't have children, all things considered, but if you did, maybe you'd understand what I'm feeling a little better," he said, trying to be as gentle as possible with the rebuke.

Her eyes narrowed, and her hands dropped to her hips. "No, I don't have kids, but that doesn't make me inhuman or unable to understand basic emotions! I understand you want to get to her, Austin, but you're no good to her dead."

He glared at her, unwilling to back down. "I'm not being mean. I'm only trying to make you understand how hard this is for me. It's killing me not being able to be there for her!"

"So, you think killing yourself trying to get there is a better idea?" she replied, eyeing his crutches pointedly.

"I have to try! That's what parents do! They walk through fire to get to their kids. I'm the only parent she has!" he near-yelled, the frustration of being laid up and essentially useless boiling over as he thought of his lost wife. His daughter only had one parent to depend on, and here he was in the middle of a pasture in the middle of Nowhere, U.S.A, forty miles from his kid.

She stomped a foot, calling his attention back to her. "I'm trying to keep you alive for your daughter!"

"Good. Great. You succeeded, but now I have to get back home," he said, trying to calm his voice.

Losing their tempers and going in circles was getting them nowhere. In the back of his mind, he knew Amanda had been right to keep him planted on her couch for the first few days. He would have killed himself if it had been left to him. But now...

"You know, if you were such a great father, looking out for his daughter, maybe you shouldn't have jumped off a bridge!" she snapped.

He rolled his eyes. "I didn't jump off the bridge."

"Oh, really, now you're ready to tell me the story?" she asked.

He wasn't about to tell her the story. Not yet.

He didn't know her and didn't know how much he could trust her. Plus, he certainly didn't want to put her life in danger. He had no idea if the people who had killed Callum would still be looking for him or not, but the USB driver was in his pocket, still incased in its protective plastic case. He wasn't sure what he was going to do with it, but something told him to hold onto it and keep his mouth shut about the damn thing.

"I fell into the water," he muttered, his eyes going back to the horses. How difficult would it be to get on and off was what worried him more than anything else.

"Whatever. Not only are you in no condition to walk or ride forty miles, but I can't leave my animals, my house, and all of my supplies untended. Look what happened when you were in the house. If people figure out I'm gone, they're going to loot my house," she said.

"They've already tried," he replied dryly.

She rolled her eyes. "Tweakers are nothing new. They're always around."

"Then stay. I'm going," he said firmly.

"You don't know where you're going," she reminded him.

"I'll find the highway and go from there," he shot back.

"Have you ever ridden a horse?" she asked, the hand back on her hip and a snide look on her face.

"Yes, Amanda, I've ridden a horse. Is that all you needed to hear?"

She smiled, but it wasn't a friendly smile. It was cynical and made him a little nervous. "Have you ever ridden bareback? My saddles were in the barn that burned to the ground the night I was fishing you out of the stream."

"How hard can it be?" he asked.

She threw her head back and laughed, harder than he'd seen her laugh before, her black hair blowing around her. "Oh, piece of cake, that's why everybody does it!" she said with a heavy dose of sarcasm.

He looked at the horse standing next to her, and then at the others contentedly grazing. "What about that one?" He pointed to a chestnut that looked significantly smaller than the black mare in front of him. And 'smaller' meant he'd have an easier time getting up on the creature's back.

"You want to ride him?"

"Are you saying he's not a good horse to ride?" he countered.

"I'm saying I ride him all the time, but you, well, you'll die if you try to climb onto his back." She grinned. "Plus, he's too small for you—at your height, you'd only hurt him."

He raised an eyebrow. "Okay, so I'm too tall," he acknowledged. "You want to tell me why I'd die climbing on his back?"

"Because Johnie's mean and fast—two things I know you can't handle."

Austin glanced back to the harmless-looking horse. "Oh."

"We can try you with this girl, maybe. Raven is a kind soul. She'll probably only try and throw you once or twice," she said with a chuckle, nearly making Austin rethink the whole idea.

He couldn't let the thought of falling stop him, though. He had to get back to his kid, and the only way that was going to happen was on the back of a horse.

"Okay. How do I get up?"

She shook her head, clearly not happy she hadn't scared him

off. "I'll take her to the porch. You can stand on the steps to get up. I'm not lifting you."

"Fine with me," Austin agreed evenly.

She walked ahead of him as he carefully moved across the wet ground. He didn't want to risk the crutch slipping and sending him to the ground. Once he made it to the porch, he used the crutches to climb the steps, only a little worried he'd tumble backwards. He'd made progress over the last few days.

"Okay, stand on your good leg, and I'll try and help you get the broken leg up and over," she instructed him.

He nodded, looking at the horse and realizing just how stupid and dangerous it was to attempt this with a leg that hadn't had the chance to heal. And they weren't even talking about how he'd get on and off without Amanda there to help him. He almost changed his mind, but an image of Savannah scared and alone popped into his mind, giving him the courage he needed to try.

"Here goes nothing," he breathed, lifting his bum leg up. Amanda held it up while he hugged the horse's neck and tried to mount the patient mare.

But, almost immediately, he realized it wouldn't work. The pain in his leg was severe, and getting worse. Then he felt the cut on his side tear and knew there was no way he could even get onto the horse without seriously injuring himself all over again, let alone ride forty miles.

"Give up?" she asked in a soft voice when he stopped actively trying to climb on.

He grunted, willing himself not to fall apart. "Yes."

She carefully moved his leg away from the horse's back, and then slapped the horse on the butt and sent it running back out to the pasture.

"I'm sorry," she whispered. "I really am. I want to help you, but you are not well. Please, will you give it a couple more days?"

He nodded through gritted teeth. "Yes."

"Do you want some pain meds?" she asked.

"Yes," he breathed out, unable to move from his spot where he leaned on his crutch.

"Give yourself a minute, and then we'll go inside," she said, no judgement in her voice.

He felt the heavy weight of defeat weighing him down. At least he'd tried, he told himself. He just wasn't ready to make the journey. Savannah was going to have to hold on a little longer. He closed his eyes, silently willing her all the strength he could muster.

"Hang tight, baby girl. I'm coming," he whispered.

11

Ben punched in the four-digit code before pushing the heavy steel door open. He dreaded giving the report, knowing he was going to be in trouble. Failure wasn't something that was tolerated. He steeled himself to be berated and possibly even killed for failing to complete his mission—there was no point in running, as he knew that would only make it worse. One never knew what to expect with the people he was working with. It was a risk he had willingly taken when he'd signed on. There were always going to be those people in the world who rose above, and that's what he'd wanted for himself. He had situated himself with a group that was one day going to rule the world. He wanted a front row seat and was willing to do whatever it took to secure it. He'd already done unspeakable things to insert himself into the group. It couldn't all be for naught.

He followed the dimly lit hall to its end, his booted feet scraping along the metal floor as he moved. He peered through the small glass window in the door. All five of the top commanders were sitting at a table, a series of maps spread out in front of them. They looked to be in a heated discussion. When he'd returned from his failed mission, he'd been informed that they wanted to see him.

Taking a deep breath, Ben knocked once and then opened the door.

All eyes were on him, making the news he had to deliver that much harder to say. The men at the table were ruthless, some of the scariest individuals he had ever encountered in his life, and he'd done time in a maximum-security prison. The murderers and rapists he'd met there had nothing on the men currently staring him down.

"What'd you find?" the man sitting at the head of the table asked in a gruff voice. His gray beard and beady eyes gave him the appearance of an evil wizard.

"I couldn't find the drive," Ben admitted, meeting the steely brown eyes.

"You searched the body?"

"Thoroughly. Searched his pockets, stripped him down and all. He didn't have it."

"What about the other guy? Who is he?"

Ben cleared his throat, uncomfortable. "We know he's a jour-nalist, Austin Merryman. He used to be one of those hotshot reporters writing whistleblower stories. Callum's phone records showed he called the guy several times. I hacked his phone and read the messages between them. He never revealed what he had, only that he wanted to meet."

"And? Who is this Merryman guy now if he's no longer a hotshot reporter?"

"He's a single father traveling with his teenage daughter. His wife died a year ago. He's been writing stories about people living alternative lifestyles. It's a lot of fluff. I don't think he's a threat," Ben insisted, hoping to allay the fears of the bosses.

"You don't think? That's an understatement. Why this guy?"

"As far as I can tell, they knew each other in college. Back then, the journalist was a bit of a crusader. I'm guessing that's why Callum reached out to him. Merryman took on tough political stories and exposed cover-ups involving politicians. Callum probably didn't know the guy had changed."

There were grunts and groans followed by more disgusted looks directed his way. "Did Callum tell him anything? Did Merryman know why they were meeting?"

"Callum didn't tell him anything in the messages, only that it was important they meet in person," he reiterated, wanting them to believe his mistake wasn't all that bad. "I didn't find any records of phone calls between them that lasted more than

a few seconds. Callum didn't get the chance to tell him what the meeting was about," he said, hoping he sounded confident.

"Does this Merryman have it—the USB that punk stole from us? Did Callum pass it off?" the bearded commander asked in a gruff voice.

Ben slowly nodded. "I believe that's a possibility. They couldn't have been together long before I showed up. I shot them both," he said, not admitting that he couldn't say for sure if he'd shot the reporter, but with the spray of bullets, he felt there was no way the guy could've been spared.

"Where is he?" came the irritated question from another man sitting to the leader's left.

"I don't know," he replied.

"How the hell don't you know?"

"He went over the side. I doubt he could have survived. The water was moving fast," he said.

"Never doubt a man's desire to survive, especially a man with a kid. He's out there somewhere. If that drive gets into the wrong hands, we've got problems. It needs to be recovered," his boss declared, sneering at him with disgust.

"I'll go back," he said. "I can start looking for the body immediately, or find him if he's not dead. But I think he is."

"Go back? Where? The bridge? Do you think he's going to be hiding out underneath it? It's been a week!" the boss snarled.

"Merryman was staying nearby. One of the messages mentioned a farm. Callum told him where to meet and Merryman said it would take him about fifteen minutes to get there. I'll go there first."

"You didn't check there already?" the voice boomed.

"I did, sir, I did. No one was in the camper. I took care of the farmer who was asking questions; made it look like a robbery gone bad. He won't be warning Merryman I'm looking for him."

The men at the table exchanged looks with one another. "This is a colossal screw-up. We have to get the drive back. We need to find that journalist."

"I'll find him. I'll leave now," Ben said, hoping they'd let him walk out of there.

They blamed him for failing to complete the mission, and it was true that Callum Barker had been his responsibility. But the guy had been smart and had managed to lose his tail for thirty minutes. By the time he'd caught up to him, it'd been too late. He had eliminated Callum, but the information that could disrupt their entire plan was out there somewhere. He only hoped it had drowned with the reporter, and that he could somehow find the jerk's body.

"No, you've done enough. We need someone more reliable on this!" the leader of their faction declared, slapping a hand on the stainless-steel table.

"Who?"

"Get me Craven," the leader growled.

"Zander?" he asked, irritated his colleague was going to get the job that should have been his.

"Yes, Alexander Craven. He'll get this handled. We can't have that intel getting out. I will not allow one man to ruin everything we've worked so hard to achieve. Phase One is complete. To stay on track, we have to get that intelligence back. If it falls into the wrong hands—" He let the sentence hang unfinished, leaving everyone to draw their own conclusions.

They all knew what would happen. They'd all go to prison for a long time, or possibly be executed for treason.

Ben turned to leave. There was no point in arguing. He knew they could decide to put a bullet between his eyes for the enormous screw-up he'd made. He'd just have to find a way to get back in their good graces. After all, he'd been a part of it from the beginning. He wanted to see it through to the end. He'd worked too hard and sacrificed too much to let someone else kick him out of the organization now—'Zander' or anyone else.

12

———

Malachi watched Savannah through the trees. She was collecting firewood for the campfire. They had been walking for several days now, and he'd thought she'd have cheered up by now, but the fact that it was so slow-going wasn't aiding anyone's outlook. They hadn't encountered anything too serious, but the information they had been picking up along the way was alarming. They'd already been warned against going anywhere near Lexington. Apparently, the city had erupted into violence a couple days after the blackout. People were fleeing en masse. The stories were bad enough that the Loveridges and their companions had decided to take a wide berth around the city, adding what would probably amount to an extra day of travel.

"Malachi?"

His father's voice had startled him, making him jump.

"What?" he asked, spinning around, feeling both guilty and afraid that his dad would see what he'd been doing.

His father looked over his shoulder, sighed, and then looked back at Malachi, slowly shaking his head. "You're tempted."

"I'm sorry."

"Son, it's okay. It's natural. Please, just be careful. I'm here if you have any questions," he said.

"I'm sorry… I wanted to make sure she's okay. I told her she shouldn't go into the woods alone," Malachi stammered.

His father smiled, patting Malachi on the shoulder. "I'll help her. Go back and help your mom make the beds for the night."

He nodded and headed back towards the area where they were setting up camp. His mother was on her knees, piling leaves and pine needles into small rows for them each to sleep on. The bedding wasn't as nice as a mattress, but it provided a small barrier between them and the hard earth that would be damp after a spring rainstorm earlier in the day.

"Hey there," she said, looking up at him.

Looking at her face, he noticed the paleness. They had little to eat, as living off the land wasn't easy. They could grow food, but not while traveling, and they knew little about wild edibles. Gretchen, from somewhere back east, had been identifying things like dandelions and some other weeds for them to eat, but it wasn't enough. They'd long since gone through the little food they'd taken from their camp a week ago, as well as what little had been left at the Little farm.

"Mom, I'll do that. Rest," he said, moving to scoop up some leaves.

"It's fine, I can do this. You can finish building that fire ring," she said, her voice weak.

Without bothering to argue, he moved to do her bidding. He kept glancing back, though, watching her move slowly. She was growing more lethargic. They all were.

He kept his focus on the fire then, until his dad came back into camp with Savannah, each of them carrying a pile of branches in their arms.

"Dad, we have to try hunting. We're starving," Malachi said.

"Son, we have no skills for hunting. None of us knows how. We don't have tools to hunt with," he replied.

"We have that revolver. Ken knows how to use it," he reminded him.

Ken stepped forward, carrying more firewood. "We've only got a handful of bullets, and we'd go through them fast trying to hunt. It's been years since I've done any hunting, so I don't know that I could vouch for my shots being true. We've got so many mouths and so few bullets... I don't know that it'd be worth it."

"Maybe we could set traps," Savannah suggested.

Jim turned to look at her. "Traps?"

"I used to watch a show, like, men surviving in the woods—they would use different types of traps to catch things like squirrels and birds and whatever they could get. They used wire or rope, making little nooses on trees or along the ground. Sometimes, they'd use a stick to hold up a heavy rock and, when the animal went under it, the rock would fall and kill it."

Malachi heard his mother gasp in shock behind him, but the idea didn't bother him—not like it might have some weeks before. He was hungry. The idea of killing didn't appeal to him, but they had to eat.

Malachi eyed Savannah, thinking about the suggestions. "Squirrels? I was thinking of something like a deer."

She put her hand on a hip and glared at him. "Have you seen a deer?"

He shrugged. "No."

"Have you seen a squirrel?"

"Okay, yeah, a lot of them," he acknowledged, frowning.

"Exactly."

He could hear his mother snickering behind them, clearly over her initial horror at the thought of killing little woodland creatures.

"Okay, I get it, it isn't that simple. Why don't we try to go into that town we saw the sign for? We could pay for food," he suggested.

"Son, nobody wants our money," his dad said gently.

"Maybe that was only those two towns. The city we're close to looked bigger on the map. They're probably still taking cash. We have to try. We have to eat!" he pleaded, hunger making him cranky. He looked to his parents, begging them to hear his words.

"Jim, he's right. We have to try. Maybe we can ask politely for handouts if they won't take our money," his mother said.

Malachi looked hopefully at his father. "Dad?"

It took another second, but the man agreed. "Fine, we'll try, but it could be dangerous. People are going to be turning on those who believe in God. You heard what that last group told us. The city is chaos."

"We won't go into the city," Malachi insisted. "We'll stick to the suburbs."

"Why would anyone turn on those who believe in God?" Savannah asked, as if it was silliest thing she had ever heard.

Jim, always the patient man, turned to her and smiled. "Because, dear, it is in times like these that the unfaithful believe God has abandoned them. They will hate those who still believe. They will mock us, and want to try and punish us. It is all written in the Bible."

She scoffed. "The Bible predicted there was going to be a blackout? I find that hard to believe."

Malachi froze in place, shocked by her blatant refusal to believe his father. His father, of all people! He was used to people coming to the tent meetings and being a little skeptical, but Savannah had seen what was happening. She had to realize things were terrible. It wasn't going to get better for a long time—if ever.

Just then, they heard the crunching of leaves and twigs, and all spun to look in the direction of the sound. It was Gretchen and the others coming back with their gatherings of what could only be called weeds. Gretchen stopped, her boyfriend Tim beside her. They looked guilty.

"Jim, Tonya, I'd like to introduce you to Bonnie and Bill," Gretchen said, stepping to the side.

Malachi stiffened when he saw a large man and woman coming through the trees. The man was probably fifty, balding and huge. He guessed he was over six feet tall and had to weigh close to three hundred pounds. The woman was a little shorter, but she was just as big. His first thought was that they had been eating well for a while.

Jim stepped in front of the family. "Hello, Bonnie. Bill," he said, extending his hand to each of them in turn.

Malachi wasn't quite as welcoming. They had encountered a young couple a few days before, and they hadn't been nearly as polite as the Loveridges felt the need to be. They had looked nice enough, but when his father had attempted to talk to them, they had cursed at them and told them to get away, brandishing a semi-automatic handgun to get their message across. He was a little weary of strangers now, despite his father's opinion that all people were good until proven otherwise. Even then, his father encouraged Malachi to see the good in all people.

Gretchen was smiling. "Bill has some beef jerky he's offered to share with us, as well as some rice. They'd like to travel with us," she added more hesitantly.

"Oh, really?" Jim asked, clearly pleased with the new additions.

His mother stepped forward. "Hi, I'm Tonya Loveridge, and it's good to meet you both. This is our son, Malachi, and Savannah is traveling with us. There are others in our group who'll return soon—we're still setting up camp."

Everyone shook hands and went through the general niceties.

"We'd love to have you join us," Malachi heard his father say, and cringed.

"Dad, can I talk to you for a minute?" Malachi said in a low voice.

His father nodded. "Sure."

"Over here," Malachi said, separating them from the rest of the group.

"What is it, Mal?"

"Dad, is it wise to bring new people into our group? We don't know them. They could be dangerous," he whispered.

"Malachi, we don't judge. We meet people we don't know all the time. We didn't know Gretchen or Tim or any of the other people we're traveling with until we did. Does that make sense?" he asked.

Malachi struggled. "It does, but... Dad, things are different. What if they're dangerous?"

Jim Loveridge put a hand on his son's shoulder as if to ground him. "I think we have to trust God's plan. Let's look at the positive side of this. They brought food. You were just saying we needed food, and God delivered."

Malachi sighed. He knew there was no arguing with his father in matters like this. His father was a faithful believer and would never turn away anyone in need. He believed in redemption for all, and loved to be the one to lead them to it. If these people wanted to join them, he'd be the first to welcome them again and again.

"Okay, but please, we have to be careful," Malachi insisted.

"Of course, son, of course," his father said, patting him on the shoulder as they returned to the group.

Bonnie was kneeling on the ground, unloading her backpack. Malachi's eyes fell on the jerky then, and his stomach immediately started to rumble. It wasn't a meal, but it was much better than the pile of dandelions he saw stacked on a piece of cardboard. He got busy building the fire ring. The sun was already setting, and he knew the chill that night would be fierce.

Savannah took over making the beds while his mother and Bonnie chatted. He got the fire going, thankful they had a lighter. He had no idea what they would do if it ran out of fuel, but that was a worry for later. He wished someone from one of those shows Savannah talked about would walk into their camp. That's what they really needed. They needed someone who could hunt, fish, gather supplies, and protect them.

With water boiled for drinking and the rest of the group returned, they all sat around the fire while his mother distributed their meager food offerings. His father said a blessing, thanking God for the food and the new arrivals. Instead of closing his eyes, Malachi stole looks, checking out Bonnie and Bill. They had their eyes closed and their hands folded together as his father spoke to God.

"So, tell us where you're from?" Tonya suggested once they had all finished their tiny dinners.

Bonnie looked to her husband. "We left Nashville a couple weeks ago. We figured we would head north."

"North?" Jim asked.

Bill took over the story. "We were in Nashville when things went dark. We thought it was a blackout, something temporary. Within a few days, we had to run. Things were terrible. Our neighborhood was overrun. We heard all kinds of rumors."

"What kind of rumors?" Malachi asked.

Bill and Bonnie exchanged a look. "There's chaos in Washington, or what's left of it. The President was killed in the attack. The Vice President is supposedly hiding out in a bunker and some of the other top-ranking government officials are in bunkers around the country. Supposedly, there's a safe haven in Seattle. They have food, water, and shelter. We also heard Denver might be a good place to go."

"Denver and Seattle?" Tonya asked excitedly. "Aren't we headed in that direction?"

Bill nodded. "It's a rumor, but it would make sense that the government would set up some kind of shelter."

"Who's in charge?" Jim asked.

Bill shrugged. "No one knows."

"Isn't there a military? Are we under attack?" Tonya asked.

"I don't think anyone knows. It does sound like this is a wide-spread problem. It isn't isolated to any one city. We thought it was just Nashville. Then we ran into some people from New Orleans and they said they were headed to Mexico. We considered going that way, as well, but we've settled on Seattle. We visited once, and it may be cold, but there's plenty of fishing opportunities and a lot of forest area for hunting. If there's a shelter there, all the better."

"That's where you're headed?" Malachi asked.

Bill nodded. "They have power and are taking in refugees, from what we've heard, but only as many as they can support. We hope to get there before they close the city to newcomers. It sounds like you're going in that direction, so perhaps we could travel together for a while—that's what we were thinking, anyway."

Jim Loveridge nodded even as Savannah chimed in, "That's a long way to go on foot."

"It is, but what choice do we have? We might see what Denver looks like, but I like the idea of having plentiful fishing grounds, as the Pacific would offer in Seattle."

Malachi sat back, blocking out the debate over locations that had come up. The news of the country's turmoil was difficult to accept. Malachi had secretly been hoping they would get to Salt Lake City and discover everything was okay. He hoped the rumors were wrong. Gossip was a tool of the devil. It could all be lies. There was a small chance they could get to the city and find everything was okay. His father would tell him to have faith, if he asked.

His eyes moved around the circle of people until he saw Savannah. She looked so pretty in the glow of the firelight, but his father was right. He couldn't let himself be tempted by her beauty. She didn't want to go to Salt Lake City with his family, and he knew she wasn't a real believer. Right then, he made a decision to never be alone with her. He'd too often found himself thinking about kissing her and knew that was wrong. He needed to keep his distance. She was not right for him, not when they'd been traveling this long and she still hadn't shown any signs of becoming more interested in their faith. He simply needed to remain pure until he could find the right girl—one who believed as he did and would not question his faith.

13

Savannah had never felt so alone in her life. They'd been walking all day, and no one would really talk to her. Malachi was keeping his distance, though she didn't know what she'd done to make him mad at her. Ever since the new people had shown up, he'd simply quit talking to her. He'd been going out of his way to avoid her, in fact. Tonya and Jim walked together, always talking amongst themselves, and the rest of the group had all divided into pairs, leaving her completely alone. And Malachi was the only one remotely near her age—she didn't understand how he could stand to be so solitary, either, or how he could be so hurtful after wanting so badly for her to come along.

Part of her wondered if Malachi was mad at her because she'd been unsuccessful in getting food on the trip into town the day before. It had been decided that her, Tonya, Gretchen, and Jim would go into town. They looked the least threatening, and Jim could be very persuasive. Savannah had tried, too. She'd begged and pleaded with several people, in a way that had made her feel pathetic, and still nobody had helped. All of them had tried. Jim had managed to get some bread from a kind old woman, but that was it. It didn't seem like Malachi could fault her for what even his mother had failed at accomplishing, but she couldn't imagine what else was going on.

When they finally stopped for the night, she decided she was going to get Malachi alone so they could talk. She needed to find out what to she had done. She couldn't stand the thought of him hating her, or even another day of solitary travel like this had been. She needed him.

"Malachi, can you help me collect wood?" she asked politely.

"Uh, I can't. I have to help my dad," he mumbled, not looking at her.

She looked around the group, and noticed Jim and Bill talking about twenty feet away from the rest of them. They were huddled together, talking in harsh, quiet voices. Whatever they were talking about had Jim very upset. Obviously, Malachi only wanted to avoid her. Too hurt to question him further, she moved away from him, pretending to be looking for brush and twigs they could burn for fire. She paused near the men, straining her ears to hear what they were talking about.

"I don't want another gun near my family. The first one was

bad enough, but that one looks far more dangerous," Jim hissed.

Savannah bent over pretending to pick something up but looking towards them. She gasped then, giving away her presence. Jim spun around to face her even as Bill tried to hide the handgun he was holding, but it was too late. Malachi had been only a few feet away, and he'd seen the gun, as well.

"Dad?" he asked, his voice revealing his shock.

Jim sighed, his shoulders slumping forward. "It isn't what it looks like," he tried to explain.

"It looks very much like another gun!" Tonya said, irritation in her voice.

"I'm sorry," Bill apologized. "This is my gun. I brought it from home. Things are bad out there."

Tonya was shaking her head. "Jim, you said no guns, and now we have enough to form an army," she exaggerated.

Savannah had to fight to keep from rolling her eyes. An army? And who knew if that first gun would even work? But this gun looked a lot like the one her father had. She didn't know specifics, but she knew it was going to be more reliable than the antique they'd been carrying.

"I know, but Bill has a point," Jim reasoned, surprising Savannah.

Everyone stopped talking and doing whatever it was they'd been doing, most of them staring at the gun as if it was a venomous snake. Personally, Savannah was happy to have a real gun in the group. It made her feel safer. Or, well, it should have made her feel safer, but she doubted any of them knew how to use the thing. That was a little scary. She did, though. She was more than confident she could handle the gun if they'd give her a chance.

"What point?" Tonya asked.

"We don't have to shoot anyone, but if we can at least look like we can defend ourselves, it might be enough," Jim reasoned.

Savannah fought the urge to do a face-palm. She couldn't let that comment go. "My dad and uncle always said that if you have a gun, you have to be prepared to use it or it will be used on you," she interjected, earning a number of horrified looks from the others.

"Do you know how to use a gun?" Tonya asked, clearly aghast.

"I do."

Bill grinned. "Have you shot a nine millimeter before?"

She looked at the gun more closely, stepping forward. "I think so. I don't know what it was my uncle had, but I shot a small gun and a rifle; I think it was a twenty-two or something like that. My uncle taught me how to load a magazine and gun safety in general," she answered nonchalantly, "and that looks like my dad's gun, which I shot once."

"Show me how to shoot," Malachi blurted out.

She raised an eyebrow. Now he was talking to her? If that was what it took... "I can do that."

"I think I'd prefer you to leave the gun alone," Tonya said, her lips pursed.

"Mom, I'll be the one who learns how. I won't ask Dad to shoot someone. I will protect the family," he said proudly.

Bill cleared his throat. "It's my gun. I'll carry it with me."

"Do you have extra ammo?" Savannah asked.

Bill looked at her more directly, and she could feel him sizing her up. "I have some."

She smiled, hoping he'd see the logic in letting her try it. "Wouldn't it be better to have a back-up plan in case something happens to you? We can show Malachi the basics. With the revolver and your gun, we need to be sure more than two of us can shoot."

"I can shoot," Ken chimed in. "It's just been a while."

"So, three of us know. I think it would be smart if Malachi knew, as well," she said, wanting the chance to prove her value to the group and also get some time alone with Malachi.

Bill nodded. "I guess we can do that. Tomorrow, I'll show him how to load and fire the gun."

Savannah didn't take offense to being excluded, nodding instead of arguing. She was getting used to it. Whether it had more to do with her being a girl or being a teenager, she wasn't sure, but this would give her something to talk to Malachi about since he was clearly interested. And, soon, they'd get to her Uncle Ennis' house. He was the one who had let her shoot at his private gun range, and he'd respect her more than this group did. They all seemed to think she was a helpless little girl, and she couldn't wait to get away from them. They could leave her with her uncle and go on by themselves. She trusted her dad and uncle to keep her safe a million times more than she trusted these people. She was simply stuck with them for now and knew that their group was better than none.

14

Austin felt every mile they had traveled over the last two days. It seemed ridiculous that forty miles felt like two thousand, but riding bareback on a horse wasn't easy. The broken leg had just made it all the worse. Now, he focused on Savannah, which was the only thing still keeping him going. Getting to her helped him get through the pain. She'd been alone for coming up on a month now, around three full weeks, and that was far too long.

He'd suffered a serious setback and become extremely ill after trying to get on the horse that first day he'd tried. Amanda had been worried enough to make him seriously concerned he wasn't going to make it. After three days of high fevers, he'd felt like he was on the mend, but it had taken that long.

Since then, there'd been a lot of healing, and a lot of arguing. He'd wanted to set off on horseback at the very moment the fever had broken, but Amanda's reasoning and his own pain had won the day. And a lot had changed in the interim. More people had shown up to try to pilfer Amanda's supplies, and she'd had to shoot her rifle in the air more than once to scare them off. As it was, two of her horses had been stolen, or maybe the mean one had run off when she'd stopped feeding him carrots and oats, if her suspicions were correct. With the barn gone,, there'd been too few supplies and no good method of protecting them while she and Austin slept, and they'd agreed it might be a matter of time before her remaining horses, Raven and Charlie, disappeared.

Even now, he wasn't sure how it had happened, but one of them had raised the idea of her accompanying him to find Savannah, taking what supplies she had along with her horses. There was nothing keeping her on the farm, and she wanted news of what had happened. He liked to think that they'd grown into enjoying a friendship also—at least, he hoped that she wasn't tagging along simply because she felt responsible as some sort of caretaker.

One way or another, the moment he'd felt like he was strong enough, he'd insisted they leave the farmhouse and go in search of Savannah. It had been a huge battle to get Amanda to agree, as she'd wanted to wait another week, but finally she'd caved in. And it turned out she'd been ready to go, to the point that he guessed she worried she was more of a target in the farmhouse than she'd been letting on, between being a single female and a veterinarian. She'd traded with Daniel, offering him some medicine and food in return for a cart and harness that she'd hooked up to her Charlie and loaded up with supplies, practically before he'd blinked.

Now, though, after three days of on-and-off travel to make the forty miles to his and Savannah's RV, he wondered if they should have taken their chances and waited another week.

"It's just around the corner," he grunted, the throbbing in his leg beating in time to his heartbeat.

"You look awful," she muttered from her horse beside him.

He shrugged, gripping Raven's mane and harness in a way that probably gave away just how much agony he was feeling. "But, I'm alive."

"Barely."

The rhythmic plodding of the horses' hooves remained oddly cathartic as they traveled down the dirt road he knew would lead him to the backside of the farm they'd been staying on. They'd encountered gangs the first day they had left Amanda's place, but not seen much of anyone since then. Fortunately, Amanda had brought along several of her guns, giving him a Glock to hold onto. Thankfully, the gang had been on foot, and only armed with baseball bats.

"We're not far," Austin told her, feeling better about their progress now that he was somewhat familiar with where they were. His eyes scanned the horizon, looking for any signs that there had been trouble on the farm.

"Up there," he said excitedly, pointing to where his fifth wheel was parked in the field next to the long driveway.

He got the horse to move a little faster then, anxious to find Savannah. He imagined she was inside writing or reading a book, just waiting for him.

"Let's get to the stairs of your RV. I'll help you dismount," Amanda called out, riding ahead of him.

He ordered Raven to stop and slid from her side, putting his weight on his good leg. Amanda dismounted Charlie nearby and grabbed the cane she had found in the back of her father's closet, giving it to Austin to use. It had been about three long weeks since he'd broken the leg. It was healing, but bearing his full weight still wasn't possible. The crutches had been too awkward to try and carry on the horse, too, and they'd decided they weren't worth their space in the cart since Austin could use the cane well enough for short distances now.

He hobbled up to the front door, trying to hop more than walk. "Savannah!" he called out.

There was no answer. He tried the door and was surprised to find it unlocked. He yanked it open, already sensing she wasn't there. The place even felt still, and he turned around without taking a step inside.

"Savannah!" he called out again, swinging around to look over the farm's land. Where was she? Even if she'd gone to the house to stay with Bob, wouldn't she have been keeping an eye out for him?

But the whole place looked abandoned. He didn't hear or see anyone. Not even the farmer's horses. He froze in the doorway of the trailer, stunned. It had never occurred to him that she wouldn't be there.

"Let me check inside," Amanda said in a soft voice.

Amanda returned a couple seconds later, handing him a note. He snatched it out of her hand and read it, his heart dropping.

"Oh no," he groaned.

"Who's Ennis?" Amanda asked.

"My brother. His house has to be at least twelve-hundred miles from here. They're walking?" he said, shock and fear making his voice shrill.

Amanda looked again at the note, patting Charlie's neck absently. "Your daughter left four notes like that, just that I saw, all saying the same thing. She wanted to make sure you'd know where she was headed—she's got a solid head on her shoulders, obviously. And at least we know she's safe and not alone."

There was a lump in his throat. What Amanda said was true, but why had Savannah left? "I'm going to talk to Bob. He owns this place, so maybe he can tell me what happened. Why would she leave?" he asked, more to himself than Amanda.

She shook her head, her eyes darting around the open property. "Let's go over to the house. I'll get the horses taken care of while you talk to your friend."

Amanda stepped in beside him without another word. He knew the drill. He wrapped his arm around her petite shoulders and let her support his weight while they slowly trudged across the driveway, the horses plodding along behind them. It was such a short distance, there was no question that limping along beside Amanda was easier than getting back onto Raven for the duration.

As they got closer, his eyes landed on a cross made from a couple of branches stuck in a rectangular pile of dirt near the barn.

"What is that?" Amanda asked.

Yet, they both knew exactly what it was. "A grave," Austin ground out the words, stating the obvious.

"Who?" she asked.

"It wasn't there before," he said, feeling dread wash over him.

They kept moving towards the house. Amanda reached out first and knocked on the door. When no one answered, she pushed the door open, going in first.

"Bob!" he called out from behind her, hoping the farmer was napping or hiding out. The house even felt empty, just like the farm itself.

"Sit down in one of those chairs. I'll check and see if anyone's home," Amanda ordered him.

Austin knew he should protest. It should be him checking the house. Nevertheless, he flopped down on the worn recliner, the throbbing in his leg subsiding a little with the change in position. He could hear Amanda moving through the house, knocking on doors and calling out. Austin's eyes roamed the living room. It was neat and tidy, with no signs of trouble. That had to be a good sign.

"No one's here," Amanda announced.

"We need to know who's buried out there," he whispered.

"It isn't Savannah. She left you that note," Amanda reminded him.

He rubbed a hand over his face. "You're right. Maybe it's Bob," he reasoned. "Why would she leave? Because he died, you think? Why wouldn't she wait for me, though?" he asked, frustrated to have made it so far only to discover she was gone.

"She said it was too dangerous to stick around here. She was smart enough not to stay in danger."

"I don't know those people she's with. She had a crush on the kid that was with them. Have you ever heard of them?" he asked her.

"Kind of. I don't think they're bad or dangerous. They're a little weird and they may try and convert her, but I don't think they'll hurt her if it's the family I'm thinking of. They've been traveling through this area for years, doing their revivals."

Austin shook his head; his stomach was in knots. "I'll kill them if they hurt her. What if they're a cult and they won't let her leave?"

"Her note said she was going to your brother's house," Amanda pointed out. "Not joining a cult."

"What if they said that to get her to go with them and have no intention of letting her go?" he shot back.

Amanda took a deep breath and looked back at him. "Think about what you're saying, Austin. There's no point worrying more about it right now—it is what it is. I'm going to get the horses settled in that barn out there, then look around and see if I can find some food."

"And then we have to get going," he muttered.

She looked at him and then his leg before turning and walking away. The forty miles getting to the farm had nearly done him in, and they both knew it. He felt weak as a kitten. There was no way he could get on that horse and ride twelve-hundred miles. The Loveridges had almost a three-week head start, too, what with all the delays Austin had encountered. He stared down at his leg, wrapped in the purple casting material Amanda had used to freshen the cast before they'd left her place. She had a real thing for the girly colors.

It seemed as if he couldn't catch a break, no pun intended. Everything was all wrong, and he had no idea if or when he would ever be able to make it right again.

"Look!" Amanda came back into the living room, holding up a blue, shoe-looking thing.

"What's that?" he asked.

"A walking boot! It might be a little small, but I can rig it to fit you. This will help tremendously. I still don't want you going for a hike, but this will help you get around and support your leg!"

Austin forced a smile, seeing she'd been thinking of him even before the comfort of her horses. That said a lot. "Thank God. You know, Bob had a lot of horses. There may be some saddles out in the barn," he said hopefully. "There's a pond behind the house also, now that I think of it. You can get the horses watered there before you put them up."

"Thanks, I was worried about that. I'll check for saddles, too." With that, she seemed to hesitate, looking around the room. "Austin, I know you don't want to, but I want you to lie on the couch and elevate that leg for at least twenty minutes. I'll put the boot on after that," she said, dropping down in front of him and pulling off his own boot, then removing his sock without asking.

He was used to her tending to him now. The awkwardness was gone, though it still made him uncomfortable when he allowed himself to think about it. At this point, she knew his body about as well as he did after three weeks of taking care of him. Now, he watched as she checked his toes and made a clucking sound.

"What?" he growled.

"Your foot is swollen again. Come on, to the couch," she ordered, helping him out of the chair.

He hopped over to the couch and collapsed into its cushions, letting her use the throw pillows to elevate his foot.

"Thank you," he muttered. "Maybe you could grab me some fresh clothes from the RV, too?" he asked.

"Absolutely. I'll be back," she said before she walked out the front door, leaving him alone in the house.

It was eerily quiet. He'd been in Bob's house several times. The old guy had always had a radio on, listening to a game or the news. He wondered what had happened to him, and if Savannah had been around when it happened. Maybe that's what had scared her off from staying. There were so many questions he wanted to ask her. He closed his eyes, hoping she was already with his brother.

Ennis would be prepared for something like this. If Savannah could get there, she would be safe—of that much, he was sure. The problem was, he didn't trust the people she had left with. He'd only met the Loveridge family one time, and he'd felt an immediate dislike for them. They were weird—it was that simple. Jim had been way too happy for his liking. The guy reminded Austin of one of those TV pastors, begging for money for a new private jet while making promises of salvation to unsuspecting people.

He hoped Savannah was smart enough not to fall for their charms. He would move heaven and earth to get her away from them. His hand slid into his front pocket, clasping the USB he still carried. If all the computers in the country were truly fried, it seemed silly to hold onto the USB, but something told him not to let go of it—not yet.

"You were right," Amanda said, coming back into the house.

"About?"

"There were a couple saddles. I'll get them taken care of and then come in to see about scrounging us up something to eat—oh, I'll grab clothes from your RV, too. Anything else?"

He shrugged, unable to focus on what he might want from the RV. What he wanted was his daughter, here by his side, safe. "We need to get moving," he said without conviction.

"There is no way you're riding anywhere today. You have to let that leg rest."

"I'll be fine," he said through gritted teeth, tired of the same old argument.

"Austin, you won't be fine. You're barely able to stay on Raven as it is. You just recovered from a serious infection. You're weak, and you need the rest. I got you here. Trust me. We'll leave in a day or two. I want you to rest," she ordered him.

He glared at her, wanting to argue, but experience told him it was pointless. She'd hide the horses from him if she had to. She'd taken the crutches away back at her place, just to keep him still. The woman was fierce. He knew he should appreciate it, but it was difficult to put up with.

"Fine, I'll sit here like a giant lump and wait," he grunted. "For a day. Two, at most, Amanda. That's it."

She grinned. "Good. I'll be back inside in a bit to see what food we have left to eat."

"Whatever," he sulked. As she walked away, he wondered whether or not she'd be willing to accompany him to Colorado, or let him take her horse. He wasn't quite sure what would happen if she didn't, and could only hope that her wanting to get off of her own farm, and accompany him this far, signaled promise for what he faced now.

15

Ennis Merryman stood in the center of his living room, staring at the window. He couldn't see *through* the window because of the steel door that had been engaged when something catastrophic had happened. What, he wasn't sure. Or maybe nothing had happened. Maybe his multi-million-dollar home had just malfunctioned and now he was trapped inside a steel box with no way out. Steel doors had dropped down, sealing him inside the home he had built to withstand a nuclear war. Some malfunction had happened, for sure, catastrophe or not, because he couldn't even disengage the supposedly man-operated escape hatch.

"I swear I'm going to sue the guy who installed this system," he muttered.

It had been weeks since the walls had literally come crashing down around him. He'd been watching TV and enjoying a cold beer when there'd been what he assumed was a power surge. The TV and lights had gone out immediately even though he was connected to solar power, which made no sense to him. And he couldn't call anyone to get an answer, either—his phone wasn't working. He couldn't say for sure what had happened, but something had shorted out the computer in the house that was supposed to have been completely protected from surges, EMPs, and everything else. It was supposed to be impenetrable.

Unfortunately, the only conclusion he could come to was that he'd made a mistake in the contractors he'd hired. He'd been warned not to go with the cheapest options, and he hadn't done it on all things… but apparently, he'd gone with enough cheap and under-the-table options to kick him in the backside. The house had been so expensive, though, he'd had to cut a few corners. Or, at least, that was what he'd told himself at the time, promising himself he'd get everything double-checked at a later date, once the initial gadget payments were all made.

This house had been his brainchild, after all. He'd used his wealth gained from working as a real estate agent to build the house from scratch. It had taken over a year to create his mountain retreat, and it was supposed to be the safest place on the planet. It was supposed to be better than the bunkers built underground by the wealthiest of the wealthy, and yet, here he was, trapped inside of his dream home. When he'd bought the land nestled on the east side of the Rocky Mountains, he'd had it all in hand—everything he'd ever dreamed of. Access to the big city while living off the grid in his own secluded part of the mountains.

He walked to the touchpad again, entering his private code and hoping something would happen.

The screen lit up. "Hello," the female voice echoed through the speakers built into the ceiling high above.

"Open the front door," Ennis said slow and clear, and for what had to be the hundredth time since he'd been trapped inside the house.

"I'm sorry, that function is not available."

He groaned, fighting the urge to slam his fist into the wall pad. "Open. The. Door," he said slowly, telling himself not to start yelling at the damn computer again. All that accomplished was a sore throat.

"I'm sorry, that function is not available."

"Argh!" he shouted, yelling at the ceiling.

"I'm sorry, I didn't understand that. Can you please repeat your request?" the droning voice asked.

Ennis took a deep breath before shutting down the system again.

"I swear, if I die in this house because I got a bad system, I will never forgive that punk kid. You're supposed to be Alexa and Siri on steroids!" he shouted at the wall pad.

The system was on power save, according the little battery on the screen, conserving energy because it was relying on battery life. But that wasn't supposed to happen because he had *solar* power, so it shouldn't be necessary. Solar. What the heck had happened to throw even that off? Already, he regretted not hooking up the wind turbine he'd had installed last year. At the time, it had seemed like a good idea to have a back-up, but it had seemed like it could wait, and everything he'd read told him solar was the way to go. So, there the turbine sat, high on the hill behind his house, currently useless.

Giving up, he walked into the huge gourmet kitchen and pulled a glass out of the cupboard, running the tap to get some water. At least that part of the house was still functional. He had a few thousand gallons of water stored in a tank high up on the hill behind the house. The gravity-fed system was enough to give him decent water pressure. There was a pump hooked up that should have worked, but it had stopped when the walls had come down.

"So much for the perfect house," he grumbled.

The power had failed—it was that simple. And, essentially, the house itself had failed in response. The wall pad was run off a small battery system that seemed to be functional as far as he could tell, but it wasn't running the house systems like he'd intended. Somewhere, something had shorted. His batteries connected to the solar panels weren't holding any juice—that much he knew for sure. He wasn't an electrician or a techy by any means and had no idea why they weren't working. He'd bought the set-up from some guy who'd claimed it was what was used in some of the super-secret government safe rooms.

Ennis was now convinced that that had been a load of crap. It had worked great when he'd tested it, but the second the main power had been cut, the system had failed. The one single window that wasn't now covered by a steel door was high up on the wall in the kitchen and dining area, and it now offered the only natural light he had in the house. It was a narrow, rectangular window meant to allow in natural light while being small enough and placed high enough not to be a security concern. It was hurricane glass, which made it impenetrable, as well.

"And that worked out really well, didn't it?" Ennis said, staring up at the window.

The two-story home was just over three-thousand square feet. It was huge, open and airy. At least, it was supposed to be airy. With the windows all covered with the protective steel sheets, it was a giant tomb. He might as well have been in a prison cell. The air vents high on the walls did little to provide fresh air, which was the point. He didn't want to be breathing in radiated particles and had had the house built to be completely sealed. The air filters that were supposed to keep him supplied with fresh air, however, had died when the power had gone out—yet another thing that wasn't supposed to happen. He knew he didn't have much longer before he ran out of air and ended up breathing in carbon dioxide. He was a dead man walking.

A hungry dead man at the moment. There was no point in dying of hunger, he mused. That was one thing he could take care of.

Ennis opened the pantry, thankful he'd spent a couple thousand dollars on the freeze-dried food he'd researched on one of the many prepper sites he followed. No skimping here. He had food for months—years, technically, if he believed the serving suggestions on the cans. He'd decided after the second day that those servings were for tiny children and not for a full-grown adult man. He was glad he'd gone overboard, too, assuming he lived long enough to get to eat the food.

Now, he grabbed a package that claimed to be biscuits and gravy.

"We'll see about that," he said, not all that hopeful that it would look or taste quite as great as the picture on the package would lead one to believe.

He followed the directions and prepared his meal, using a minimal amount of his propane to heat the water on the stove. Propane would eat up the oxygen in the room. He couldn't spare much oxygen. As he sat down at his large, elegant dining table, he stared up through the window. He saw the rocky mountainside the house was built against and little else. His house was in an idyllic location, way off the beaten path, surrounded by mountains and some of the most beautiful scenery in the world.

It was his dumb luck that he'd happened to be at the house when it had malfunctioned.

He had no idea how he was going to get out, or if he would. His investment in being able to ride out the end of the world with all the creature comforts money could buy was backfiring in a big way. He was alone and trapped. Would anyone come looking for him? It was hard to tell and might depend on whether or not something had really gone wrong in the world, or whether his house had just gone bad.

Assuming it was just his house, there was still no knowing. His brother was gallivanting around the country and would have no idea he was missing. His clients would think he'd skipped town and find a new real estate agent. He had no one else to miss him, really. The isolation hadn't been intentional. It had just kind of happened, he mused. One day, he'd been a handsome, driven, twenty-five-year-old man with the world at his fingertips, with plenty of time to find a wife and start a family… and then, one day, he'd woken up at forty-one, divorced and alone. Wealthy, yeah, but alone and a little less handsome.

"Don't do it, Ennis," he said, knowing he was headed to his own pity party if he kept up with that line of thinking.

He finished his meal, impressed by the flavors even if the

texture was a little wonky. It was better than starving. He used minimal water to clean up the single dish he used—refusing to eat out of the bag, as the package suggested—and headed upstairs to take his daily sponge bath and change into clean clothes.

16

Nash Gladstone added a few more branches to his small campfire before propping his metal cup on the makeshift burner he'd created to boil the water he collected from the stream. He had no idea how long he'd been in the forest, but was guessing it had to be a little over two weeks. Before that, he'd been trapped inside a mine for at least a day, or possibly two, he guesstimated.

Someone had to be looking for him. His mother would be worried sick. Where was the forest ranger? Where was the search party? Hell, where was anybody? He'd been trapped in the mine, apparently abandoned once he'd gotten separated from the small group he had come out to explore the abandoned mines with. When he'd finally found his way out, he'd discovered his group had disappeared on him—so much for them being worried sick.

"Great friends, Nash," he mumbled to himself, already knowing what his mother would say.

He stared at the fire, mesmerized by the flames, his mind drifting back to the moment his world had literally gone black. He'd been deep in an old mine, exploring one of the tunnels on his own when everything had gone dark. The generator that had been running the lights they'd had temporarily installed for their exploration had died. He'd waited for someone to restart it. When that hadn't happened, he'd known something was off. He'd pulled one of his emergency glowsticks from his tactical vest and cracked it, lighting up the tunnel he'd been in.

He'd called out for the other three people who were part of the geology group he'd joined. No one had answered. They'd ditched him, or they were dead. He wasn't sure which even now. When he'd finally made it out of the mine, it had been to discover he was all alone on the mountain. He'd gone back to the camp to find it empty, as well. He'd tried using his phone to call for help, but it wouldn't turn on. The two-way radio was dead, as well. The flashlights that had been left behind were also fried.

And it all added up to one conclusion that Nash couldn't deny. He was too smart to deny it.

In fact, he was a genius. People hated that about him, but nobody could argue against him being smarter than the average eighteen-year-old. Heck, he was smarter than the average adult with decades of life under their belt. It was his curse and his blessing at the same time to have been born with an IQ that doubled that of most people. That being the case, it had taken him less than five minutes to figure out what had happened.

It had been an EMP. He hadn't felt an explosion, true, but he'd been underground, and it was possible it had been muted. There were a number of possibilities about the why, he knew, but none of that mattered. It had happened, and he needed to get to safety. For now, though, he'd been left wandering through the forest, trying to find a way back to civilization with the hope that he was wrong, and that everything would be fine once he got back to the city. Without GPS or the benefit of a map, both of which had disappeared with his so-called friends, he'd gotten himself lost in the unfamiliar mountains.

For today, though, he was about done. The fire before him was a small one—all he needed to purify the water he'd collected from the small stream he'd settled down beside tonight. Every day, he walked until it was almost dusk. Then, he would make a fire and settle in for another night of sleeping under the stars. The fire gave him a small measure of comfort and helped scare off the creatures that came out at night to eat. He did not want to find himself on the menu of some hungry bear.

He'd finished off the last of the food he'd collected from the abandoned camp three days before. As a result, hunger was a constant distraction. He had to find food and real shelter. He didn't want to be alone, either. Community was important in a situation like this, he reasoned. He'd studied primitive cultures and knew they survived because they had each other to lean on. There was strength in numbers. He needed the protection of a group or he wouldn't survive. No matter how smart he was.

He stared at the small bubbles forming on the bottom of the metal cup and waited. He was thirsty and anxious for a drink, even if it would be warm water, having long since emptied out his canteen while walking that day. As soon as the first large bubble rose to the surface and plopped, he used his shirtsleeve wrapped around his hand to pull the cup from the flames. This would be his first drink—he'd have a few more after it, and then re-fill his canteen. For now, he placed the cup on the ground and waited for it to cool enough that he could drink it down.

Finally, he stuck his finger inside, testing the temperature before bringing the cup to his mouth to take a long drink. Water was his everything at this point. It helped fill his empty belly, at least offering some illusion that he wasn't as hungry as he was.

"And, repeat," he commented to himself, dipping his cup back into the stream. It wasn't a fast process, but he needed to stay hydrated, and he couldn't afford not to boil the water.

That night, he told himself that he'd find another person the next day and didn't allow himself to think about the fact that this was what he'd told himself every night before he went to sleep. It had to happen at some point.

In the morning, he repeated his ritual with the water, hydrating and then kicking out his small fire before he set off once again, heading east, knowing he should run into a town at some point. The canopy of tall pine and fir trees provided nice shade, but it was a warm day. He could already feel sweat trickling down his back.

He stopped at the top of a steep hill and took a long drink from his canteen while using his vantage point to get a look at the surrounding area. Unfortunately, the dense trees made it difficult for him to see far at all. He was sliding his canteen back into the side pocket of his pack when something glistened, catching his eye.

"What was that?" he asked aloud.

He moved his eyes slowly over the area where he'd thought he'd seen something metallic. He blinked several times, looking down the hillside. It couldn't be.

"Is that a house?" he whispered.

In another second, he was convinced he was staring at a roofline. Nash started making his way down the steep hill, little rocks sliding down in front of him, reminding him to take it easy. He couldn't risk falling and hurting himself. The closer the got, the more jubilant he grew. It was definitely a house or a shop. The square building looked to be made of steel. There was a deck off the west side, but no way to get to it since the house was set into the mountain. There were also steel doors over what he assumed had to be doors that led onto the deck from the second story.

His position on the hill put him directly above the house. He could jump onto the roof from where he stood, but doubted that would get him a welcome from inside. Instead, he moved a little further down, intrigued by the huge house that resembled a fortress. He stopped moving when he saw the window. It seemed odd and a little out of place, but he ignored it, heading down the hill to look for a door. There was a small porch, but the door was sealed off.

He turned to walk back up and around the house, looking for another way in. Noting a black SUV sitting in the driveway, he realized there was a good chance someone was inside.

"Hello?" he called out, wondering if he could be heard through the steel walls.

He went back to what he assumed to be the front door and used his open hand to pound on the door. "Hello!"

A banging sound on the other side of the wall was his response. Someone was inside.

"Hello! I need help! Let me in, please! I'm not going to hurt you!" he shouted, waiting for the door to open.

There was more banging in response. Nash leaned his ear against the door, listening intently.

"Locked!" the muffled shout came through.

He could hear more talking, but the walls were too thick to allow for any clarity. He couldn't understand what was being said. An idea popped into his head. He hurried back to the hill and climbed up to where he'd seen the window. It appeared to be the only window left unprotected.

Thankfully, he was a tall guy, and was able to hold onto the ledge of the hill with one hand and pound on the glass with his other.

"Hey! Over here!" he shouted.

Within seconds, a forty-something-year-old man with dirty blond hair appeared in the fancy kitchen.

"Hurricane window!" the man inside shouted.

Nash leaned back to a more comfortable position, glad to be able to hear the man clearly. "Unlock the door, please! I'm not a threat!" he promised, even as he realized that someone who was a threat would be just as likely to say the same.

The man was shaking his head. "I can't! I'm trapped inside!"

Nash stared at the man, but his panicked face suggested he was telling the truth. How did a person get locked inside a house?

His brain started whirring, putting together all of the little pieces of information. The house was obviously some kind of massive panic room, but something hadn't gone to plan. The EMP must have short-circuited the electrical system in the house. So many people wanted safe rooms and bunkers, whether they needed them or not—though, now, he guessed that most did—but most folks didn't have the first clue about how to get one set up. Most contractors who claimed to be experts didn't, either, and obviously this guy had fallen prey to some false promises. And this guy had bought one hell of a false promise. The steel doors and windows would have to be electronically opened and closed, which meant there was no way they were going to be able to move them without brute force.

He let out a long sigh, looking at the window and judging it to be less than two feet high. It was a skinny window, made for light and not for entering or exiting. And he was a skinny guy, but the last thing he wanted to do was get stuck in a window high above the ground. Plus, what good would it do to get himself trapped inside this crazy house?

"Help me get out!" the man shouted.

Nash looked back at him, frowning. "How?"

"I don't know." The man backed away from the window, getting down off of whatever he'd climbed up on so that Nash could once again see the gourmet kitchen inside. Man, was he hungry.

Nash pushed away from the house and sat down on the hillside, staring into the house he couldn't get into. He could see a dining table and chairs within the kitchen, and imagined there would be a bed and a comfortable couch, as well. The man looked healthy enough, too, and probably had plenty of food and water inside.

He stared at the window, his mind working out different options for breaching the secured house. Even if this wasn't his problem, he couldn't abandon this guy to die inside a steel box. He was going to find a way in. The guy's life depended on it.

17

The mission was clear, and Zander remained confident that he would succeed where his colleague had failed. Failure was not an option in his mind. He'd been well trained by the Marines for several years before being selected to join MARSOC, where he'd excelled, blowing old records out of the water. His training had put him in position to be promoted within the organization, and he had the skills and ability to see any mission through to the very end. He would stop at nothing to finish, either.

"This is where he went in?" Zander confirmed, turning to look at his colleague.

Ben nodded silently, scanning the water.

Zander could see the fear in his eyes, and suspected he knew what was coming next. That was fine with him. Zander wasn't interested in prolonging the man's suffering. He wasn't a complete animal. Without hesitation, he raised the Beretta he'd been carrying and shot Ben in the head, ending his employment with the organization and sending him off the riverbank and into the river. There was no room for failure. Ben's mistake threatened the entire operation. Death was the only fitting punishment.

He slid the Beretta back into the holster on the side of his rib cage and stepped onto the covered bridge. The bloodstain on the old wood was testament to death. That was where Callum had died. His eyes moved over the bridge, looking for signs that the journalist had also been killed. There weren't any, though the wood rail and flooring were freshly splintered by the bullets Ben had used.

Zander shook his head. "Amateur."

Ben had made a mess, and left behind a great deal of evidence. Fortunately, no one would be looking for shell casings or following the ATV tracks back to the road. The country had bigger problems to worry about than searching for a missing journalist and scientist.

Zander squatted, looking through the shabby rails that were meant to keep people from falling over the edge of the bridge. The river wasn't quite as violent as Ben had described it. It had been a few weeks, though, and the mountain run-off had subsided some—it might have been worse before, Zander knew, and so he'd give Ben the benefit of the doubt there.

Yet, the fact was that Zander's instincts told him that the journalist was alive. Ben hadn't found a body—not washed up on the bank or caught by trees or rocks—and he'd supposedly talked to a number of people who had property further downriver, searching for the lost journalist under the pretense of having a friend who'd fallen out of a boat. Nobody had reported a body, or even a half-drowned stranger needing help. There'd been no sign of the man.

Maybe Ben had been right, and he'd injured him, but Zander didn't think the man had been hurt enough to keep him from moving on his own. He was willing to bet money that he needed to search the man's RV for signs of where he and his daughter might have fled. If the journalist was smart, he would be long gone—but that didn't mean he couldn't be found. Ultimately, that's what Zander expected to happen. In this new world, a smart man would pack up and move if someone had tried to kill him, and it sounded as if this Austin was a smart man. Just not smarter than Zander.

Back on the highway, riding on horseback, Zander set his destination as the farm where the journalist had been staying.

And the trailer was right where Ben had described. Zander could see it was empty. He checked it out, finding evidence of the daughter—including a framed picture of a happy family. He smashed the glass frame and snatched the picture out, sliding it into his pocket. A note indicated she was with a family named Loveridge, and going to an uncle's house in

Colorado. He left the note where it lay. He'd do some more checking of riverside properties, closer to where rocks might have caught up a body—maybe he'd even look for offshoots from the river, where the body could have gotten side-tracked —and he'd check at the nearest hospital, but if the journalist didn't turn up, the information in the note would lead him to the girl. And if he could get the girl, he knew her daddy would come running, assuming he was alive. Zander thought he was, and his daughter would be a good bargaining tool. He headed over to the house and did a cursory inspection. Someone had been there after Ben, but they were long gone now.

"Idiot," he grumbled, irritated that he was following a cold trail because Ben had taken so long to report in. One way or another, it wouldn't matter. He wasn't going to give up until he found Austin or his body. Unlike his former colleague, Zander didn't fail. He would complete his mission. And if anyone got in his way, they would die.

18

Amanda rolled to her side on the lumpy mattress she had taken for her own. It was better than the hard ground, she reminded herself, which was exactly what she'd probably have been sleeping on that night if Austin had gotten his way.

Thinking of that, yet again, she wondered if she was crazy. She'd just met this man, and while it was clear that her farm wasn't a safe harbor—not when so many people had known her as a vet, and one who lived alone—did that really mean she should be pairing up with him, traipsing through the country after his teenage daughter? He'd been right the night before, saying she didn't owe him anything, so why did she feel like she did, just because she'd pulled him out of that water-heavy stream? Why did she care?

The questions had kept her up for much of the night but hadn't changed anything. She had no destination for her own life now, and the world was changed. Until she had an idea of what she wanted for herself, helping him seemed like a better option than sitting around or searching blind for somewhere she'd be safe. For the time being, at least, she'd keep helping him.

But that didn't mean she had to be a pushover and watch him kill himself in the process.

The man insisted that they start heading north to his brother's house. He was desperate to find his daughter, and while she could kind of understand his need to make sure his kid was safe, she couldn't get her head around his willingness to sacrifice his own life. He needed rest, now, or he might as well not bother with the journey.

Hadn't he ever flown before? The flight attendants gave a very good example of why parents had to take care of themselves before taking care of their children. Austin didn't seem to understand that. He wasn't thinking clearly. If something did happen to him, he was going to leave Savannah in the world all alone. The way Amanda saw it, if he took some time to heal and get his body back to being one hundred percent, or at least closer to ninety percent—heck, she'd settle for eight percent, the way he was acting—then he could find Savannah and be with her for years to come. That's what Savannah needed.

Giving up on further sleep, Amanda let out a long sigh, staring out the nearby window with its sheer, shabby white curtains hanging over it. Austin couldn't see reason. He was thinking with his heart and not his head. She was already mentally preparing herself for another exhausting day of listening to him complain about how badly they needed to get going.

She'd gotten him to stay at the farm for two days. There was no way she was going to get a third, and she knew it. At least his leg would be in much better shape with the boot she had found. The wound in his side was essentially healed, no sign of infection to be seen.

With the sun silently beckoning her to get out of bed, she threw her feet over the side and opened the door, listening for signs that Austin was awake. He had wanted to sleep in his trailer, but she'd convinced him to sleep in the house to protect her. Of course, it was he who needed the protecting, but she couldn't tell him that.

"Good morning," he said, coming through the front door as she cleared the hallway.

As she'd expected, he'd already been up and moving around. "Good morning," she replied evenly. "Feeling good, I take it?"

He nodded, meeting her gaze. "It's time we get going, Amanda. If you're coming with me, that is. I packed a few changes of clothes, got my trusty Glock 19, and raided the pantry for anything I could find, which was basically nothing more than a little salt and some Johnny's seasoning. I think Savannah must have cleared the rest out," he finished.

"Understandable. We'll need to find food," she pointed out.

"I know, but it isn't like we can run down to the gas station. We need to get moving and search the stores on our way. I take it you haven't changed your mind? I was worried you would," he admitted, his face going more serious.

She let herself smile. "You need help with that leg of yours, and I don't seem to have anything better to do or any safe home to call my own, so I figure I might as well. Doesn't mean I'll let you starve me," she added. "Did you have anything else in that trailer that will be useful?"

He smiled, but shook his head in answer. "I had some matches, a few lighters, candles, and I grabbed the rope I kept on hand. That's about it."

That was a start. "I bet there's a lot more that could come in handy on the road in there. Do you mind if I look?"

He shrugged. "If you think it will help."

"What about a pocket knife?"

He reached into the front of his dark jeans and pulled out a Leatherman. "It's not going to be useful for gutting an animal or stabbing an attacker, but it has its uses."

She grinned at the sight of the tool—the morning was looking up. "Excellent. Duct tape? Plastic?"

"I might have duct tape, but I doubt there's any plastic."

She nodded, her mind whirring with a long list of things she wished she could get her hands on. Her camping gear had been limited. She never camped out. And Austin had been living in a luxury home on wheels and wasn't prepared to actually rough it. The farm they were on had been looted, as well, leaving slim pickings to choose from.

"Garbage bags?" she asked hopefully.

"Maybe. What are you looking for exactly? What's this obsession with plastic? You planning on burying a body?" he joked.

"We're probably not going to find an empty house to stay in, so we're going to need shelter."

He waved a hand. "We'll be fine. It's plenty warm."

This man really was low on survival instincts, she realized. "It isn't that warm. Not at night, Austin. And we need to prepare ahead of time."

"We're headed northwest in the midst of summer, and we'll be at my brother's before it turns cold. We'll be fine," he insisted.

She had to clench her teeth together to keep from snapping at him. "All the same, if you have a tarp or something, that would be helpful. We'll take a couple blankets from here. I'm guessing that the closer we get to the Rocky Mountains, the chillier the nights will be. I'd prefer not to sleep directly on the ground or have my stuff getting wet. We need to keep the matches and blankets dry, hence the need for the plastic. We should double-check here to make sure there are no matches hidden in drawers, too, just in case."

"Fine, and I think I have a small tarp in the storage area. What else?" he asked, frustration evident in his voice.

"We can't carry a lot of water. Do you have any of those reusable bottles?"

"Probably a couple. Savannah was always buying new ones," he replied.

"Good, then we'll need them." She stopped, trying to brain-storm what was worth carrying and what would just be added weight and cargo. "I don't know," she murmured, her brain going through a catalog of survival skills and trying to think of what was needed.

"My brother will be well-equipped to handle this situation," Austin promised, leaning against the wall near the door. "He spent millions outfitting his house to survive the apocalypse. He's one of those prepper types. All we have to do is get there," Austin insisted.

She scoffed. "Oh, piece of cake. What is it, a thousand miles? Two thousand?"

"We've got horses," he shot back. "My daughter's walking."

"And we're going to be riding through towns and cities that have been left completely disrupted. Don't forget that. It isn't going to be a straight shot down the highway. We're going to have to stay off the main roads. We're going to have to do our best to go undetected," she reminded him for what had to be the tenth time.

"I know. I got it. But, Amanda, standing here arguing isn't doing us any good. I'm ready. Let's go search the trailer again and go," he said, turning and awkwardly walking out the door on his booted foot.

She watched him leave, dreading the coming days. She'd made her decision, but what lay in front of them wasn't going to be easy. What would have happened if she hadn't seen him in the river? Would she still be on her own farm, or would she have already left, just the same—maybe even sooner, without Austin there. In reality, she knew her house would have been overrun, given some time. She felt capable of handling herself, but she wasn't so naïve as to believe she was a superwoman able to fend off an army of looters. And she'd been a clear target. Eventually, her home would have been overrun, and she would have been on her own. Maybe without a horse, even, let alone two horses and a capable—well, mostly capable —companion.

She walked out the door, following Austin's dusty trail back to his RV. He was the lesser of two evils, she supposed.

After tossing his trailer, she'd gathered a box of trash bags, soap, and a small bottle of bleach.

"Are you sure we need to keep pulling that cart along with

us?" Austin asked as he saw the growing pile of supplies beside his RV. "It slows us down."

"It isn't like a covered wagon. It's a small cart. Charlie can pull it fine as long as we keep it light, and barely notice it. There's stuff that would be hard to carry without it—a pot for boiling water and extra blankets, to name a few."

He cursed under his breath. "I get it," he muttered, "but I wish we didn't have to keep to the roads."

"You don't need a map to get us to Colorado," she pointed out, remembering how excited he'd been to discover that Savannah hadn't taken his road atlas.

"Yeah, yeah, yeah, whatever," he grumbled, pushing open the door of his trailer and nearly falling down the metal steps.

She bit back a laugh, watching him hobble towards the barn. He had a way of swinging his left leg wide instead of just stepping forward. She was sure it was the bulk of the walking boot making him walk so awkwardly, but it provided a little entertainment for her. Once again, she trailed behind him, her stomach growling loudly.

Back at the barn, she studied the old cart they'd gotten from Daniel, noticing it was in rougher shape than she'd realized. At least, now that she was considering how well it would hold up if they asked it to go all the way to Colorado. Still, the wheels looked good, and that's what really counted. "Do you think we could reinforce it a bit?" she asked.

Austin studied her, his blue eyes boring into hers. He finally let out a long sigh. "Yes, I can fix it up a little. There was some scrap wood in the barn."

She smiled, loving that he had some handyman skills. He'd told her he had made a living as a handyman before the writing thing had really taken off for him. That was going to come in handy. At the very least, it certainly couldn't hurt.

"Good. You do that, and I'll go pack up the food we brought from my place. I'll make those eggs we collected yesterday, too, and get some protein in our bellies before we set out."

He nodded absently, his focus already back on the cart as he walked around it, kicking a tire with his good foot and evaluating the wood situation. She looked back and felt confident he could make it sturdier so that it wouldn't slow them down a bit. It would also give him something to do while she made something to eat. She was starving.

19

Savannah's heart pounded harder against her chest, her feet slamming against the pavement of the highway they were running down. They couldn't stop. It was too dangerous. Tears continued streaming down her face as she did her best to keep up with Malachi, who ran just a few steps ahead of her. His long black hair was streaming behind him, giving her something to focus on.

Then, she made the mistake of turning to look back, and saw that the man with the gun was way too close.

"Malachi! He's coming!" she screamed, infusing as much strength as she could into her muscles to carry her away from the danger.

"Run, Savannah! Don't stop!" he yelled, not turning back.

She could hear the heavy breathing coming from Gretchen beside her, and glanced to her right and saw the woman's terror-stricken face.

"Run," Gretchen gasped out, "just run!"

Savannah pushed herself harder, veering off to the left and following Malachi into the trees when he made a sudden swerve. Branches slapped her in the face, scratched her bare arms, and threatened to trip her as she pushed through, not slowing down for a second.

They burst through to the clearing within seconds of one another. Jim Loveridge was standing over the campfire, his eyes going wide when he saw them, and Gretchen skidding in just behind them.

"What happened?" he called out at the same time that the man following them broke through the trees.

Malachi had already lunged into the makeshift tent they'd made with two blankets and emerged a second later, holding the gun Bill had brought along.

"Get out of here!" Malachi shouted at their pursuer, holding the gun up and aiming at the stranger.

Savannah rushed in behind Malachi. Her lungs burned as she struggled to pull in a breath. Gretchen came to stand beside her, bending over with her hands on her knees, sucking in air. Everyone was silent but for their thundering breath—even the man who'd pursued them was fighting to catch his breath and speak now that he'd caught up to them. Malachi stood staring down the stranger, closer than any of them to the man's gun, up until his father stepped forward.

"Whoa, there, what's going on?" Jim asked, holding his hands up as he moved to stand between his son and the man who had chased them into camp.

"Dad! He's trying to kill us!" Malachi warned, gesturing for his father to stand back.

"Everyone, put the guns away," Jim said calmly.

The man with the gun waved it back and forth angrily. "Are you kidding? No way! We want you out of here!"

"I think there's been a misunderstanding. Let's everyone put the guns down and have a chat," Jim tried again.

Savannah watched the scene, her eyes wide with real fear and her legs still shaking from the running and the terror she had felt earlier. She felt like she was going to throw up, and was fighting to keep it together.

"Dad, they tried to kill us," Malachi said, a touch too loudly to sound calm. "They blame us for what's happening," Malachi finished.

Savannah nodded her support, but it wasn't as if anyone was paying attention to her.

Jim took a small step towards the lunatic waving the gun. "Sir, let's talk, shall we?"

"Get away from me! You're one of them! The revivalists we heard about!" the man screamed, stepping forward instead of back, so that he was only ten feet away from Jim Loveridge, and his son with Savannah and Gretchen behind him.

Jim stopped moving, his arms up in the air. "Okay, alright, I'll stay right here. Can you tell me what's going on? What is it you think we've done?" he asked in a soothing tone.

Savannah watched the man visibly relax a little. "People like you, we don't want you around here."

"People like us?" Jim asked.

"They burnt all the churches, Dad!" Malachi interrupted.

"Because there is no God!" the man shouted back, erupting again and pointing his gun at Jim. "We have to eradicate all of you if we want to survive! Your crazy beliefs are what's going to kill us all!" the man finished, his gun veering sideways to aim directly at Malachi.

"Son, I need you to keep quiet and let me handle this," Jim said quietly.

Savannah agreed with Malachi's father. It had been Malachi who'd incited the mob in the street, getting upset over the church burnings. Malachi had opened his big mouth and nearly gotten them all killed.

"That boy, he called us blasphemous!" the man spit out. "But how can you love a God who does this? How can you still believe there is some higher power? We're all going to die, and it's because your God is letting it happen! And here he comes, telling us we're sinning and blasphemous. But he's wrong. There's a new law, where those who obey will be taken care of. How dare he! It's not us, man. It's people like you, you're all going to die," the man raved. "It's that simple, we know it, and there's no room for religion here."

Jim turned to look at his son, scowling before turning back to the mad man with the gun. "I'm sorry my son said such horrible things. We believe in a kind, loving God. Could we maybe talk about what the Bible says about this time of trouble we're in?"

The man's eyes went wider, and he screamed his answer, "No! I don't want to hear another word about the Bible or your God!" He stared around the group, and then his eyes went back to Jim Loveridge. When he spoke again, he was hoarse from shouting, and looked as wide-eyed as he ever had, the gun still firm in his hand. "I was a good man. I lived a good life. I attended church almost every Sunday. But my family is dead! My baby girl, dead! What kind of God kills a man's family? I have no love for your God. None of us want to hear it. Get out of here, and take your preaching with you. I'm going to let you live because I don't believe in killing, but you better watch your back. There are others out there who are not so kind. We've been given a choice, us or you people," he warned. "And if your boy comes back to our town, it'll be him who's responsible for whatever happens. If he weren't so young, he'd already be dead."

Jim nodded, his lips tight. "Thank you. We appreciate your kindness. I understand your fear. We won't bother you anymore."

Savannah wanted to rage and scream. The man had not been kind. He had nearly shot her! The mob had chased them out of town, screaming ugly things at them, chasing them with shovels and bats and throwing rocks at them. She kept her mouth shut now, though, watching the man disappear into the trees.

Malachi lowered the gun, his hand shaking so badly that Savannah worried he was going to accidentally shoot himself in the foot.

"Where's Mom and the others?" Malachi asked, his eyes darting around their makeshift camp.

"They went down to the stream to collect some water," Jim answered.

"We have to get out of here—now!" Malachi near-shouted, panic slipping back into his voice.

Jim reached out and put his hands on his son's shoulders. "Relax. Tell me what happened."

Malachi sucked in a deep breath. "We went to the first church we saw, just like you told us to. It was burned to the ground, Dad. Actually, the whole block was burned. We found out a plane had fallen from the sky and landed right on the church. We kept walking and found another church, but it had also been burned to the ground. Every church we found was burned. There was a little old lady, kneeling in the ashes at the Baptist church. I asked her what happened, and she told me… it's so horrible…" Malachi choked on his own words, breaking off, and Savannah had to turn her eyes away, facing back to the trees in case the man changed his mind.

"What is it, Mal?" Jim urged him on.

Malachi shook his head, overcome with emotion, and finally Savannah cleared her throat and took over the storytelling. "The woman said, when the plane dropped out of the sky, it killed a lot of people. It landed right on top of a bunch of houses. At first, they thought it was a freak accident. The woman said they started to believe it was some kind of sign because the plane landed on the church. She said the people lost their minds and started blaming God. There are a lot of rumors out there."

"What kind of rumors?" Jim asked.

Savannah looked at Malachi. She couldn't quite bring herself to tell him.

"Dad, they're killing people who are caught worshipping," Malachi whispered.

Jim flinched. "What? Why?"

"I don't know. The old woman said there was a group of about ten men who stormed into her church and began beating the people who were inside. Then, they burned it to the ground. They said they had to do it, or they would be killed by the men in the black uniforms."

Jim finally seemed shaken, more so than when he'd confronted the stranger a few minutes before. He shook his head and then asked, "I don't understand. There's a group actually telling these good people to do this?"

Savannah nodded. "Yes. That's what's so weird. Didn't you hear that man? There was a poster on a light pole. There was a bunch of stuff about following the 'New World Order.' Those who did would be saved, but they couldn't worship anyone else."

Jim looked stricken. "It's just like the Bible said," he whispered.

"We have to go, Dad. They're crazy! They're going to kill us all," Malachi said, his eyes pleading with his father.

Jim closed his eyes before meeting Malachi's again. "You're right, we must go. It isn't safe for us here. Gather up the blankets and supplies. We need to move while there is still light."

"Why are they doing it?" Malachi cried out.

Jim hugged his son before stepping back. "The people are mad and angry. They're lashing out. They have to blame someone, but what's happening is nothing new. Refer to your Bible, son. How many times have God's people been blamed for famine and death? Whoever is spreading such filth must have a hidden agenda. We know better. We know the truth and will not be misled."

Malachi stared at him for a moment, and then turned away to do as told. "You're right. I should have realized. I'll fold the blankets and gather our things," he said.

Savannah breathed a huge sigh of relief. She wanted to get as far away from the city as possible. She had never seen anything so crazy. She'd seen riots on TV, yeah, but never realized how dangerous an angry mob could be. She had truly thought she was going to be murdered in the street for traveling with people who were staunch believers in God.

It was all so unreal. She glanced around the little camp they had set up yesterday afternoon. Jim had insisted they stop, and they had. He'd been in the mood to preach, and said he felt the calling to speak to the people in the city. They'd had some success in a small town they'd stayed in a few nights back. The people had been kind and open to hearing his sermons. They had been provided food and given some to take with them. Jim had claimed it was God providing for them, and nobody had questioned stopping again to try for the same results.

But the city people were clearly not of the same beliefs. Jim had once again claimed God had told him the people in the city needed to hear his words. Now, Savannah cringed at the memory of that conversation. Either God was trying to get them killed, or Jim needed to check his frequency, because somewhere along the line, the message had gotten screwed up.

The Loveridge family had thought they could set up a camp and hold one of their revival meetings here, hoping to earn more followers to strengthen their group while getting more supplies. And it had nearly gotten them killed. Savannah, Malachi, and Gretchen had gone into the city to invite people to the meeting just like they had in other places they'd stayed over. They had assumed the people in the city who chose to come to the revival would bring a potluck meal like the last camp they had set up. That plan had seriously backfired, and Savannah could only hope Jim Loveridge would remember it when he next wanted to stop and give a sermon.

"Can I help?" Savannah asked Malachi.

He looked at her, his eyes still wild from their experience. "I've got it."

"Malachi… are you okay?" she asked him.

He looked around, but he didn't meet her eyes. "I'm fine."

She nodded sadly, not really surprised by his aloofness. He'd barely said a few words to her in the past couple of weeks. He went out of his way to avoid her, it seemed. The only thing keeping her going was the fact that she knew they were close to her uncle's house. At this point, she couldn't wait to be rid of Malachi and his crazy family. They were going to get her killed if she wasn't careful.

20

Austin wasn't thrilled with the slow progress they were making. The cart had been one thing when they'd only been going to his trailer and Amanda had felt the need to bring along some things for that short trip, not knowing what might happen to her farm after she left, but now? Now, it was really holding them back. It was a cumbersome burden that required wide paths and made it impossible for them to cut through steep, narrow trails that would have shortened their journey. Amanda insisted it was a necessity, and that they had to stick close enough to roads to know where they were going anyway, but he couldn't help being frustrated.

"Seriously, I'm going to cut this thing loose!" he growled when the cart bumped its way through a rocky ditch, their gear bouncing and threatening to fall out yet again.

"If you tied the stuff down better, it wouldn't fall out!" she argued. "You're the one who's always in such a hurry that it's a haphazard job."

"I used all the rope I had!"

She ignored his rebuttal and kept trudging along up the hill. They had moved out of the mountains and were heading into the Midwest, but the journey was tiring for them and the horses.

Austin let Raven come to a stop beneath him and took a deep breath. The hill they'd just crested gave them a nice view of the valley below, though. It felt like the first real milestone they had reached.

Amanda stopped beside him atop Charlie, and gestured down toward a town further down the hillside. "We can try and trade for some food down there," she commented.

"Fine."

They continued on in silence, the only sounds being the horses clip-clopping feet and the cart squeaking as it bounced along behind them. The sound of the horses' shoed feet slapping against the hard ground had become his constant companion, filling the gaps of silence. Though he knew he should be grateful to her, Amanda had actually been on Austin's last nerve for some time. He was sure he was riding hers, as well. The latest argument had been about using the paved highway to travel. She refused. The highway was too hot, according to Amanda. It was one of the many complaints she had about their journey west, but using roads while avoiding the highway meant a lot of zig-zagging, and many more chances to run into people who might mean them harm. It was a catch-22 that she didn't seem to acknowledge, and yet she hadn't stopped complaining about how dangerous it was since they'd left the farm over a week ago.

"There's someone on the road up there," she said in a low voice.

Austin's eyes scanned the horizon, spotting the person hunched down in tall, dry grass. He pulled his gun from the waistband of his jeans and slid the safety off. Amanda did the same. They had encountered little trouble on their journey thus far, but the people they had spoken with to do some trading had told them how bad things were in the cities.

The young man who'd been hunched in the grass jumped to his feet when he heard them coming. Both his hands went into the air. "I don't want any trouble," he said, his eyes a little wild.

Austin looked down to see what he had been messing with on the ground. "What is that?" he asked, unable to identify the bulk through the thick grass.

The young man had sandy blond hair that looked like it hadn't been washed or brushed in weeks, and this close, it was clear just how young he was, and how little an apparent threat. His cheeks were hollow, a clear sign of starvation, and he looked terrified. Austin studied him closer and guessed that the kid was probably in his late teens—not much older than his own daughter.

"It's my little sister, sir," the boy replied, his voice wavering.

Austin looked at Amanda, and he saw the second her guard went down. She was a bleeding heart and couldn't pass up the opportunity to help someone—especially a child. Heck, he was proof that she couldn't turn down a chance to help a stranger.

"Amanda," he warned her, but it was too late; she was already sliding off the saddle, holstering the gun she'd held in her hand.

Austin stayed in his saddle, his own gun aimed at the boy in case he tried anything funny.

"What's wrong with your sister?" Amanda asked, approaching the bundle on the ground.

The boy watched Amanda, his apparent terror seeming to bleed away into exhaustion now that they'd become less threatening. "She's sick."

"What kind of sick?" Amanda asked.

"I don't know. She got real sick a couple days ago and isn't getting better. I thought it was the flu, but her fever is real high."

Austin watched as Amanda knelt in the grass, the top of her shoulders and head all that was visible as the dry grass rustled in the breeze. He could hear her murmuring in soft tones, and knew she was talking to the girl.

"How old is your sister?" Austin asked.

"She's eight, sir," he replied, his eyes focused on Amanda.

Austin lowered his gun, no longer worried that the boy was a threat—his eyes were only on his sister and what Amanda was doing. Austin pegged him for the son of a farmer, which brought up the question of why the kid was so far out of town alone with his little sister.

"Where are your parents?" Austin asked, keeping an eye on Amanda.

The boy looked up, his blue eyes going empty. "They're dead, sir."

Austin inwardly winced. "I'm sorry to hear that. Did they pass recently?"

"Yes."

Austin nodded, thankful that the boy's tone was flat instead of grief-stricken, at least. Maybe it was shock, but it made the conversation easier. "What's your name?" Austin asked.

"Beck, and that's my little sister, Janie. Our parents were killed a few days ago. He was a pastor... and they killed him," the boy suddenly sobbed out. Without warning, he collapsed onto his backside, sitting beside Amanda and his sister in the grass as he cried.

Austin dismounted, lost for words. Leaning on Raven, he wiggled his toes in the walking boot to get the circulation moving again before he hobbled towards the kids and Amanda. Reaching them, he put a light hand on the boy's head, and waited for the sobs to subside as he watched Amanda continue whispering to the girl she was examining.

"I'm sorry to hear it, truly. But who is they?" Austin asked quietly.

The boy looked at him then, and there was so much sorrow and pain in his eyes that it hurt Austin to see it.

"The bad ones. The ones who are blaming God for this black-out," Beck said.

"Blaming God?" Amanda asked, looking up from where she was helping the girl to sit up.

Beck nodded. "They say God is to blame for this. My dad, he was a pastor. We were at church, and these men burst in. My dad, he asked them to leave. They shot him in front of the whole congregation. Everyone. My mama, she screamed and ran to my dad. They shot her, too," Beck said, his voice flat and hoarse from sobbing. "They killed a whole bunch of other people, too. I hid underneath a pew; covered Janie with my body. I thought they were going to kill us all. Before they left, they said they would kill anyone caught worshiping the evil God responsible for all this."

Austin was listening to the words, not thinking much about it until a horrible realization popped into his head.

"Beck, I'm looking for my daughter. She's traveling with a group—they're a religious group of sorts. Have you seen them?" he asked, struggling to find the right word to explain who they were. Austin didn't know who they were, though— not really. They had no denomination, so far as he knew. He knew their names and that was about it.

Beck shrugged blankly. "I don't know. We've had a lot of people come and go."

"What are you doing out here?" Amanda asked, lifting Janie in her arms.

Austin looked at her, wondering what she thought she was doing as she walked past him, carrying her tiny bundle and heading for the cart. He moved, walking behind her, Beck right on his heels.

"It was too dangerous at the farm," Beck said from behind Austin.

"Too dangerous?" Austin asked, going around Amanda to move some stuff out of the way in the cart. There was no arguing with her, clearly, and this little girl wasn't walking anywhere on her own. Even Austin understood that, no matter how it slowed them down, they couldn't leave Beck on the side of his road with his sister in this condition.

Beck stared at Amanda and Janie as the vet settled his little sister among some blankets and then answered, "They came and took everything. I ran away in the middle of the night."

Austin nodded. It was a familiar story. People were being pushed out of their homes or killed by those who had no qualms about using violence to get what they wanted. It would have happened at Amanda's farm eventually.

"Tell me about your sister," Amanda said, steering the conversation back to the ailing little girl.

Beck walked to the side of the cart, reaching his hand in to hold his sister's hand. "She just got sick. I don't know what happened."

Amanda was in the cart now, pulling off the heavy black trash bags they had used to cover their supplies, protecting them from view as well as the weather. She grabbed her bag of medical supplies.

"I need water," she muttered, glancing up to Austin.

Austin moved to grab the canteen from his saddle. She took it and made Janie take a few sips.

"What did you two eat, before she got sick?" Amanda asked.

Beck shrugged. "Not much. We had some of my mom's

canned soup a few days ago, but we haven't eaten anything else since then."

Amanda nodded. "Did the soup taste funny? Did you get sick?"

"No," he said firmly, and then he paused, glancing again at his sister. "Well, it did taste kind of funny, but it was cold. I let Janie eat most of it," he said in a soft voice.

Austin reached out and put a hand on the boy's shoulder. "You were being a good big brother."

"Did I make her sick?" he demanded, looking from Austin to Amanda.

"No, like my friend said, you were being a good brother. She'll get better, but you just have to be careful about canned goods now, okay? I think she might have some food poisoning. I have some medicine that's going to help make her feel better. She needs rest and fluids, and I think she's going to be just fine," Amanda assured him.

"Are you a doctor?" Beck asked.

Amanda smiled. "Kind of. I'm a vet, but I grew up on a farm, and my mother's canned food made me sick enough times to recognize food poisoning."

"Do you have family or somewhere to go?" Austin asked.

"My uncle lives a few miles away. I was on my way there."

Austin and Amanda exchanged a look. He gave a subtle nod, agreeing to what he knew she was asking. There was no way to refuse, after all.

"We'll give you a ride over there," Amanda said.

"You will?" Beck asked, his voice betraying his shock.

"We will. Get in and tell us the way to go," Austin said, moving back to climb into Raven's saddle.

Austin looked at Amanda once she'd mounted Charlie, and she smiled. "Thank you."

He nodded, frowning to think that she'd believe he could abandon some kids like this on the side of the road. "I'm not unfeeling. I'm not going to leave a couple kids out here."

"Good. We might not kill each other yet," she joked.

He rolled his eyes, shaking his head. "Don't count on it."

She laughed and clucked her tongue, spurring Charlie and the cart into movement. The cart jerked forward and they set off once again. Austin remained on high alert after hearing the story about the townspeople turning on those who believed in God. That was a scary situation to be in, and he couldn't imagine being in the position of these kids. It made him even more worried about his daughter and the religious nuts he knew she was traveling with. Hopefully, they were keeping their heads down and not spouting off all their religious jargon.

"Right up there," Beck called out, pointing to a small white house in the middle of a large wheat field.

A man emerged on the porch, a long rifle hanging at his side. It was a silent show of strength without appearing overly threatening.

"Is that your uncle?" Austin asked.

Beck jumped out of the cart. "Uncle Art!"

"Beck?"

"It's me! Uncle Art, Janie's sick!" Beck called out, running across the field and into his uncle's arms.

"Where's your mom and dad?" Austin heard the uncle ask as they got closer, and his heart squeezed.

Beck threw his arms around his uncle's neck, apparently unable to answer, and Austin pulled his horse to a stop, giving Beck and the uncle a few minutes of privacy as Amanda went on with Janie in the cart. He could hear the uncle's sobs and imagined how he would feel if it had been his brother Ennis who'd been killed in such a brutal fashion. They weren't exactly close, but it was unfathomable.

"Come on, sweetie," Amanda said to the little girl who was sitting up in the cart.

"I can carry her," Austin volunteered.

"No, not with your leg. You don't need to be putting any extra weight on it," she lectured him, already taking the girl in her own arms.

He wasn't going to argue, he guessed, knowing the damage he could do to himself and the girl if he fell. Instead, he walked along behind her as she headed toward the porch.

"I'm Austin, and this is Amanda," he said, introducing himself to the uncle.

The man nodded, still clutching Beck. "Thank you so much for getting them out here."

"Do you have food and water?" Amanda asked.

The uncle hesitated, apparently stuck for words.

"For the kids, not for us," Austin supplied, knowing that that was what Amanda had been asking. "Your niece has a touch of food poisoning, it seems."

The man breathed out relief, and nodded thanks. "I do."

Amanda smiled, settling Janie into a chair on the porch. "Great, she needs to start with something light—rice, apple-sauce, maybe some toast," Amanda said, forgetting that bread might not be an option, and that toasting it the traditional way was definitely not possible. Still, from the look on his face, the man seemed to understand.

"Can I give you something for your trouble?" Art asked them.

"No, thank you. We need to be on our way."

"Where you headed?" he asked.

"Out west," Austin replied simply.

"That's a long way. Are you headed out to Denver?" he asked.

Austin raised an eyebrow, immediately suspicious. "We'll probably pass through. Why do you ask?"

Art shrugged, his eyes on Beck and his sister. "I heard a few other folks are headed out that way. Supposed to be some kind of refugee camp or something."

"Really?" Austin and Amanda asked in unison.

"That's what I heard. I don't believe it for a minute. I'll be staying right here," he said.

"I'm looking for my daughter," Austin said. "She's traveling with a group of people who are headed that way. They're a religious group of sorts."

"Oh?" Art asked.

"Maybe you saw them?" Austin asked hopefully.

"Loveridge family?" he asked.

Austin felt his own eyes widen as he grinned. "Yes! You saw them?"

"It's been a couple weeks. They said they were going to Utah. They were trying to recruit people to join them. Which one is your daughter?"

"Savannah. Brown hair with blonde highlights—petite teenager," he said, anxious for any news at all of his daughter.

"She was with them alright."

Austin nearly dropped to his knees. "She was okay?"

"Looked fine to me. They gave a service and then moved on the next day. She kind of hung back. I wondered what her story was. I asked her if she was okay. To be honest, I didn't much care for the leader and was a little worried she was being held against her will, but I didn't get the impression that was the case once I spoke to her. She assured me she was fine," Art said. "Just didn't fit in."

Austin fought down the emotions rolling through him. "Thank you for talking with her. I can't tell you how good it is to hear she's okay. I've been worried sick about her."

The man stepped down off the porch away from his niece and nephew, gesturing Austin to the side for a quieter word. "Listen, I don't want to worry you, but what happened to my brother, that's been happening all over. I told my brother to be careful, but he wouldn't listen. Those heretics are roaming savages," he said, shaking his head. "I had no idea my brother had been killed. I would have gone into town to get the kids."

Austin nodded, his throat tight. "Thank you for the information. Take care of yourselves," he said, taking one last look before moving back to the horses.

Amanda quickly re-secured the gear in the cart and climbed into her saddle. They waved goodbye and headed back toward the town they'd seen and bypassed in favor of getting these kids to their new home. Austin felt lighter now, elated to know Savannah was in good health. Well, two weeks ago, she had been. He prayed Loveridge was keeping his mouth shut.

He'd kill the guy if he put his daughter in danger.

21

Austin and Amanda plodded along. He couldn't dismiss the feeling of foreboding he felt, more and more, the closer they got to the town spread out below them. They'd passed a sign announcing that the town had a booming population of ten thousand residents. It wasn't exactly a metropolis, but Austin hoped there was still some scavenging to be done. They were running critically low on food, and trade was their best method of getting food since they had to keep moving.

Amanda was confident she could hunt for wild game, but Austin just wasn't willing to stay put long enough. He wanted to keep going. Now that he knew they were trailing behind Savannah, he was energized to keep pushing harder. He could deal with his aching leg—what he couldn't deal with was being separated from his daughter for much longer. Plus, they had an advantage of being on horseback while the Loveridge crew was on foot. Once again, he couldn't help thinking that the cart was only slowing them down.

"We need to think about leaving the cart," he started.

"No."

"We'll be able to move faster. We can trade it for some food," he reasoned.

"Austin, the cart is allowing us to carry more supplies. It's keeping us off the ground at night. We're making good time, and the cart isn't slowing us down that much," she said irritably, her eyes remaining focused on the town ahead of them.

"It isn't your kid we're chasing. I think you'd feel differently if you were in my shoes," he grouched.

"I'm sick of you using that excuse. I'm with you, and that should mean something. I do care about you finding your daughter. Can't we leave it at that?"

He opened his mouth to argue but snapped it shut almost immediately, squinting into the distance and urging Raven forward. He'd been right, he saw after a moment—they were being greeted. "Up ahead," he said, just loudly enough to be heard over the cart.

She nodded, having just spied the men who were stepping onto the road. "Crap," she muttered as several more people joined the few men who'd already gathered in their path.

They drew their horses to a stop at the very edge of town, facing off with the group ahead of them. "We don't want any trouble," he said.

A man stepped forward. "Nice horses."

Amanda's hand went to the weapon on her side, and Austin mentally willed her to leave it be. They were outnumbered and would never make it out of a face-off alive.

"We're passing through," Amanda said.

"What about the cart? What's in it?" the man asked.

"Personal stuff. Nothing of any value," Austin replied.

"I'll be the judge of that," the man shot back.

And with that, they were quickly surrounded by the group. They watched helplessly as the man and a few of his cronies started pulling trash bags aside, picking up the pots, blankets, and the extra changes of clothes they had. One of the men grabbed Amanda's medical bag and opened it.

"What's this?" he asked pointedly.

"I'm a vet. Those are my supplies," she replied.

Austin watched the faces of the people who were essentially holding them hostage. The revelation of her profession changed things. He could see it. And while he couldn't quite put a finger on what was happening, it was clear that there was an undercurrent of malice here—enough to send a shiver down his spine as he waited to see what would happen next.

"A vet, huh?" one muttered.

She nodded. "Yes."

"Does that mean you know how to work on people, too?"

She shrugged. "I know the basics."

The group exchanged looks then, and Austin knew Amanda's confession had been a grave mistake.

"Why don't you come with us? We have someone who could use your attention," one of the men said.

Amanda looked at Austin and then back at the man. "I can do that. In return, I expect you to leave us be and let us pass through."

The first man grinned. "Sure."

Austin could see the lie written all over his face. "Amanda…" he hissed.

It was too late, though; she was being pulled off her horse. One of the group members carried her bag. She turned back to look at Austin, and his eyes locked with hers. He moved to get off the horse then, but was stopped.

"She'll be fine. You don't need to worry about her," a tall man said, putting his hand on Austin's leg.

"I'd like to go with her," he argued.

"I said, she'll be fine."

Austin looked up and saw Amanda being led around the corner of a building. Glancing around, he took in the restaurants lining the street—diners and fast food joints that would probably have been raided already. They were just on the outskirts of the town. To the side, away from it, he could see a line of trees signifying the river they'd been running parallel to for a while.

His mind was already searching for an escape route. Through town and into the heart of it was not an option.

"Where is she being taken?" he asked, unable to see her any longer.

"Why don't we go have a drink?" the man asked in return.

"A drink?" Austin echoed.

The man chuckled. "We're not completely uncivilized here. The bar is open!"

Austin knew it wasn't really a request—he was being ordered into the bar. He had a feeling he was about to be relieved of his gun, too. As long as they didn't search him, though, he would be okay. The Glock from Amanda's house was secured in his walking boot.

Austin dismounted and grabbed the reins of both horses,

leading them to a park bench on the sidewalk in front of the bar. The cart clunked along behind them. He looped the reins over the bench's armrest, not really securing the horses in case they had to make a quick escape. That done, he followed the man into the bar. It took his eyes a minute to adjust to the darkness inside as he looked around, expecting to be jumped at any minute.

"Look, I appreciate the offer, but I'd prefer to stick with my horse," he said.

"Relax. She's fine. Have a drink," the man ordered, bellying up to the bar and gesturing to the man behind it.

Austin took a deep breath and found a seat close to one of the few windows in the place. He was able to see down the street to where Amanda had disappeared. There was one of those emergency clinics on the right-hand side of the road, with only a single building next to it. He had a feeling that was where they had taken her.

He glanced back to Raven and Charlie, and their cart—nobody was bothering them or their supplies at the moment.

"I should get the horses some water," he muttered.

"Just hang out a minute," the man answered, taking a seat across from him.

Austin sized him up. The guy was big—like, linebacker big. With Austin's bum leg, exhaustion from traveling, and a lack of real food, Austin didn't think he stood a snowball's chance in the desert if he got into a physical altercation.

"So, is someone sick?" Austin asked casually.

"You could say that."

"Injured? Shot?" he asked, pressing the man for information.

The guy chuckled. "Yep, got himself shot. Messed with the wrong old lady."

Austin raised an eyebrow. "Really?"

He nodded and sat back as the man from behind the bar came out with a bottle of whiskey and two glasses. The man across from Austin poured each of them a shot, sliding the glass over to Austin as the bartender left them alone once again. Austin took the shot, one eye closing as the cheap whiskey washed down his throat. There was nothing friendly about this situation, though, despite the man's attempts to make it appear so.

"Your friend—a real vet, huh?"

Austin shrugged. "I guess. I don't know for sure. That's what she said."

"You don't know her?"

He shook his head, wanting to play off the relationship. He sensed malice, and his instincts were telling him to keep it casual. The situation was not as it seemed. This drink in a bar was nothing more than a distraction.

"We met recently, and I offered to travel with her," Austin explained.

The man was quiet for a few minutes, slowly drinking down his liquor before pouring himself another shot. Movement outside caught Austin's attention. It was two more men, younger and wearing camo. One of them made a hand signal. Austin's head snapped, looking at the man sitting across from him.

"Well, I believe we have relieved you of your burden," he said with a smile.

"Excuse me?"

"You can take your horse and some provisions, and go ahead and ride out of here," he said, as if he was granting Austin some huge gift.

"I'll wait for my friend."

"No, you won't. You'll leave, just like I told you to."

Austin studied the man's face, his beady eyes cold and dangerous. He wasn't going to win this round. It was more than likely that there were people situated behind the bar, just waiting for him to argue, and even more outside. He was outnumbered, and likely outgunned.

"You want to tell me what's going on here?" Austin asked, working hard to keep his voice casual.

The man grinned and gestured down to the clinic Austin had guessed they'd taken Amanda to. "It's not difficult to figure out. Your friend, the good doctor, she's going to be sticking around here for a while. We'll need those medical supplies she's brought along. You can take a horse and keep moving to wherever it was you were headed. I think we're being rather generous. You don't want to insult us by refusing our offer."

Austin swallowed, glancing at the men outside. "You're keeping her against her will?"

He looked back to an evil smile.

"She's a doctor. Don't they swear an oath to take care of folks?"

Austin fought the urge to roll his eyes. "She's a vet. I don't think she made an oath to be held hostage to take care of a dude who got shot because he was up to no good."

"Same difference."

Austin wasn't going to win. He looked outside, noting the intersecting streets and the clinic where he suspected Amanda was being held before looking back at the man. He took note of the empty lot behind the clinic, too, making a point of not looking too obvious as he surveyed the area by trying to give equal attention to everything in sight, from the clinic to the abandoned convenience store and fast food joints.

"Alright. I guess I have to see your point. I'll take the deal and head out," he said.

"Perfect. Why don't I help you sort through the stuff and see what all you need and what we'll need here?" his so-called friend said, standing.

It wasn't a question, but a statement. Austin was going to lose both his gear and his partner.

They walked out of the bar. The two young men who'd been on the other side of the road drifted across and began pulling at the bags in the cart. In the end, Austin was allowed to keep his canteen, some of the jerky and nuts they had, and some basic gear. The cart was staying, along with Amanda's horse, Charlie. He didn't put up a fight or argue.

Austin climbed onto Raven and rode out of town, not looking back. He could feel them watching him. There was a stand of sagebrush and locust trees up ahead, about three miles past the outskirts of town, and he'd head there; it would provide some cover.

He only allowed himself to glance back once, about two miles out, and the men had already walked off at that point. He faced forward again, and guided Raven into the trees and dismounted, giving himself a minute to think.

Amanda had given away too much information about herself —they should have foreseen how valuable someone with medical knowledge would be, and that she'd be held captive if someone got the opportunity. The moment she'd opened her mouth, Austin had known it was too much. Now, he had to decide if she was worth the trouble of trying to save. It was hard to put it in those terms, even in his own mind, but he had a bum leg and his daughter was counting on him. If he went back, there was a good chance he would be killed or taken prisoner himself. He was only one man against what appeared to be a good-sized group of people who would all be armed. They hadn't taken his Glock, which meant he had two hand-guns. Amanda's rifle had been deemed hers, which by default meant it had become theirs, and therefore he hadn't been allowed to take it.

If he was captured or killed, he would never see Savannah again. His dad heart was telling him to get back on the horse and keep riding. His sense of right and wrong was telling him he couldn't leave Amanda behind. She had saved his life, and she was only out here because of him. He owed her.

"Crap," he muttered, rubbing a hand over his face.

He wasn't a hero. He wasn't trained military. He knew nothing about covert operations. How in the world was he supposed to rescue her? Raven gave a soft neigh as she moved to a patch of green grass and began to munch. He watched the mare, realizing that, with only one horse, they were going to be on foot. Catching up to Savannah would be extremely difficult, or impossible—they'd just be heading to his brother's and hoping she'd stopped there. He could feel himself practically being torn in two over the decision now and had to tell himself that it wasn't an either-or thing. He wasn't choosing Savannah over Amanda if he left, or choosing Amanda over Savannah if he stayed. He was just… changing the timeline. And that was what he had to do, he realized.

He couldn't abandon Amanda.

He'd have to go in under the cover of darkness. He could find his way back to the clinic, though there was a chance she wouldn't be there. She could be held anywhere, but the sooner he went back, the better a chance he'd have that she was still there. Streaks of orange were already racing across the sky, telling him nightfall was coming soon. He was only going to get one chance to save her.

With his mind made up, he sat down and got comfortable, waiting for it to get dark.

Austin made the decision to leave the horse about a mile outside of town. Raven was too loud, and would draw attention to himself. He removed the walking boot, as well, testing his weight on his leg before putting on the boot that had been hanging from his saddle. It felt good to wear a real shoe again, at least. He needed to be covert and unencumbered, and the boot was neither of those things. Meanwhile, as it had gotten darker, he'd come up with a plan and hoped it would work. The clinic was fairly isolated, and he'd taken a wide berth coming up behind where he estimated the clinic to be, the empty lot directly in front of him.

There was only a sliver of a moon in the sky, which made navigating difficult, but it also served to help him stay hidden. He squatted behind a car, straining his eyes to see clearly. He hoped he was in the right area as he dashed across a road. It was eerily quiet, making every step he took sound much louder than it actually was.

He heard a horse neighing and froze, looking behind him and expecting to see Raven following him. She wasn't there. He moved closer to the building he could see outlined in front of him and heard the soft sound of a horse again. His eyes re-focused, and he realized it was Amanda's chestnut, Charlie, tied to a dead streetlamp outside the clinic.

Either Austin had some really good luck, or it was a trap. Did they know he was coming back? Austin raced to the back of the building, pressing his body flat against it when he heard men's voices.

"I don't know anything about horses," one of the voices said.

"That lady doc won't take care of Tim if we don't bring her the horse," another voice replied.

"Side of the road seems like a dumb place for a horse."

"You want to take it inside, make it a bed?"

"Shut up. I just want to know what the hell we're supposed to do with the thing. Ain't like none of us are planning on traveling."

"I don't know. I guess we watch it and make sure it doesn't run off."

Austin had to smile. Amanda could be extremely demanding and difficult. He was glad to know she was giving them a hard time, and having Charlie right there could prove very useful for a quick escape, assuming Austin could even get to her and the horse without getting shot. Now that he knew there were two men outside, he had to assume she was probably being guarded inside the clinic, too.

He pulled his Glock from where he'd placed it in his waistband, his other gun now resting in a side holster. Weapon ready, he began sliding along the wall, feeling for a back door. He knew there had to be one. Finally, his back connected with a door handle. With a deep breath, he tried it, hoping it would be unlocked. His luck wasn't that good, which meant he was going to have to go through the window he could see a couple feet down, or else go around to the front.

He moved to the window and rejoiced when he found it about halfway open. Someone was taking advantage of the cool night air. He imagined the clinic would be hot and stuffy with no AC and few windows in the building, so it made sense, but it also worked to his advantage. He removed the screen before leaning his head inside and listening carefully, and immediately picked up on Amanda's voice. She was talking with someone in what he'd come to refer to as her doctor voice.

Without wasting another minute, he put the gun back in his

waistband and hoisted himself through the window. Not trusting his bum leg to catch him, he let himself down gingerly, but his leg was holding out better than he'd hoped. Amanda had been right that he must have been giving it more exercise than he'd realized, just by riding. Inside, he moved to the room's doorway and froze, listening intently to make sure no one had heard his entrance. Amanda was still talking. She was close by.

Austin could make out a desk and what looked like a shelf. He was in an office, the door wide open. The clinic looked to be pitch black beyond the door, which was going to make his rescue mission all the more difficult. He stood against the doorway, listening to Amanda's voice, and then he stepped out. With one hand on his gun and another pressed against the wall, he slowly followed the wall through the darkness, using it as a guide.

He came to a closed door and paused with his ear against it. Amanda had stopped talking, stealing away his impromptu guiding light. His eyes darted back and forth in the darkness, but he could see and hear nothing. Standing still wasn't going to help him find her, though. He kept moving until his hand hit air. He reached out, waving his hand around, and realized he'd come to another hallway. He turned, peering down the black hole that was the hall, and saw a faint glow near the ground about ten feet in front of him. He put his finger on his gun's trigger, readying himself to shoot.

Amanda's voice came through the darkness then, much clearer and louder. She was in the room. He took small steps, using his free hand in front of him to check for any obstructions before getting to the open door. Gingerly, inching his face out, he carefully peeked into the room, praying no one was guarding the door.

With the candlelight in the room, he first saw Amanda, her hair pulled into a ponytail as she used a cloth to dab at a man's stomach. The man was facing away from them. He could see no one else, though he couldn't be sure without stepping inside. Taking a chance, he slid in.

Amanda spun around, her eyes going wide when she saw him. "What are you doing?" she hissed.

He held a finger to his lips, shushing her.

"He's unconscious," she grumbled.

"Guards?" he asked in a whisper.

"Out front."

"Let's go," he said, not wanting to spend another second inside the clinic.

She looked back at her patient and, for a second, he thought she was going to tell him no. After all this, though, there was no way he was leaving her here to fend for herself just because some dirtbag had gotten himself shot. He'd pick her up and carry her out of there if he had to.

"Gun," she requested.

He gave her her own Glock and quickly told her how he'd gotten in, and how they'd get out. Together, they moved back down the hall and towards the office.

"Go," he hissed when they got to the window.

She'd jumped up and out the window in mere moments. He was about to follow her through when he heard a shout behind him. He spun around to see light flooding the hallway.

"Come on!" Amanda hissed.

He moved up onto the ledge and was trying to figure out how to land on his good leg when he heard the first gunshot.

Automatically, he jumped, falling to the ground on impact. Amanda reached for him, helping him to his feet.

"Get them!" he heard a male voice shout.

Footsteps were already pounding towards them from the right side of the building.

"Go!" he shouted at Amanda, who dashed to the left, heading for the street.

The last place he wanted to go was into town, but his exit was blocked. Amanda raced around the corner of the building.

"Charlie!" she cried out.

Austin turned, aiming wildly and firing off a couple rounds at whoever was giving chase before hurrying after Amanda's slim figure. He rounded the corner and found her already on horseback.

She reached out a hand, yanking him up as she kicked the horse into movement. More gunshots rent the air, followed by more shouts and bullets whizzing past them. Austin turned, keeping himself mounted with his legs and with one arm wrapped around Amanda's waist as he unloaded his magazine into the darkness, having no idea if he had hit his targets or not. There was no aiming involved—this was about escape and living to fight another day.

"I'm out!" he shouted over the sound of the horse galloping down the paved city street. He turned back to face forward, feeling Amanda hunkering down to urge Charlie on faster. The horse wasn't used to having two adults on his back, or to running at this speed, but he was doing an admirable job of suggesting he was—Austin wouldn't have bet the horse could run this fast.

As THEY MOVED from the road onto the grass skirting the trees, Charlie kept to a full gallop, nearly bouncing Austin off the back. Austin wrapped his other arm around Amanda's slim waist, holding on for dear life as she guided the horse further away from town, only slowing when Austin directed her to move into the trees ahead.

"I don't think they're following us," Austin breathed out on a long sigh.

Amanda slowed Charlie to a walk before pulling him to a full stop. "I'll walk. Did you lose Raven?" she asked.

"No, I left her in a grassy area right around here," he said, his eyes scanning the dark surroundings.

Amanda put her fingers to her lips and gave a piercing whistle, nearly deafening him.

"What'd you do that for?" he asked angrily.

"Raven will come if she can," she replied easily.

"And so will the guys that were just holding you hostage," he snapped, wondering if she was going to sabotage all of his efforts.

Amanda laughed, the sound both familiar and welcome, even as tense as he was.

"Relax, those guys don't have horses. They weren't all that organized, either. I could have walked out of there on my own," she said.

"Oh, really?" he asked, nudging her shoulder with his gun to remind her who'd been doing the shooting and had a weapon.

She looked over her shoulder at him, her face going more serious. "Thank you for coming back, Austin, really. Admittedly, I probably couldn't have walked out, but they weren't really doing a great job of guarding me, so I was hoping."

Austin nodded as she slipped down to the ground and then helped him off Charlie's back, as well. "I think they were playing at the bad guy thing with no real experience at actual kidnapping."

"I figured out I'd made a huge mistake telling them I was a vet. I played the dumb girl routine and pretended to be completely naïve to what was happening and it worked well enough, though I don't know how long it would have lasted. They left me alone with my patient, assuming I wouldn't try to escape. They told me you were getting some rest in one of the houses. I knew they were full of it—I saw you leaving on Raven, out a window—but pretended otherwise," she explained.

He nodded again. "Smart move. They ran me out of town. They kept the cart and most of the supplies," he told her.

"I should have known better," she muttered, leaning back against a tree and watching Charlie beginning to nibble on grass.

"We know better now," he assured her.

Amanda whistled again, the sound cutting through the night air. "Listen!" she told him, just a moment later.

Austin cocked his head to the side, listening to whatever it was she heard. "Holy crap," he said with surprise.

It was the sound of hooves, running fast. Seconds later, the black horse emerged from the shadows, going straight for Amanda. Amanda wrapped her arms around Raven's neck, nuzzling her before holding her steady for Austin to climb on.

"Let's get out of here," she said, mounting Charlie and clicking her tongue to begin moving her own horse through the trees.

22

Savannah observed the horse Jim Loveridge had managed to get with a great deal of apprehension. She wasn't fond of horses—not now, not ever. They were so incredibly big, and their mouths were huge, and their teeth even bigger. When she'd told the Loveridges about the horses on the Little farm, she'd had no intention of going with them and actually having to ride one of the things or share the same air. At best, horses were pretty from a distance, or in pictures. Up close and personal was a different story.

Tonya Loveridge currently rode the horse. She'd been growing weaker every day. Jim had used his charm to talk a family into giving them the horse—in return for prayers, of all things. They'd stayed a night at the farm and been given a nice meal, too. The stay had been a welcome surprise after being met with such hate in some of the towns they'd passed through.

Truly, Savannah couldn't understand why the Loveridges refused to keep their faith a secret, knowing that admitting to being Christians could get them killed. Couldn't they just focus on traveling for now, and then focus on their faith once they got back home?

Yet, the one time she'd broached that suggestion, it had opened a whole can of worms and a really long sermon she didn't ever want to revisit. Since then, it had been easy to decide she needed to keep her mouth shut. Especially with the growing divide between her and Malachi making things ever more tense and uncomfortable, there was no reason to stir up extra trouble that would make her stand out as even more of an outsider within the group. And she was perfectly capable of keeping her opinions to herself. Soon, they would be at her uncle's, and then she would never see the Loveridge family again. Although, she would miss Malachi a little… just not as much as she would have thought, back when they'd first started out. Now, traveling closer to him than usual, she couldn't help glancing at him when that thought crossed her mind. As if sensing her gaze, he looked back at her.

"You don't have to be afraid of him," Malachi told her, gesturing to the horse being led by Jim. "You're watching him like he's going to turn into a monster," he said with a small grin.

"I rode a horse once. I fell off," she said, summing up her reasoning as shortly as possible. Every time she gave up on

Malachi, he opened up a conversation that made her remember how she'd felt about him before the journey had started. She didn't need that. Better to keep things simple, and keep him at the distance that he'd been keeping her at.

"You know what they say about falling off a horse," he said with a friendly smile.

It was little moments like this that were driving her crazy. Why couldn't he make up his mind deciding how he felt about her? She sighed, as much because of his erratic treatment as because of the subject of horses. "I know what they say, but I think whoever *they* are don't know what it's like to fall off a horse. If *they* did, they might think twice about giving such horrible advice."

He chuckled, looking at the old mare that, truth be told, did seem about as gentle as they came. "My mom is doing fine, and she's not a great rider."

"Are you?" Savannah asked—despite having just told herself that she wouldn't invite more connection with the handsome teen beside her.

He shrugged. "I've ridden before. My grandparents used to have horses. When I would stay with them, I got to ride quite a bit."

"Why did you stay with them?" she asked.

"When I was younger, my parents didn't always like to take

me on their long trips. I'd stay with my grandparents. When I was about seven, my grandparents started joining my parents on the road. It became a family thing," he said with a wistful tone.

She smiled sadly, thinking of Eli. "I bet that was fun."

"It was. It's hard to believe it's all changed now."

She knew he was thinking about his grandpa and couldn't help feeling sorry for him. She wasn't sure what to say to make him feel better, and thought it best to just be quiet and walk along beside him. She'd casually closed the distance between them, not even thinking about it. He didn't seem to notice they were within hand-holding distance, though, and she wasn't going to point it out.

"I'd like to learn, maybe," she said after walking in silence.

"What?" he said, turning to look at her.

She flushed, not quite sure where the statement had come from. But if the Loveridges were right, and the world had changed for good... knowing how to ride a horse could be important. "I'm not saying I love the idea of it, but I can see how learning would be smart. At least trying it. Maybe... maybe you could show me how to ride? The basics?"

He smiled, his brown eyes meeting hers with a warmth that sent butterflies into her stomach, just like it had back when they'd first met. "Great. When we stop for the night, I'll give you your first lesson."

She grinned, as excited about the change in routine as anything. And he was right—maybe there was nothing to be scared of if the horse was this docile, so much so that Tonya could ride him. And it would be so nice to get a break from walking. Her feet hurt from all the traveling, but she knew every step was getting them a little closer to her uncle's place. She was hoping her father would be there, waiting for her. The sensible part of her told her it was next to impossible that he'd get there before they did, but with all the stopping they'd been doing, it was a hope she held onto. Plus, she knew that her dad knew how to ride—he'd been trying to get her on a horse since they'd parked at the Little farm, and she'd been refusing him constantly. If he'd found a horse to ride, couldn't he have gotten ahead of them somehow?

It wasn't long before she noticed the distance between her and Malachi was back. He'd somehow ended up leading the pack. Gretchen was on the horse now, and Jim was in deep conversation with Bill behind them. Once again, Savannah walked all alone in the middle of the group.

Tonya dropped back to her, as if sensing her thoughts, falling into step beside Savannah.

"How are you doing?" she asked.

"Me?" she asked, not a little surprised.

Tonya laughed. "Yes, you, silly. You seem melancholy."

"I'm fine. I'm a little tired. I'm sure all of us are."

"Yes, we are. But God gives us strength when we think we can't go on," she said in a soft voice.

"I suppose."

"Savannah, I know you're feeling all alone. I don't want you to feel that way."

Savannah smiled. "Thank you. It's hard not to, though."

Another minute passed before Tonya spoke again. "Are you and Malachi getting along okay?" she asked gently.

Savannah nodded automatically, and then shook her head. She honestly had no idea what to say to that. "I guess. I think we're all a little stressed."

"You'll have to forgive him. We, his father and I, have put a lot of pressure on our son. I think we may have given him the wrong impression."

"About what?" Savannah asked.

Tonya took a deep breath. "We have talked with Malachi a great deal about what we expect from him. I know you're not familiar with our beliefs and our ways, but we love our son and we want him to grow up to be a good man who will one day fill his father's shoes. It takes a special woman to give up her home and her worldly belongings to follow a husband around the country."

Savannah went quiet for several seconds. She wasn't quite as naïve as Mrs. Loveridge clearly suspected. "You don't think I'm good for him," Savannah said.

"It isn't that, honey, not at all. It's just, you're a beautiful girl, and we don't want Malachi to forget those values we've instilled in him. You are both young, and we know how powerful such feelings can be. We only want to be sure the two of you are making good decisions. Being out here, living like we are, it can confuse things. I'm not your mother, but I can be a shoulder for you to lean on. We're all here for you. If you want to talk, please come find me," she said, touching Savannah's hand.

"Thank you," Savannah muttered. None of what Tonya had said had surprised her, but it hadn't exactly been a comfortable chat, either. She'd settle for friendship with Malachi, instead of his attitude toward her running hot and cold, but she couldn't deny there'd been stronger feelings there before, and not that long ago. But it wasn't like she'd ever been thinking about marriage, and maybe that was the difference. Maybe the Loveridges jumped right over dating to exchanging rings, in which case she and Malachi had never been on the same page.

Tonya drifted away after a few minutes of companionable silence, leaving Savannah alone once again. She thought over everything Tonya had said, going through it piece by piece. It did explain Malachi pulling away, but it also made clear she wasn't good enough for their precious kid. She got it.

She just couldn't wait until she could get to Uncle Ennis' house. There was more walking to come first, though.

It was late in the day and they were setting up camp when Malachi walked over to her. "I can give you that riding lesson now," he said with a smile.

She shrugged, the prospect less tempting than it had been earlier. "I'm fine. We have things to do."

"No, we don't. My mom said I should show you how to ride."

Savannah hesitated, still hurt by the declaration that she wasn't good enough to be with a Loveridge. Then, a surge of stubbornness ran through her and she pushed Tonya's words aside. Learning to ride was more important, and she preferred that Malachi show her over anyone else.

"Okay, but not fast. Don't let go."

He laughed, his hair blowing in the wind. "I won't. I'll be right there with you."

They walked together to where the horse had been tied to a tree. It pawed at the ground as they approached.

"I don't think it likes me," she said, hesitating all over again.

Malachi reached out and petted the horse's nose. "He likes you fine. Come on—I'll help you up."

She grimaced, but allowed him to help him fit her foot into the stirrup and then give her a lift upward so that she could swing over and into the saddle. "This is so high," she squealed, holding onto the saddle horn with both hands.

"You'll be okay. Relax and take the reins in your hands," he instructed her.

"I don't want to let go," she whispered.

"It's okay, Savannah. He's not going anywhere unless we want him to. He's been walking all day and he's just waiting for you," Malachi said in a calm voice.

She nodded tightly, feeling her whole body tense at the prospect of holding the flimsy reins instead of the saddle, which at least seemed a little sturdier. "Okay, but I don't want him to run."

"I'll walk alongside you. Relax your body and enjoy the ride," he said.

She held on as the horse began to move through the clearing they'd reached, her heart pounding as she got used to the movement, finally relaxing her hips and allowing her body to sway back and forth. True to Malachi's word, the horse stayed at a steady walk and didn't seem inclined to do anything more. "It's not so bad," she said with relief.

"I told you. Now, you take the reins on your own. I'll walk beside you, but you're leading. Tug right or left to steer him."

"What about when I want to stop?" she asked.

"Just pull back on the reins."

She took a deep breath. "Okay. I got it," she said, taking hold of the reins and feeling more in control, even once Malachi's hand left them.

It was both freeing and exhilarating at the same time. The horse's easy walk was rhythmic—almost soothing in a weird way. Suddenly, she couldn't believe she had been afraid of riding a horse. This was actually kind of fun. She looked to her left to talk to Malachi then, and saw he wasn't there. She twisted in the saddle, and saw him about twenty feet back, standing with his hands on his hips and grinning from ear to ear as he watched her.

"I knew you would be a natural!" he called out.

"You weren't supposed to leave my side!" she hollered, and then she was jerking forward and clenching up as she lost her balance, the horse having turned suddenly beneath her.

The horse must have taken it as a sign that she wanted to go faster. It set off at a rocky trot, bouncing her in a way that suggested it was trying to rock her out of the saddle. Every-thing Malachi had told her left her head. Panicking, she tried pulling on the reins while digging her heels into the horse's sides to hold on, but she couldn't bring herself to lift her hands from the saddle to really tug backward—she was too busy hanging on. The next thing she knew, the horse was racing across a wide-open field.

"Savannah! Slow down!" she heard Malachi shout behind her.

"Malachi!" she screamed, dropping the reins and grabbing the saddle horn with one hand and the horse's mane with her other, leaning forward and just hoping not to fall.

"Hold on! Don't let go!" she heard him shout, but his voice was far away.

She didn't dare look back. She was barely holding on as it was.

"Whoa, boy, whoa!" she screamed, but he only seemed to go faster.

All she could do was hold on and hope it would stop on its own. And then he sped up instead, and she looked up ahead and saw a fence and what looked like a cliff beyond it.

"Oh no, please, please stop," she pleaded with the horse.

The last thing she remembered was screaming as she was launched through the air, blackness swallowing her up as her body connected with hard ground.

23

Nash stared at the glass of the hurricane window in the kitchen, judging the thickness of it. It was thick. He couldn't throw a rock through it and expect it to shatter. It was going to take more effort than that. Common sense told him the center would be the weakest part, but with this type of glass, that didn't make much difference. And even if he could break the window, which was a big if, he wasn't sure he could get the man out. No. There had to be another way.

Meanwhile, the man inside was staring at him. Nash shook his head, telling the guy that this wasn't going to work. There had to be another way in. He climbed back down the hill and walked around the house, studying the structure. The steel walls came down over the windows—that suggested there was a pully system and some type of gears. All he needed to do was reverse the direction of the pullies. He walked back to the stoop, where one of the smaller steel walls covered the front door. This was his best chance at getting in.

He pressed himself against the wall, looking up and trying to find the mechanism, but it wasn't visible. He was going to need to make a lever to ratchet up the heavy steel door if he had any hope. His mind was already whirring, trying to think outside of the box. He'd aced physics in high school. This was nothing more than a simple problem that could be solved with a simple solution—if he could only think of it, and then come up with the right tools.

He walked up to the door again, cupping his mouth to hopefully project his voice. He doubted it would work, but he had to try.

"I'm going to make a lever!" he shouted. "Hold on!"

He looked around the property, hoping to find a crow bar. Finally, his eyes hit on the SUV and he grinned. The tire iron would work if he could find the right fulcrum. He pulled up the handle of the SUV, happy to find that the vehicle was unlocked. That would save him the trouble of smashing the window, though he imagined that the guy inside couldn't have objected, given his situation.

"Hey! What are you doing?" a male voice shouted.

Nash froze before spinning around to see a man walking up the drive. "Who are you?" he asked the newcomer.

"The better question is, why are you breaking into my friend's car?"

"Your friend?" Nash asked, checking out the man standing about ten feet in front of him.

He was of average height, with a thin build. His dirty blond hair looked truly dirty, but remarkably he had no real facial hair.

"My friend Ennis lives here. Why are you here?" he asked, obviously trying to be intimidating... but failing miserably.

"Your friend is trapped in that house. I'm trying to figure out a way to get him out. He asked me to help," Nash explained.

"Trapped?"

"Yep. Those doors are solid, and he can't get out. I was going to use the tire iron to try and pry the door up."

"Will that work?"

"I don't know. I guess we're going to find out. I'm Nash, by the way," he said, extending his hand.

The other man stepped forward, taking his hand in a puny grip. "Wendell Carter Nills the third," he announced, as if they were in some conference room setting up a business deal.

Biting back a laugh at the guy's attitude, Nash nodded, finding it more than a little odd that the guy used his formal name like he was a member of the royal family. He tried not to judge entirely off first impressions, but the reaction in this case was undeniable. Nash immediately disliked him. But he wasn't the one who needed rescuing.

Ignoring his distaste for the new arrival, Nash focused on the problem at hand. "Great. Well, I need a fulcrum," he said, turning back to dig through the SUV in search of the tire iron.

When he found it and pulled it out, however, he realized he didn't need a fulcrum at all. He had a jack. It made perfect sense!

"What's a fulcrum?" Wendell asked for the second time, Nash having ignored him the first.

"Never mind. We don't need it," he explained, pulling the jack out and holding it in the air.

He couldn't believe he hadn't thought of it earlier. He blamed the lack of sleep and lack of food. He was tired, hungry, and hoping like crazy that the house had running water for a hot shower inside. Or a shower in general.

Upon reaching the door, though, he realized he still needed a fulcrum. The steel door rested flat against the cement stoop.

Wendell loomed behind him. "How's that going to work?

"I need a rock—a steel ball would be better—but I need some-thing to help hold the door up high enough to slide the jack under it once we pry it up with the tire iron," he explained. "A rock will serve as a fulcrum so I can get the leverage I need.

Wendell looked at him like he was crazy, but sprang into action. There were plenty of rocks around, but they needed one that would hold up to the weight without rolling around. When they finally found one that worked, Nash got to work with the tire iron and his fulcrum, getting the door up a few breaths at a time before pushing the rock closer and closer until the door was high enough for the jack.

"Push it under," he grunted.

With the jack under the door, he slowly pried the steel up, inch by slow inch.

"Ennis!" Wendell shouted.

"Wendy?" a muffled voice came through the door.

Nash heard the man next to him curse before answering, "Yes, it's me, Wendell."

"What are you doing here?"

"Can we work on getting you out before you two catch up?" Nash growled.

"Sorry," Wendell mumbled.

"Ennis?" Nash yelled.

"What?"

"I need you to open the door. Will it open?" he asked.

He listened to the door rattling. "No!" Ennis shouted back.

"Get a screwdriver and take it off the hinges!" Nash shouted, finally beginning to grow frustrated with the ineptness of the people around him.

"The hinges aren't inside!"

"Then take off the door knob!" he shouted, slamming his fist against the steel.

"You're testy," Wendell commented.

Nash stood up to his full height, towering over the other man. "I'm testy because I'm trying to help the guy and I would appreciate a little help in return. I can't do it all myself."

Wendell took a step back. "Relax, Ennis will get it."

A few minutes later, they heard the door knob being jimmied, and then the door opened.

"It worked! I'm free!" Ennis said, popping his head out from under the steel door.

"Be careful! I don't know how sturdy that jack is, man. We need to find a way to get the door all the way up or support it better," Nash advised him.

Ennis was already shimmying under, stepping into the bright light of day, his arms wide as he spun around.

"Thank you!" he said, stepping forward to shake Nash's hand.

"You're welcome. You have food and water in there?" he asked.

"I do, and you're welcome to it. I'm going to stay out here for a minute. I'm Ennis Merryman, by the way."

"Nash Glasdstone. Happy to help. If you don't mind, I'm going in. I haven't eaten in a while," he said, looking between both men.

He knew it was bad manners but really didn't care. He was tired, hungry, and thirstier than ever. He dropped to the ground and began shimmying under the door, hoping the jack didn't slip. That would be just his luck, to get so close to food only to be killed after saving a man.

"Wendy, I can't believe you're here," he heard Ennis say to his friend.

He wasn't sure why he kept calling him Wendy, but assumed it must be a term of endearment, although Wendell hadn't looked like he appreciated the nickname.

"I came out to check on you," Wendell said. "I'm hungry, too, and if you don't mind, I'd like to raid your kitchen with that kid."

Rising on the other side of the steel, Nash moved on through the house, briefly glancing around the wide-open space with its high vaulted ceilings. It was a nice place—something he'd have expected to see in a fancy mountain retreat. Décor didn't concern him, though. His focus was on food and water, and nothing else. When he got to the kitchen, he pulled a water bottle from the fridge and drained it.

"I've got freeze-dried meals in the pantry," Ennis called from behind him.

Nash turned around just as the other two men came into view again. "This is a nice house," he commented.

"It's a great house. It was designed to ride out the apocalypse. Something malfunctioned, though, and the thing locked me in. I had no way out," he muttered, opening a thin door that matched the woodgrain in the kitchen. "Thank God you came along, man."

Nash's eyes nearly bugged out of his head when he saw the assortment of food in the pantry. "Man, I'm hungry," he commented, taking a step forward. He'd take anything this guy would give him.

Ennis pulled out a large can that claimed to be spaghetti and meatballs, setting it on the counter before moving to the tap and filling a pot with water. Nash watched in awe as he set the pot on the stove and manually ignited the pilot for the propane burner.

"It'll be a couple minutes," he said before moving to a cupboard and pulling out two bowls.

"How do you have running water?" Nash asked. That option hadn't even occurred to him.

"Gravity. I have a large stock tank up on the hill behind the house. I can get about three gallons a minute. It's enough to run the shower," he explained.

"Do you have hot water?" Nash asked, hope blooming inside him.

"I do. Not a lot. It's a solar hot water heater; holds about twenty gallons," he said.

"Do you have power?"

"Well, that's the tricky part. I have some power, but somewhere, something malfunctioned. I think the batteries for my solar power system are fried. I'm running directly off the solar panels. When it's dark, I have no power. I don't know the specifics about the electronics, but I'm guessing I don't have enough juice to run the mechanism that powers the doors," he explained.

Nash nodded, certain Ennis had guessed right. "This is still pretty cool. You live up here all the time, or did you come up here after the disaster?"

"I live here."

"Wow. Nice."

"After you eat, I'll give you the grand tour. I spared no

expense and have all the gadgets and gizmos a prepper could want. Unfortunately, I think I got taken on a lot of this stuff and it's all pretty much useless," he grumbled.

Nash was anxious to see the house, but more anxious to eat and shower and sleep, in that order. Ennis filled the two bowls with a scoop each of freeze-dried food before pouring hot water over the top. Nash couldn't wait the full minute for the food to turn into a delicious meal, however. He dug in, listening to Ennis and Wendell talk.

"You walked all the way out here?" Ennis asked his friend.

"I did. Anything for an old friend," Wendell replied.

"Thank you. I really appreciate you thinking about me," Ennis said, beaming.

Nash studied both men from his seat at the end of the counter, feeling better now that he'd had a few bites and telling himself to take his time. Truth be told, he had a feeling the real reason Wendell had made the long trek out to the house had a lot more to do with his own survival than worrying about his friend. Nash had seen the pantry, and he'd be willing to bet that Wendell had seen it at some point in the past. The house was built with a doomsday situation in mind. Wendell was probably hoping to crash with his friend, or maybe worse. There was something about him that put Nash on edge. He'd watch his back around the guy until he could get a better read on him, but for now, he was going to fill his belly and rehydrate. After all, the way he saw it, Ennis owed him for saving his life. He doubted his buddy Wendell would have figured out how to get that door open.

"Can I take advantage of that shower?" Nash asked when he'd finished eating.

"Of course. I've got a bathroom upstairs and downstairs. It will need to be a quick shower—a Navy shower as we call it," he joked.

"A Navy shower?" Nash asked, a little worried he was about to say they had to share the shower, but he followed behind Ennis anyway, his legs and feet exhausted from days on the move. "Get in, turn on the water, get wet, and turn off the water," Ennis explained. "Lather up and then rinse. If you do it right, you'll only use a gallon of water. With your size, maybe two."

"I can do that," Nash said, not caring if it was a one-gallon cold shower now that the idea of real bathing was before him.

Ennis gave him the grand tour of the bathroom, complete with radiant heat that ran off a boiler. It was plenty warm in the stuffy house and the heater was unnecessary, but in the winter it would be nice.

When Nash had finished showering and putting on his dirty jeans—having opted to give his underwear a quick shower, as well—he wrung out his shirt and hung it over the shower curtain rod along with his socks before moving back down the hall, taking in the abstract art hanging on the wall. It wasn't his thing, but it looked expensive. He moved down the stairs, taking in the fine furnishings and realizing that, whoever this Ennis guy was, he was wealthy. Or, he had been when money had mattered. If Nash was right and they were dealing with an EMP, that would seriously change the world as they knew it.

"How was it?" Ennis asked.

"Awesome. Thank you so much. I can't tell you how good it felt to wash away the sweat and dirt," he said, moving to take a seat on the couch.

Wendell looked at him, staring at his bare chest and sneering. Nash raised an eyebrow, essentially asking the dude what his problem was. He was in good shape and wasn't ashamed of his body. Clearly, scrawny Wendell was a little jealous. He'd have to get over it. Nash was too tired to care if the guy didn't like it.

"You're welcome. It's nice to have company after being locked in here for so long. What's it like out there?"

"Bad," Wendell jumped in.

Nash shrugged. "I was in a cave. I had one run-in with some guys who said it was pretty rough in town. I heard a plane crashed down somewhere on the other side of the mountains and started a forest fire."

Wendell, clearly not wanting to be left out, chimed in. "I was in town. It's ugly. People are looting and things are dangerous. They're killing each other, man. There's some military faction that's moved in and is trying to take over. I figured I'd wait until things settled down before I went back."

Ennis got up from the couch and was moving into the kitchen when he called out to his so-called friend. "Is that why you came out here, Wendy?" he teased.

Nash saw the man's face twist in rage. It was alarming. When Ennis turned back to look at his friend, though, Wendell's expression morphed into a friendly smile.

"I was worried about you. I figured I'd check on you, stay for a day or two, and then head back," he said easily.

Nash doubted Wendell had any plans of going back to the city if danger was involved, but Ennis chuckled, clearly not realizing his friend was shooting daggers at his back. Nash rubbed a hand over his face, too tired to worry about the drama between old friends.

"Did you want to shower, Wendy?" Ennis asked, coming back into the room with a glass of water.

"Yes, that would be nice. I've got a clean change of clothes to change into," he said, gesturing to a backpack and shooting a look at Nash.

Nash looked down at his naked chest. "I wasn't planning on the apocalypse. My stuff is mostly at a hotel in the city," he explained. "I have a small pack outside, but the stuff in there's dirtier than what I was wearing when I got in here."

Wendell rose from the couch. "I know where the bathroom is. I'll use the one downstairs," he said, shooting Nash a look that said he was more important because he knew where the bathroom was.

Ennis sat down, a smile on his face.

"How long have you known that guy?" Nash asked.

"Since high school. He was the guy who was always there, you know? Like, you turned around and there he was. He was a decent guy but didn't have a lot of friends. My brother and I kind of took him under our wing," Ennis explained.

"He's, uh… different," Nash said.

Ennis laughed. "He's an acquired taste. He doesn't mean any harm. I think he just wants to be accepted."

"I guess."

"Come on, you can't be that far out of high school. You have to know what it's like," Ennis prodded.

Nash knew what people thought of him. "I'm eighteen, but I've been out of high school for a couple years. I graduated early—already earned my bachelor's degree."

Ennis raised both his brows, his eyes widening in surprise. "You one of those prodigies?"

Nash shrugged. "I don't play a musical instrument, but I do know things."

"Good to know. I'll bet you'll be handy to have around."

They chatted a bit more about where they'd come from and briefly talked about their families, offering each other the proverbial small talk. Eventually, Nash noticed movement out of the corner of his eye and looked up to find Wendell standing in the hallway, listening to them talk. He looked angry—violent, even. A cold shiver ran down Nash's spine. Wendell was definitely one to keep his eye on.

24

Z ander jumped off the horse and moved towards the edge of the stream. There was a lot of disturbance on the ground. A hose was tied to a tree, telling him that someone had gone into the water. Most likely, that someone had been fishing out an injured person. Finally, it seemed he'd found signs of Merryman after days of searching. With every passing hour over the last few days, he'd grown madder and madder at Ben. But this looked like progress.

It had seemed like a longshot to question people at the properties along the river, but finally he'd hit pay dirt when someone had told him they'd seen a body rushed by in the rapids on the night of the EMP—the old woman he'd spoken to had been guilt-ridden, and her family had thought she was hallucinating. Zander hadn't disillusioned them, but had spoken to her at length. Not far beyond that property, the combination of rapids and a powerful stream shooting off from the river had led him here. Luck, maybe, but it seemed to be offering him the proof he needed that Austin was alive rather than drowned.

Zander walked towards the house, noticing what looked like the skeleton of a small airplane and the rubble of a burnt-out building. He kept moving towards the house, his gun in hand, ready for anything.

Quietly, he climbed the steps onto the porch before turning the door handle. It was locked. That had to be about the dumbest thing he'd ever heard of, all things considered. The window to the left had been smashed, a curtain billowing through the open space. He shook his head and climbed through the window.

"Come out, come out, wherever you are," he called out.

No one answered, and no one came out. He searched the house for inhabitants and found it was empty. With the home cleared, he started a more thorough search, looking for signs his journalist had been there.

Buzzing flies swarming a trash can drew his attention first, and he used a spatula to move stuff around until he found bloody bandages.

"Gotcha!" he said with a grin, sure he was on the right path.

Knowing he was in the right area, he began searching the living room again. He dropped to his knees and looked under the couch, searching for the USB drive or any other clue that would lead him to his quarry. Between the couch cushions, he found a wallet wedged in and forgotten. He opened it and saw Austin Merryman's driver's license photo staring back at him.

With proof that he was on the right track in hand, he tossed the house, looking for food or other supplies before rushing back out with little to show for it. He had found business cards telling him the owner of the house was a vet. The burned building and the fenced-in pasture told him she'd probably had horses. It stood to reason that they had left on horseback. Merryman had been injured, obviously, but Zander couldn't know how extensive the injuries had been or when they had left the farm.

He paused in the gravel driveway, putting himself in the man's shoes. He would have gone back to the trailer in search of his daughter first. By now, he might well have moved on to search her out at his brother's house, and getting back to the RV would mean a delay of two days, if not more, given the forty-mile distance. No—it made more sense to set off for Colorado, and cut cross-country as he did so. He could ask for word of the Loveridges' passing as he traveled. Worse came to worse, he'd travel more quickly than the injured journalist and collect his daughter for leverage.

He smiled. "I'm coming for you now," he whispered.

With renewed confidence that he was going to succeed in his mission, he headed out. It was time to find the Loveridges.

Traveling northwest through the afternoon, he determined that he'd stop at the first town he came to and see whether there'd been any indication of the exact path the Loveridges were taking. Just knowing whether they were stopping as they passed towns or traveling straight through would be worth the time.

Near toward evening, he reached a gas station on the edge of a small town and slipped down from his mount to stretch his legs. The shelves had been picked clean, predictably enough. He grabbed a small jug of motor oil that remained, knowing everything had a use and thinking to put it in one of his saddlebags. Walking out, however, he noticed a bulletin board on the wall. There was a flyer tacked dead center, announcing a tent revival hosted by Jim Loveridge and family.

He smiled, shaking his head. "You're making this too easy."

He took down the picture of the happy, smiling family from Salt Lake City, Utah, and laughed. If the family didn't drop the girl at her uncle's house, for whatever reason, he'd still know where to find them, and by extension her. And if Zander knew the type, the Loveridge family wouldn't be going quietly— whether this flyer had been tacked up at the gas station before or after things had gone dark, it signaled that they advertised their presence. Chances are, that wouldn't change as they moved northwest. They'd be preaching from any pulpit they could find. Zander doubted they'd be moving very fast, either. Maybe the journalist was already well on his way to catching up with them if he and the vet were also traveling cross-country, but Zander suspected they'd stick to roads, and maybe Austin's injuries would slow them down, as well. Either way, he had no doubt anymore that he'd catch either the man or his daughter. Which happened first was of little consequence. The daughter would be spared if he reached Austin first, or she wouldn't be.

"Easy prey," he told himself as he headed back to his horse.

25

Savannah woke up suddenly, jerking up into a seated position and looking around the dark room she was in. For a brief second, she thought she was in her room at home—but she wasn't that comfortable. Instead, she was on the cold, hard ground. Moisture clung to her skin, too, and she could feel jagged rocks poking through the mat she was on.

She reached up and rubbed her aching head, her fingers moving over a large knot on the back of her head. That's when she remembered everything. The horse had thrown her! All the more reason to hate horses anew.

"Relax," a woman's voice came through the darkness.

At first, she thought it was Tonya Loveridge or one of the other women in the group, though the voice sounded unfamiliar. Savannah blinked several times, making out the shape of a person not far from her. "Where am I?" she asked.

"I can't tell you that," the unfamiliar voice replied, and now Savannah was sure this wasn't anyone she knew.

"Why?" she asked when it seemed the woman wouldn't say anything more revealing.

"We're in hiding," the voice answered simply.

Savannah stared back at the shape, wondering if this was some sort of sick joke. Melodrama, much? "From who?"

"Them," the woman answered, so that Savannah nearly had to bite back a derisive laugh—it was as if the woman was trying to create mystery where none had to exist. "The people who are out there spreading lies. We're doing what has to be done, and it has made us targets," she continued.

Savannah was thoroughly confused and annoyed. "Who is spreading lies?"

"The people who claim God will save them. There is no God, Buddha, or any other deity."

"Oh," Savannah breathed out. That was it then. She'd been picked up by the group of people responsible for the killing of so many innocent people simply because they were praying and believed in a higher power. Like the man who'd confronted them earlier, this woman had lost her reasoning or fallen prey to some crazy man's persuasion.

When Savannah remained quiet, the woman added, "Those people deserve to die! They brought this down on us!"

"I should probably get back to my—" she stopped, unsure what the right word would be.

"Your...?" the woman asked.

"My parents."

"Who are your parents?" she asked.

Savannah heard movement behind her then and realized they weren't alone in the dark. "Where are we?" she asked again.

"You're safe. Where are your parents?" the woman pressed.

"I don't know. I don't even know where I am," she pointed out the obvious. "I got bucked off a horse, and that's the last I remember. We were traveling."

"We only want to talk to you. We heard there is a band of missionaries traveling through the area. They are holding services and trying to recruit more followers into their cult. Are you with them? Or, have you seen these people? We have to get them before they get us," the woman explained, suspicion apparent in her voice.

"Why would missionaries want to hurt you?" she asked.

"It's us against them!"

Savannah gulped down the lump in her throat, wishing that, at the very least, she had some light to see by. It would have made all of this far less strange and menacing—the way this woman talked, they might as well be in an old horror movie where half the people had gone crazy. And yet, this was the world they were in? Where this woman and whoever she was with were hunting missionaries? There was no doubt in Savannah's mind that they were talking about the Loveridge family. She'd known Jim had made a mistake by being so vocal in his love for God and the Bible. He'd drawn too much attention to himself, and now they were all being hunted. In fact, she'd been caught.

"I haven't seen them," she lied.

"Maybe your parents have?" a male voice suggested from behind her, causing her to jump and squeal.

"I don't think so," she squeaked out, suddenly all the more terrified that they'd discover who she really was and execute her like they had so many others.

"Why don't we get her some water?" the faceless male voice replied.

Savannah's heart was pounding in her chest now, fear making her shake, the hair on the back of her neck standing on end. Then, at a moment's notice, the area flooded with light, hurting Savannah's eyes. She squinted, looking around her and realizing she was in a cave.

She watched the woman who had been talking to her move

away from the covered cave opening. She returned a minute later, leaving whatever it was they were using for a door open, flooding the cave with light. *A blanket maybe*, Savannah thought—nothing that was hard to move, anyway.

"What time is it?" she asked.

There was a soft laugh. "We don't tell the time anymore. It's morning. You've been asleep all night," the woman told her.

"I have?" she shrieked, terrified the Loveridges would have moved on without her.

"Will your parents be looking for you?" the man asked.

Savannah scoffed. "Of course!" But, watching the woman's face, she realized she had said the wrong thing.

"We'll keep you safe with us," she said, not looking at Savannah. That didn't seem like a good sign.

"I can walk," Savannah pointed out. "I'll go ahead and go find them. Thank you for taking care of me last night," she added with what she hoped was a friendly smile. Then, without another word, she tried to get to her feet—only to have her arm yanked back down by the man behind her. She spun around, staring into cold, dead eyes.

"You'll stay here," he said firmly.

Savannah froze, trying to think of any way to persuade him to let her go, but he'd been so insistent... nothing came to her. "Okay."

A minute later, she sipped water from the plastic cup she'd been given, her eyes watching the woman and staring out the cave entrance. She could see nothing but trees beyond the opening, but realized that she was going to have to escape, and soon. The Loveridges couldn't come looking for her—they'd be slaughtered.

"I'm going to lie down if that's okay? I'm feeling a little dizzy," she said, putting her hand up to her head and swaying —hopefully, not too obviously.

"Lie down and get some rest," the woman said gently. "You took a hard fall."

Savannah lay down, resting her head on what felt like a coat folded over several times. She could feel a zipper and buttons digging into her head, but didn't acknowledge the discomfort. Instead, she went completely still, feigning sleep. It wasn't long before she heard the man get up and walk out of the cave, and the woman following him. Savannah opened her eyes, watching them as they huddled together outside of the entrance. They were talking in soft whispers. She couldn't hear what they were saying, but she had a feeling the woman was trying to help her. She'd play on that.

The woman came back into the cave as the man walked away, pulling what looked like a heavy blanket over the entrance again and plunging the cave into darkness. Savannah could hear her heart pounding in her ears. She could sense the danger around her and knew she had to escape. She had to warn Malachi and his family.

Humming filled the silence in the cave then, coming from the woman. The sound was soothing, and Savannah almost fell back to sleep but forced herself to stay alert. She would likely only get one chance, and she couldn't afford to miss it.

An idea popped into her head. She stirred, pretending to just be waking up. "I need to go to the bathroom," she murmured.

"Oh, uh, let me see what he wants to do," the woman replied, getting up and moving towards the entrance.

Once again, Savannah got a look at her surroundings. There were blankets spread around the cave. She was lying next to what had to be a firepit for cooking. Blackened rocks were in a circle with a pile of twigs and branches piled up nearby against the back wall of the cave. She guessed the inside of the cave was about the size of a large living room, but more long than square. There were six makeshift beds, not counting the one she was on.

"I'll take you," the woman said, coming back into the cave.

Savannah pretended to struggle to get to her feet, swaying when she stood and making a show of reaching out to the wall for support. She wanted this woman to think she was weak, injured and unstable. Focused on staying in character,

Savannah only shuffled along as the woman led her out into a wooded area. There were three men standing off to the left, skinning a deer. Savannah cringed at the horrific sight of it, the animal hanging dead from a heavy tree branch.

"This way," the woman said, leading her in the opposite direction of the men.

With Savannah gripping onto random trees as they moved, as if seeking support, they walked about ten feet into the trees before the woman stopped.

"Here?" Savannah asked.

"Yes."

Savannah hesitated, glancing back toward the cave as she leaned more heavily on a tree. "Can we go a little further? I can still see the men," she pleaded.

The woman looked back. "Fine, but not too far. He'll get mad."

Savannah nodded. "Okay."

She kept moving, slowing leading the woman away now and trying to put as much distance between her and the men as she could. Her eyes scanned the terrain, looking for the best route to take when she made her break for it. She was definitely going to run.

"Here, this is far enough," the woman ordered her.

Savannah moved to go behind a tree. "Can you turn around, please?" she asked sweetly, making sure she was leaning on a tree when she did so.

The woman watched her for a moment, hesitating, but finally did as requested. And the second her back was turned, Savannah took off.

"Stop!" the woman shouted.

Savannah kept running, not bothering to look behind her. She ducked her head, dodging tree branches and twigs as best she could. She had no idea where she was going, but knew that getting away from the people who'd been holding her was the first priority. What felt like ten minutes passed as she sprinted away from the cave, though she knew it probably wasn't that long. Soon enough, as her breath began coming in snatches, she saw open space up ahead and pushed her body to move faster, breaking through the trees and finding a road in front of her. She recognized the area as the same place she had walked along yesterday with the group. She dug deep and found the energy to pick up her speed now that she wasn't impeded by trees in her path, crossing over it and into the trees on the other side, where she veered right to run parallel with the road.

"Stop! Stop!" the woman was screaming behind her.

Savannah took a chance and looked back, but there was no way the woman would catch up to her. The woman had already fallen back, nearly out of sight and still in the trees on the other side of the road, and Savannah had youth and an athletic body on her side. She kept running, through and beyond another small clearing, until her lungs felt like they would explode. She slowed to a fast walk then, her arms pumping at her sides as she searched for Malachi and his family.

The sound of a horse neighing on the other side of the road drew her attention. She gathered her strength, and started running again.

"Savannah!" Malachi shouted from somewhere to the right.

She turned to see him sprinting towards her.

"Malachi!" she said, relief pouring over her as she skidded to a stop.

"You're alive! You're okay!" he said, throwing his arms around her.

"We have to get out of here! They're chasing me. They'll kill you if they find you!" she exclaimed, pushing the words out through her raw throat.

"Who?" he asked, grabbing her hand and leading her away from the road as they began jogging together, him pulling her along.

"I don't know. They want to kill your family. They were asking me questions about you all," she said, gasping for air again. He squeezed her hand, and she squeezed back, pushing herself to keep up with him. In seconds more, though, she was able to stop.

"Mom, Dad! She's back!" Malachi called out.

Tonya and Jim and the rest of the group were all sitting around, reading the Bible of all things. Savannah wanted to shake them and scream at them. Why hadn't they been out looking for her?

"We told you God would answer our prayers!" Jim said with a warm smile as she and Malachi came to a stop just beyond their circle.

"We have to get out of here! They're following me, and they will kill you!" Savannah burst out, wanting to run and not stop until she reached the safety of her uncle's house.

"Slow down, take a deep breath, and tell me what happened," Jim said, only now bothering to stand up.

Savannah sucked air into her deprived lungs, and then burst out with her story. One by one, the group rose as they listened, moving to pack up their campground, though Jim and Tonya remained seated.

"We have to go, Dad," Malachi said.

Savannah furiously nodded. "Now!"

"Let's say a prayer and then we'll go," Jim said, finally heeding Savannah's warnings.

For her part, Savannah could practically feel the gang she'd met with breathing down their necks. That didn't change even as he kept praying, and at the very second he said 'amen,' Savannah was on her feet, ready to run like the wind.

Fortunately, despite Jim's calm outward appearance, she could tell he was scared. Within minutes, they were traveling again, and walking a lot faster than they had been before. Everyone was quiet as their eyes darted back and forth. Savannah had only counted four people in the group that had held her, but knew there were probably more. And the dead deer said that the other group had guns and knew how to shoot to kill.

"We need more weapons," Savannah whispered to Malachi.

"My dad will never go for that."

"We have to be able to defend ourselves!" she insisted. "Two guns isn't enough!"

"What do you suppose we use for another weapon?" he asked. "It's not as if we can pick guns off of a tree."

"We could make spears with tree branches or get heavy branches to use as bats."

Malachi thought about her suggestion for a moment before nodding. "I'll talk to my dad," he said, stepping up his pace to move ahead to talk with his father.

Savannah watched their exchange but wasn't surprised when

the man shook his head. His stubbornness was going to get them all killed.

She wasn't about to go down without a fight, though. She might only be a fourteen-year-old girl, but she was tough. She knew how to shoot, too, and would take the gun from Bill if she had to. Tim had the revolver, but those two men carrying guns didn't make her feel safe. She'd seen the way Bill handled the gun and knew he wasn't experienced. She doubted he could hit a moving target—maybe not even a still one, if it wasn't close. Uncle Ennis had always told her a newbie with a gun was far more dangerous than a trained sniper, and she had no reason to doubt him.

For now, however, she'd arm herself with a spear—no matter what Jim said about it. She knew Bill had a folding knife and asked to borrow it as they moved. With that in hand, she picked up a branch about four feet in length and began to sharpen one end as she walked.

"That's a good idea," Bill said. "When you're done, I want to make one for my wife."

Jim had seen what she was doing but didn't try to stop her. The scowl on his face made his thoughts on the matter clear enough, but maybe he understood they were past the discussion point on this matter. Malachi had already begun scouting the area for his own branch, as well as picking up medium-sized rocks and sticking them in his pocket. Savannah finally saw Jim do the same. Soon, all of them were armed with sticks, crude spears, and rocks. It wasn't much, but it was all they had. As they moved, of course, Jim regularly assured them God was their real protector.

Savannah wasn't going to argue with him, but she preferred having an actual weapon in her hand in case God was busy.

26

Malachi did his best to encourage his father to keep moving when he talked about settling in and making camp for the night; his father had said they'd walk on into the night, but then they'd come across a field that had remnants of potato plants. It had nearly been picked clean, though, and there was no protection in the open field. He believed Savannah, and knew she was scared. He was, too. They'd seen what had happened at the church and had been hearing the stories of the executions happening all over the area. It wasn't safe for them. Worse, he now realized that it had been stupid and naïve of his father to openly preach when they knew it was dangerous.

"It's getting dark," Savannah whispered from beside him.

"Do you think we should stop for the night?" he asked.

"I don't know. I don't know what to do," she replied, her voice laced with fear.

"Malachi, we've been walking all day. We need to rest," his mother said.

He took a deep breath. His mom and dad were both looking to him for guidance instead of the other way around. They were way out of their element—that was becoming more and more clear to him as each day passed—and had no idea what to do. Malachi was just glad his mother seemed to be in better health. The temperatures had been warm, and fortunately, they'd been able to do a lot of flat-ground walking as they'd crossed prairie land with lots of corn, wheat, and bean fields covering the landscape. They'd also passed a sign earlier in the day announcing that they were two hundred miles from Denver. It felt like they were so close, knowing how far they'd come. He wanted to get there and be done, but knew this last part of the journey was going to be long and hard as they steadily climbed in elevation.

"Okay," Malachi finally said, "let's find somewhere to rest for a bit, but no fire. We can't alert them to where we are," he said.

"Someone should keep watch," Savannah chimed in.

He nodded. "I will."

"You can't stay up all night. We'll all take shifts," his father said.

Malachi was glad that his father wasn't arguing as he scanned the area that was quickly fading into twilight. The problem was that they'd moved into flat country. There weren't a lot of trees to provide cover.

"Over there," Savannah said, pointing to a corn field just a bit further into the distance, beyond the near barren area of potato plants.

"It's the best we're going to find out here," Malachi said.

The group dragged their feet as they cut across the one-lane dirt path the farmers would have used to get to the fields. Huge watering circles stretched across the wide expanse. Seeing them, Malachi remembered that they'd gone through the last of their water earlier in the day. He knew they were all on the verge of dehydration and would need to find water first thing in the morning.

"Bill, do you think you could open that end?" Malachi asked, pointing to the huge sprinkler in front of him.

Bill studied it. "I can. I'll use a rock. There should be water left in there. We'll need to boil it, though."

"No fire," Savannah chimed in.

Malachi looked at Bill. "Do you think it will be safe to drink?"

Bill hesitated, mulling it over. "I don't know if it's worth the risk without boiling it," he muttered.

"I'm thirsty. I'll drink whatever I can," Bonnie grumbled.

"It's irrigation water. It isn't safe," Jim chimed in.

Malachi weighed the risks and made the decision. "We'll get the water and boil it with a small fire." He glanced to Savannah and could see she wanted to argue, but they needed water. She nodded once after meeting his eyes, and he hoped his expression communicated that they'd keep the fire as small and as brief as possible.

The corn stalks were only waist high, but they'd provide some cover should that group still be following them. Malachi hadn't seen or heard them since Savannah had returned, but they couldn't be sure there weren't others out there, or even that the original group wasn't still following them. His father might have doubts, but he believed her when she said they were searching for them. For that reason, he knew they had to hide as best they could.

The fire was quickly made, using some of the dry, dying corn to fuel it. The single pot they had meant it took much longer than he was comfortable with to get enough water boiled for everyone to get a drink, though.

Once everyone had quenched their thirst, they kicked a heavy layer of dirt over the fire, completely extinguishing it. Then, Malachi took a seat on the soft earth at the edge of the corn-field. Everyone else was behind him, already fast asleep in beds made on the hard ground, stalks sprouting up between them. His eyes searched the area, looking for any movement in the dark. There was a strange feeling in the air that he couldn't quite explain. He could practically feel the danger lurking, hiding in the darkness.

His shift went slowly, and then he had trouble sleeping after passing the responsibility on to Bill. Nearly as soon as he lay down on his own mat, it seemed he was hearing Bill approach the mats to wake up the next watchman. That decided it then. There was no point in his lying here awake while someone else could be sleeping; he might as well be the only one to go sleepless.

"I'll take watch," he said as he sat up.

"It's your dad's turn," Bill whispered.

"Let him sleep. I'm already awake. I want to watch the sunrise," Malachi assured him.

Malachi sat down in the same spot he'd been at the beginning of the night. He stared at the horizon, the first glow of light from the sunrise already showing itself in the distance. He was just admiring the beauty of it all when the hairs on the back of his neck stood on end. It was the only warning he had.

A gunshot rang out, and a split second later, he felt a bullet buzz past him.

"Stay down!" he shouted, hearing the crack of what he guessed was a rifle.

He dropped to his stomach.

"Malachi!" his mother screamed.

"Stay down!" he shouted.

"They're in there! Get them!" a male voice shouted, his words followed by the sounds of pounding footsteps.

In a flurry of movement, the people behind him all got to their feet, their makeshift weapons in hand as they prepared to take their sticks to a gunfight.

"Bill! Bill!" he heard Bonnie scream.

"Shh," he hissed, not wanting her to alert their attackers to her specific position.

"He's dead!" she screamed.

"The gun, where's the gun?" Savannah cried out, the sound of her voice indicating that she was on the move.

He could hear the crunching of corn stalks being trampled from all around them. Malachi aimed his spear outward, ready to attack his unseen enemy.

Suddenly, there was a flash of movement a few feet to his left. He spun around, his spear pointing outward as he jabbed at the shadowy figure advancing on him. He could hear his mother sobbing in the background, crying out for help, and the sound of his father praying for protection. Before he could think to respond, Malachi was hit from behind by something hard and stumbled forward, barely catching himself from falling face first to the ground before he spun around again and jabbed his attacker with his spear. The feeling of hitting a human was sickening.

Still, he heard the scream and pushed harder, silently praying for forgiveness as he tried to kill the person. When he felt no more struggling, he yanked his stick back and went in search of his family, scattered throughout the cornfield.

"Leave us alone!" he heard Savannah shout a second before a loud shot rang out, telling him he was close.

"Savannah!"

"I'm here!" she yelled, bursting through the corn, her image backlit by the faint pink and orange glow radiating from the rising sun.

"Watch out!" he cried, seeing a man racing towards them.

Savannah spun around, raised her arm, and fired the gun in her hand. The man dropped to the ground.

Malachi didn't get much time to think about what had happened; he was hit from the side and tackled to the ground. He swung out, punching and kicking with everything he had.

"Get off him or I'll shoot," Savannah said in a low voice.

The bearded man that was on top of Malachi stopped hitting

him and jumped to his feet, backing away as Savannah aimed Bill's gun at him.

The relief of being saved was short-lived. Another shot erupted from the rifle, and then he heard his mother's scream.

"Mom!" he cried out, racing towards the sound.

Savannah's warning to stay back echoed through the air, quickly followed by the loud boom of the gun she was hold-ing. There was another shot then, and then a lot of yelling. Malachi spun around, looking to see who was still standing.

"They're leaving," Savannah announced, running towards Malachi.

He scanned the area and saw Gretchen consoling Bonnie. He couldn't find his mother anywhere.

"Mom!" he shouted again.

He could hear her sobbing, repeating his father's name over and over again.

"There!" Savannah pointed deep into the heart of the field, to directly underneath one of the giant sprinklers.

He raced towards the spot, now glimpsing his mother on her knees. Savannah was right behind him, and she skidded to a stop with him when he came to a dead stop upon seeing what had his mother so upset. His father lay against her lap, blood trickling out of his mouth, his chest awash in bright red blood.

"Dad?" he whispered.

Savannah stood beside him, and he looked at her, tears filling his eyes before he spun and rushed to drop down next to his father. His mother was rocking back and forth, a low keening sound slipping through her lips as tears poured down her face.

Malachi reached for his father's hand. "Mal," his father whispered in a voice so low Malachi could barely hear him.

"I'm here, Dad, I'm here."

"Take care of your mom. Get her home," he grunted.

"Dad, please, please don't leave us," Malachi begged him, gripping his hand and then his arm, trying to bring more awareness back into his eyes, but they were going blank already.

His father gave his hand a weak squeeze before going lax, and Malachi knew he couldn't do anything else. He could only stare at his father's lifeless body and weep. His heart broke fully in two as he listened to his mother wail behind him. She sounded like a wounded animal, her voice breaking as she prayed to God not to take her husband.

When he could see straight through the tears, he looked up, meeting Savannah's eyes and seeing the tears sliding down her cheeks, as well. She'd tried to warn them. She had told them what was coming. He only wished they would have listened better. They should have run instead of walked. He hit the ground with his fist—furious with God, the world, and the men who had taken his father. He wished he could stab them all.

It was Savannah who had saved those of them who'd survived, he realized. She had gotten the gun and not hesitated to shoot. If she hadn't taken the gun, they'd all have been slaughtered in the cornfield, their bodies left to rot.

"I'm so sorry," she whispered.

He shook his head. "You saved us."

"They got Tim," Gretchen wailed from behind him.

Malachi looked over his shoulder, watching the woman coming towards them. She froze when she saw his father's body, her eyes widening with fear.

"It's okay," he assured her. "We'll be okay," he lied.

He looked back at his father's dead body, his heart filling with rage as he silently vowed to get revenge. He knew it was wrong, but in this moment, he didn't care. He wanted the ones who had hurt his father to pay.

27

Austin's lower back ached, and he felt pain in his inner thighs from spending too long on the back of a horse. They had been riding at a rigorous pace for days. Every person they encountered along the way, they asked about the traveling band of missionaries. Each time, he was buoyed by the news that they were gaining on them. He was hoping that, today or tomorrow, they would finally catch up.

Jim Loveridge was moving slow. He'd been holding mini-revivals, which both infuriated and terrified Austin at the same time. They'd heard about the horrors happening all over the Midwest. People who worshipped God were being prosecuted and blamed. There was a dangerous undercurrent getting stronger and stronger each day, pressing tension higher. Somewhere, someone or some group was feeding the hate. They'd even heard rumors about certain religions offering sacrifices, which infuriated others. It wasn't safe to express one's religious or personal spiritual beliefs any longer.

"We've got to be close," Amanda said from beside him, her horse trotting along the paved road with that maddening clip-clop he'd even begun hearing in his dreams.

"Wow, would you look at that," he said, taking a moment to appreciate the beautiful countryside spread out for miles and miles in front of them.

She laughed. "We are officially in Kansas," she joked.

He smiled as they headed down the last hill he could see around. "It won't be long before we're in the Rocky Mountains, and it will be a homerun from there."

"Going through or over the mountains is going to be difficult. There's probably going to be snow up there," she added quietly.

"You think?" he asked.

"Maybe," she replied.

They'd been getting along a lot better, having come to an understanding that they needed one another. The companionship had grown more and more important to both of them, and two sets of eyes were better than one. Austin was constantly watching for threats, and he knew Amanda was, as well. They'd taken no one at face value since their encounter in the not-so-friendly town. Everyone was an enemy until proved otherwise.

"I wish that corn was a little more mature," Amanda commented.

"You and me both. That snake we had for dinner last night wasn't all that filling."

She laughed. "No, but it was something. When we stop tonight, we'll look for prairie dogs. I'm sure they're prolific around here."

"Oh yeah, prairie dog," Austin groaned. "I cannot wait for the day when I can walk into a restaurant and order a T-bone steak with all the extras."

"Don't think about food; you're only making it—" Amanda stopped talking, pulling Charlie to a halt.

"What?" he asked, his hand on the butt of his gun.

"Blood," she said, pointing to the side of the road.

A few steps down the road, he looked down and saw the dark pool that was still tinged with red, telling him it was relatively fresh. He looked around for the source of the blood and saw nothing. They both started moving ahead again, slow and steady, ready for anything.

"More." He pointed to a spot in the gravel where there was a larger pool.

"And crosses," she murmured.

Austin looked up, following her line of sight to where three wooden crosses made from sticks were poked into the ground within a small clearing torn out of the corn stalks. If they hadn't been mounted on horseback, they'd never have seen them.

"I want to check it out," he said, his voice thick with emotion.

He knew they weren't all that far behind the Loveridge caravan, and his heart pounded in his chest as he slid off Raven, landing on his good leg and moving slowly to where the crosses stood. The sound of a crow circling above the cornfield sent a shiver of terror down his spine. He moved into the corn, the feathery tops tickling his bare arms as he moved.

"Austin, wait, let me check," Amanda said, rushing past him and turning to put up a hand against his chest, pausing him mid-step.

"I have to know," he croaked out.

"I know, I understand, but let me look, please?" she asked.

He nodded. "Hurry."

She turned around and started moving, coming to an abrupt halt at the crosses. He watched her hand rise up to cover her mouth, and then she turned, her face gone pale.

"Oh God," he groaned, his feet stuck in place. His legs felt like lead.

"It's not her," she said, shaking her head. "But she was with them."

He felt air rush out of his lungs as relief washed over him. "Thank God."

He moved towards Amanda then, his legs shaking as feeling moved back into them. He cursed under his breath as he looked at the three crosses with names carved shallowly into the wood. The dead men had been buried in shallow graves, and skin was showing through the dirt that scavengers had already begun plying at. The middle cross bore the name 'Jim Loveridge.'

"Do you recognize the other names?" she whispered, as if the sound of their voices would disturb the dead men.

No, but I'd have no reason to."

"We should go," she whispered.

He turned, not saying a word, and walked back to where the horses were waiting on the road. There were no less than a million thoughts running through his mind as he mounted Raven and tried to figure out what the deaths meant.

"We need to hurry," he said, his voice devoid of emotion.

"I understand. We're close, Austin, really close," she assured him as she kicked Charlie into a walk beside him.

"What if—" He couldn't finish the sentence.

"Don't say it. Someone put those crosses up. We have to believe she was one of the survivors," Amanda said, infusing what sounded like fake confidence into her voice.

Austin glanced at her, knowing her well enough by now to know that she was only saying the words. She didn't actually believe what she was saying.

"This isn't going to get any better," he blurted out.

"What isn't?"

"The world we're living in. There's a serious divide happening here. What kind of person could kill another man like that, simply because he believes in God? I'm not a religious person, never have been, but I know plenty of people who are. They will never give up what they believe, no matter what it might cost them. Jim Loveridge died for what he believed. Even if the power comes on tomorrow, that hate and distrust is still going to be there. How can one side forgive the other?" he asked.

Amanda shook her head, but reached out to brush her hand against Austin's arm in support before she answered. "I don't know, but I'm sure the violence and fear are caused by the uncertainty of our future. Once power is restored and we have law enforcement again, this won't happen," she insisted.

He scoffed. "You ever been to the Middle East? Ever watched what's been happening over there for decades? It's one of the oldest fights in the history of mankind. Depending on what you believe, it goes back for thousands of years. Religion's what's caused many a war."

She was silent for a minute. That was fine. He knew he was right. He'd seen it all firsthand. It was ugly, and it didn't simply go away. The hate bred and manifested in new generations. And whatever was happening in the country was a lot more than a lack of electricity. The hate was rampant.

"Let's focus on getting Savannah, and we'll worry about saving the world later," she said, trying to lighten the mood.

They both gave their horses a little kick, urging them to pick up the pace. For all he knew, Savannah was only a few miles ahead. He had to get to her.

28

Amanda was doing her best to hide her fear. She didn't want Austin to know just how terrified she was. Finding the bodies yesterday had been bad—really bad. They'd decided to stick with the highway, avoiding the interstate, but there was no telling how the Loveridges were traveling; the best they could do was head toward his brother's and hope to overtake them. Meanwhile, they'd come across people camping in fields with little to nothing to eat. A few of them had had shelters, but Amanda was convinced it wouldn't be long before they became sick and died.

The towns they'd encountered were full of hate and animosity. She was convinced that, if there had been an aerial view, there would have been a clear, divided line between the two factions that were developing in the wake of the EMP. There were those who believed in a higher power and those who believed that the death and destruction were some kind of Biblical plague, which was kind of ironic considering that those who didn't believe were essentially blaming a higher power. Threaded throughout both groups, though, there was one common belief.

"Did you see that sign painted on the side of the building?" Amanda asked as they walked alongside their horses, giving the creatures a break.

"I did. What do you think it means?" he asked.

"*True Patriot* could mean a lot of things. It seems like the further west we go, it's a lot less about hating the religious people and a lot more about hating the government," she said.

Austin nodded. He'd not been very talkative since finding the preacher's body the day before. She knew he was worried sick about his daughter. She'd never met the girl, and she was worried for her safety.

"It could be old," he muttered.

"Old?"

"We're in the heart of America. People out here are big on patriotism. How many American flags have we seen waving?"

She scrunched up her nose, not buying the explanation. The paint had looked new. The young men and women hanging around the building hadn't looked the part of the typical gung-ho patriots she had seen before the EMP. There'd been something a bit more sinister about them.

"I suppose. I think the horses are rested enough. We can probably ride until nightfall," she said, hoping to buoy his spirits some.

"Fine," he grumbled, pulling Raven to a stop and climbing on her back.

They set out at a fast walk, wanting to cover as much ground as possible.

Every time they came upon a group of people or passed through a town or city, they asked about Savannah. They'd stopped referring to the Loveridge group as missionaries and revivalists. It always sparked more questions than answers, and seemed to put people on edge. Now, they described the group based on what they'd heard early on, and Savannah in particular, and got what information they could.

They'd been traveling for what Amanda guessed was several hours when something looked out of place on the road up ahead. She slowed her horse, hissing at Austin to do the same.

"What? What's wrong?" he asked.

"Look up there," she whispered, gesturing up ahead.

"Amanda, there are cars and trucks all over the roads. We've seen hundreds," he grumbled, not bothering to slow Raven or take out his gun.

She shook her head, staring at the government-issued Humvee. "That one is wrong."

"What do you mean wrong?" he asked, frustration coming through in his voice now.

The hairs on her arms were standing up and her sixth sense had begun screaming at her. Something was off, no matter what Austin might think.

"Austin, trust me, something is off."

His blue eyes looked sideways to meet hers. He nodded once, telling her he believed her. "Move slow," he ordered in a low voice as they moved up the road towards the Humvee, the front of the vehicle slammed into the back end of a large van truck.

"Why?" Austin asked.

"Why what?" she snapped, her eyes scanning the area.

"Why do you think something is off?"

"The Humvee is crashed into that van, like it was trying to go around it and didn't make it. Look at the other cars. They're in lanes, and they have tons of dust and dirt stains on them. Those cars have been sitting here since it rained. Now, look at the Humvee—it's a little dusty, but not like the others," she explained.

She glanced over at Austin, watching the realization come to his face. "Government plates," he said, pointing to the back of the crashed rig.

She smiled. "The government is intact. They're probably bringing aid! I bet it's the National Guard," she added, excitement racing through her as she nudged Charlie, urging him to go faster.

"Amanda, wait. We need to be careful," Austin said, pulling Raven to a stop.

She did the same, dismounting and looping the reins over a side mirror on a big Chevy truck. Together, the two of them approached the Humvee, Amanda on the left and Austin on the right; both of them had their guns drawn, ready to shoot if a threat appeared.

"There's a body," Amanda called out.

"I've got one on the passenger side, too," Austin replied.

"Back seat!" Amanda called out.

Austin approached the rear of the vehicle, his gun still out as he reached for the handle and pulled it open. A man dressed all in black slumped to the side, nearly hitting the pavement. Austin caught his shoulder, holding him up while he slid his gun to his back.

"He's alive," he called out.

Amanda raced around the vehicle, hooking her arms under the

man's unconscious body and gently pulling him out while Austin grabbed his legs. They laid him on the pavement while Amanda quickly took his vitals and then began assessing his injuries.

"He's in bad shape," she said, defeated.

"What's this uniform they're all wearing?" Austin asked, moving the man's black jacket to the side.

"I don't know. There's no name or patch indicating what branch they're with."

Austin ran his eyes along the man's clothing, shaking his head. "Nothing."

"He's not going to make it," she whispered, her fingers moving back to take the pulse at his neck.

"What do you think happened?" Austin asked, noticing a lack of obvious injuries.

"Brain trauma is my guess," she said, pointing to the blood trickling out of his ear.

Austin looked at the crashed vehicle. "They must have been going pretty fast to kill all three of them on impact. These rigs are meant to withstand a lot."

"Let's check the Humvee; maybe we'll find out where they were going," she said, getting to her feet.

The front seats were ignored. The blood and gore from the two occupants slamming into the windshield wasn't something either of them was interested in touching. Blood-borne diseases were still a concern.

"There are boxes back here," Austin called out with excitement.

Amanda hoped it would be a case of MREs and water, truth be told. She rushed to the back and pulled open one of the flaps on the first medium-sized cardboard box.

It was full of flyers. She pulled one out as Austin did the same. As she read the banner, her blood ran cold.

"True Patriot," she breathed out.

"What the hell is this crap?" Austin growled, flipping through a sheaf of the flyers with a look of sheer disgust on his face.

He tossed the flyers to the ground and started digging deeper into the box.

"This is bad," Amanda said, her brain reeling as she read the message of hate and violence detailed on a brochure she'd picked up from the side of the box. It was calling for action from those who considered themselves to be patriots. It asked people to join the crusade against those who had torn the country apart, promising a salvation of sorts for those who helped clean the earth.

"I don't understand," Austin muttered, pulling out another

flyer and reading the smaller print again as if he'd read it wrong the first time.

"They're telling people to kill people! This is where the religious crap is coming from! This is someone trying to destroy the country from the inside out!" she realized.

"We'll never make it through this if the entire population of the United States is fighting each other," Austin said, his lip curled in disgust.

Amanda continued reading the message, an icy shiver of dread snaking down her back, making her physically shudder. "The enemy of my enemy is my friend."

"What?" Austin asked, looking up to meet her eyes.

"Is it too crazy to believe someone is spreading this filth because they want to be seen as the savior of sorts? By pitting people against one another and creating an enemy that has to be eliminated, the people distributing this are creating a loyal following."

Austin looked thoughtful for a moment. The bushy beard growing in from a lack of shaving made him look even more scholarly, but it didn't bring a smile to her face now like it sometimes did.

"It's a tool Hitler used, and many dictators before him," he said. "Again, look at the Middle East," he murmured as if he were talking more to himself than her.

"Who? Who would do this? Do you think the people behind this flyer are also behind the EMP?" she asked.

She'd said it without thinking, but he was quick to agree, nodding so easily that it shocked her. "I do."

"Why?" she demanded.

He pointed to the box. "How would anyone print these flyers post-EMP?"

Her mouth dropped open, then shut. "Oh."

"Things are going to get a lot worse. I'm sure there are more guys just like this, traveling around and handing out flyers inciting violence. Look at this," he said, reaching forward to grab another box, then pulling out a bottle of water from a case tucked inside.

Her eyes widened. At least she had been partially right. She pulled at the corner of another box in front of her, yanking the flaps back to find MREs and tiny bags of nuts, like the kind an airline would hand out. There was the True Patriot logo on every package and every bottle of water.

She started shaking her head. "This isn't the usual military-type rations," she muttered, ripping open another box and finding small personal packs of shampoo, wet wipes, toothbrushes and toothpaste. There were hundreds of the little packs.

"What do you think all this is?" he asked, surveying the back end of the rig filled with boxes.

She took a deep breath, wishing she could be wrong. "It looks like humanitarian aid packs." She swallowed. If she was right, that meant that people in charge were using the guise of humanitarian aid and gifts to back up a message of hatred— bribing people to turn against men and women who might as well have been their neighbors.

"What if they're handing these out with the flyers?" Austin asked, reading her fear. "They're buttering people up, pretending to be helping while they're recruiting," he said, tossing one of the personal packs to the back.

"This is bad."

"Which is why I need to get to my kid. We're not far from my brother's property. We're probably a day's ride away if we get moving now."

"Austin, we need to load up as much of this as we can. This is too good to leave behind," she said, already calculating the weight.

He put his hands on his hips, staring at her and shaking his head. "I already know what you're going to say, and the answer is no."

"Austin, we aren't going to be any help if we're dead. We need the food and water," she insisted.

"We take enough for a few days," he said flatly. "I don't want to walk, and I know you're going to say that our weight and the weight of the goods will be too much for the horses. It'll take too long to walk, though, and honestly, my leg is already sore," he told her.

She groaned, wishing she could find a way to argue—she didn't want to leave any of this behind. What if it took longer than planned to get to his brother's house? She felt pulled between taking too much and slowing them down, and not taking enough and moving fast, but possibly running out of food and water. She closed her eyes, knowing this was a compromise she had to make.

"Fine. We use the shoestrings from their boots, tie the water bottles together, and wear them around our necks, and we can hang a few more off the back of the saddles. The saddlebags will hold a few MREs. I guess washing my hair isn't a big deal, but I am taking one of those packs for myself," she said firmly.

He smiled, his blue eyes dancing. "I think that's reasonable. Those little bottles don't weigh much. Take a couple. We could use the plastic bags for something, I'm sure—maybe trade the toiletries for food."

"I think we should burn those flyers," she added, feeling defiant.

He shrugged, lifted the box out of the back end of the

Humvee, and walked a few feet away from the stalled vehicles on the road. He ripped a few of the paper flyers before pulling the lighter out of his pocket and igniting the edges. Amanda came up behind him, both of them staring at the box as the flames slowly grew, engulfing the papers and eventually the box, sending up thick black smoke.

"Let's get loaded," Austin said after a moment more passed. "I want to get out of here. I think we definitely need to stay off the roads. I don't want to know what these guys are like when they're alive and breathing. We'll search the rig for anything else that might be usable and then we're out of here," he said, walking to the man lying dead on the road and going to work at removing the long laces from his boots.

Amanda took the first shoestring and tied it around the top of a water bottle. They worked in silence, looting some gum from one of the men and searching for weapons.

"Why don't they have guns?" she asked, finding it strange.

"Judging by that leg holster on the front passenger, I'd say they did have guns. Someone got here before us and took them," Austin replied, removing the holster and putting it on his own thigh.

She took a second to admire the holster—or, rather, the leg the holster was attached to. "I like it," she said, grinning.

He looked up from where he'd been testing the fit of his gun in the newly-attained holster. "You like what?"

"The holster. You look very mercenary, commando-ish," she said, for lack of a better word.

He gave her a strange look. "Thanks. I think."

"I'm going to see if I can wear the one the other guy has on."

He nodded, going back to searching the man's pockets. She grabbed the leather strap with the tips of her fingers, wishing it weren't wet with his blood. For lack of other options, she wiped it against the cloth of the man's pants. Sucking up her discomfort over looting a body, she put the strap on her right thigh, tightening it as far as it would go and neatly sliding her gun into place. She took a couple of steps then, testing the weight and feel before going back around the vehicle to help Austin load the horses up.

He turned and pointedly looked at her leg, smiling when he saw her new accessory.

"What? It will be a lot easier to grab in a hurry," she said, shrugging a shoulder and feeling a little self-conscious.

"You look like Lara Croft," he said with a small laugh.

She looked down at her leg. "Works for me. Lara Croft is a badass."

They each drank two bottles of water before heading out, wanting to hydrate as much as possible without having to carry extra water, and then they dug into the MREs and stuffed their faces before downing another bottle each.

"That should be enough calories and water to keep us going for the rest of the day," Austin commented with a satisfied sigh.

She nodded. "I get it. You don't want to stop and eat."

"No, I don't," he said.

With as much as they could carry loaded onto the horses, they set off, heading away from the main roads. It was clear that they were dealing with a lot more than a loss of power. Someone was purposely stirring the pot and creating more drama, which Amanda feared would result in the country imploding from the inside. At the very least, she guessed that was the faceless group's intention.

29

Savannah settled into her makeshift bed alongside a couple of the other revivalists. The ground was hard and a little damp, and her legs were aching after a long day of climbing uphill. She hadn't known it was possible to keep climbing upward for so long. Malachi had assured her they were close to her uncle's, but she worried that he only wanted to make her feel better. She was so exhausted, it seemed impossible they were actually going to reach her uncle's house within the next day or two.

Now, she closed her eyes, willing her brain to go to sleep. The aches in her body were distracting, drawing her attention to even the smallest discomforts, but she tried to picture her uncle's face and think about the big house she remembered visiting in the past. There were extra rooms and beds. *Real beds.* She was looking forward to sleeping in a bed, away from bugs and dirt.

Thankfully, everyone had been moving a lot faster in the last two days—it meant more progress, though it had left her sore. She wasn't alone, though—not in her discomfort or in her fears. The tone of the group had been subdued after losing Jim, Bill, and Tim. She kept seeing their bodies in her mind every time she closed her eyes.

Malachi had barely made a sound, only speaking to tell them all that they had to keep pushing on. They stayed far away from any towns and chose to forage for plants and some of the wild berries they came across. That was one good thing about going uphill into the mountains. There seemed to be a lot more food for them to pick at. Thinking of that, she felt herself begin to drift off, and renewed her resolve to fall asleep and stay asleep for as long as she could.

When she was awoken some time later, the sky was darker, with only a few stars in the sky that she could see. She'd made her bed under some very tall pine trees, using the needles to keep her off the ground as much as possible. She lay perfectly still, wondering what had awakened her, her eyes open and trying to see through the inky blackness of night.

She heard someone moving. "Malachi?" she whispered, wondering if he was taking watch.

She knew he hadn't been sleeping much and had been taking

extra shifts, choosing to let the others sleep. There was another rustling sound from behind her. She quickly sat up, wondering if it was a bear or some other wild animal.

"Malachi, is that you?" she hissed again.

Her answer was a big, warm hand being clapped over her mouth, silencing any further questions. Definitely not Malachi. She squirmed, reaching her hands back to claw at her attacker's face. Her actions didn't make a difference, and suddenly she was yanked to her feet and dragged backwards. Savannah kicked and twisted and tried going completely slack like her dad had taught her, but her dead weight wasn't enough to slow down her kidnapper. She judged it to be a man, his hard, muscular arm around her waist in a vise so tight that she could hardly breathe. Combined with the hand over her mouth, somewhat blocking her nose, she felt like she would pass out from a lack of oxygen.

"Shh," her captor whispered close to her ear.

He continued dragging her across the rocky ground, away from the group. She began stomping her feet, slamming her heels into the ground, trying to wake someone up.

Who was on watch? Why weren't they trying to save her?

An icy shiver of dread slid down her back. What if her kidnapper had killed Malachi or whoever was on watch? She began to scream behind the hand with all the strength she could muster, and bit down hard on the fleshy palm, earning her a brief reprieve.

"Mal--!" she screamed, only to have the hand slap over her mouth again, quieting her scream.

"Savannah?" she heard Malachi call out in the distance.

Tears had filled her eyes and begun sliding down her cheeks when she saw the shadow of a horse. There was no way Malachi would be able to save her or stop this man from riding away with her, and she couldn't even scream out to let him know where she was, or what direction she'd be taken in.

With one hand fisted in her hair, the man released her mouth as he climbed into the saddle with one easy, quick move.

"Malachi!" she screamed again, taking advantage of the release of her mouth.

"Savannah!" Malachi shouted in response as she was pulled up onto the horse in front of the man.

The horse was kicked into a fast trot, and then a canter, leaving Savannah to hold on for dear life. She could hear Malachi's shouts mixed with the others in the group as she was carried away.

"What do you want?" she choked out.

"I want to talk to your daddy," he said in a cool voice.

"Dad? How... how do you know who I am or who my dad

is?" she demanded, convinced the man had her confused with someone else.

"I know. I've been following you since Kentucky. Your dad will come and save you, don't worry," he said, laughing suddenly into her ear.

"My dad's alive?" she asked.

"You better hope he's alive," the man replied.

"Why my dad? I don't understand. What do you want?" she cried out, hating that she sounded so weak and whiny.

He didn't answer her for a long time as he navigated the horse back to one of the paved roads the group of revivalists had been working so hard to avoid. Eventually, the canter slowed to a trot, and then a walk, and then he finally spoke.

"He has something of mine. I want it back. I expect he's going to be on his way to find you. I beat him to you, so you'll bring him to me. When he gives me what's mine, he can have you back," he replied casually, as if he were talking about a transaction instead of a hostage trade.

Savannah tried to imagine what her father could have in his possession. She was elated to have someone telling her he was alive, but this man could be crazy. It didn't make sense that her father would know someone who would kidnap young girls in the middle of the night.

"I think you have my father and I confused with someone else," she said, hoping to talk some sense into the man.

He chuckled. "I don't get confused. Your father is Austin Merryman and he's a journalist. You're his daughter, Savannah. I found your note, Savannah. I know you're going to your uncle's house outside of Denver, which happens to be very convenient for me, because that's exactly where I'm headed."

If blood could have frozen and left her alive, hers just had. She felt cold, deadly cold, and it had nothing to do with the nighttime temperatures. This man knew who she was. He'd been to their trailer and he was after her father. The thought terrified her.

"Please don't hurt my dad," she whispered.

He laughed again. "I don't care if your father lives or dies. I want what's mine. He can hand it over and walk away or die. I don't care either way, but I will get it back."

"What! What does he have?" she shrieked.

"You don't need to worry about that. You better say a prayer or chant or whatever it is your friends taught you to do. If your dad doesn't show, you're going to be meeting the big guy in the sky or whatever you believe," he said in a low growl. "He's got some time to come after you, but not forever Especially not when you're being this much of a pain. You should learn to be quiet."

She had the sudden urge to vomit. "I'm going to be sick," she muttered.

"Don't get it on my leg or my shoe," he replied without slowing his horse down.

With that casual answer, her situation slammed into her. This man wasn't like the crazy people in the cave. He seemed far more dangerous. She could feel the evil rolling off of him in waves. Escaping him would not be easy, but that didn't mean she wouldn't try. She was not a quitter, she reminded herself. The thought of her father being alive and on his way to her buoyed her hopes, too. She had to get away from the man to keep her father safe. She didn't believe him when he said her dad would be able to walk away from this after agreeing to the trade. She wasn't well-versed in bad guys, maybe, but she'd seen enough movies and read enough books. The chances of him letting her and her father walk away after he got whatever it was he wanted seemed very unlikely.

30

N ash hadn't looked forward to hiking back to the mine, but now that he knew exactly where the house was located, he felt convinced he could be back by nightfall. When he'd headed away from the mine originally, he'd set off in the direction opposite Ennis' house, to the campground and beyond it, before really deciding on what direction made most sense, and he'd gotten turned around at least once after that point. The way the crow flew, it should only be a half-day's walk, and the maps Ennis had had stored in the house pretty much confirmed that. Nash was happy to be getting away from Wendell also, and glad Ennis had agreed to go along for the hike, claiming he needed to stretch his legs after being cooped up in the house for so long.

"You're sure you can get that wind turbine to work?" Ennis asked for at least the tenth time.

Nash nodded as they walked along a narrow path through thick pine trees. "Yes. The wind is always blowing around here at least a little. With the way that turbine is positioned high up on the hill behind your house, we should get a steady breeze."

"It will work like the solar power system?" he asked.

"Yes, but unlike the solar panels that can only run actively during the day, and then store power into a battery, the wind turbine will run all night. We'll have power around the clock," Nash replied.

"Enough to run the refrigerator? I think we need to conserve as much propane as we can. If we can switch to electric instead of propane, that will help," Ennis said.

Nash mulled it over. "Do you really need a refrigerator?"

"I do have a lot of meat in the freezer. We're going to need that if this thing lasts a long time."

"Do you hunt?" Nash questioned.

Ennis chuckled. "Let's say that I've been hunting and I can shoot, but I've never actually gotten anything. I can't say I've ever really wanted to, either. It was so much easier to go to the store to buy the meat I wanted."

Nash imagined that most folks had felt that way before, but things had changed. "We'll need to hunt, but I have zero experience in that department."

"We have enough meat in the freezer to last us a while. That combined with the freeze-dried food in the pantry should be enough to last us a year; give us some time to learn to hunt if we need to. I have a hydroponics system set-up, too, but I've never actually bothered to get it up and working," he confessed.

That excited Nash. "Really? I've read about those. I think I could get it going."

"Then by all means, go for it. We'll need the fresh veggies. That dehydrated stuff doesn't have the same flavor," he grumbled.

Nash laughed. "I think there are a lot of people who would be more than happy to eat the dried stuff if they had it. Do you have seeds?"

"I do. I bought a huge supply of heirloom seeds."

"Why would you buy them if you weren't going to plant them?" Nash asked, the practical side of him unable to keep the question in.

Ennis chuckled. "I liked to call myself a prepper. I went to all the shows and bought just about everything I could get my hands on, but I will admit, I don't know much about the actual survival part of it. I read a lot, and keeping a supply of heirloom seeds was recommended. I bought more than I could ever possibly need because it seemed like a great deal."

Nash burst into laughter. "And the hydroponics?"

The man looked a little embarrassed now. "Another thing I was told I should have."

Nash nodded in understanding, not wanting to look a gift horse in the mouth. "I'm sure we'll figure it out."

"I have some books and stuff that should help," Ennis added.

"Good. I'm thinking we'll need to grab some extra cables to rig a better pully system for that door, too. We have to be prepared for people trying to come and take the supplies. I want to be able to raise and lower it, and, quite frankly, I don't trust those rocks we've got piled up not to slip."

"If you get consistent power running, the electronics might work again," Ennis replied.

Nash looked at him, raising one eyebrow. "Do you really want to count on that? I, for one, do not want to get trapped in that house, especially not with your buddy. I'm pretty sure he'd turn cannibal and eat me first."

Ennis laughed. "He's an odd duck, but harmless."

"I'm sure that's what everyone thought about Dahmer, too," he quipped, though he was only half joking.

They walked on in silence after that, weaving in and out of the trees and up the mountain towards the mine.

"Is that it?" Ennis asked, pointing up ahead to a gravel road.

"Yep!"

They picked up the pace, following the road to the mine entrance. There were several pickups in the makeshift parking lot out front. The doors were all open now, as well, and there was trash strewn about, signifying the vehicles had already been looted.

"What were you doing up here?" Ennis asked.

"Some buddies and I were exploring the old mine. It's what we do. I'd been scheduled to go to school this fall to get my doctorate in geology. I was spending the summer traveling around, checking out old mines and doing a little spelunking," he replied.

"Spel... what?" Ennis questioned.

"Spelunking. We go into caves and, basically, explore."

"Hmm, right. Doesn't sound like a lot of fun to me, I gotta tell you."

"It's interesting to see the different layers of the earth. I love it. I guess I won't be going to school in the fall now," he muttered, still having a hard time accepting that fact. All that hard work he had put into graduating early, skipping over things like prom and high school football games in order to get ahead in life, only to be put right back on a level playing field with the rest of the population.

"How are we going to see in here?" Ennis asked, coming to a dead stop in front of the mine.

Nash pulled out his last glowstick. "This."

"Of course. I have some of those in my stash at home, as well. I didn't think to bring any."

"It's okay. I always come prepared."

Ennis burst into laughter. "I'm the prepper, and I showed up unprepared."

Nash shrugged, grinning. "This is my area of expertise. You can show me how to hunt and how to use all those other gadgets you have around the house," Nash told him, patting him on the shoulder before cracking the glowstick and illuminating the tunnel.

"I'll do my best, but I have to admit, I ignored all the advice from real preppers. I never took half that stuff out of the packages to learn how to use it. I honestly figured I'd never need it."

"Then why do you have it?" Nash asked, moving into the mine.

"I guess it made me feel better, safer. I knew I was ready for the apocalypse. It started after nine-eleven. I realized then how vulnerable we really were. Then, when Hurricane Katrina hit and all those people were stranded in New Orleans without food, water, or even the ability to take a shower, it kind of spiraled from there. I started going to prepper conferences and conventions, buying up all the stuff I saw. I didn't want to be one of the helpless," he explained.

Nash turned to look at him and smiled. "I'm glad you did all that, man, because you saved my bacon."

Ennis chuckled again. "Not like I did all that with you in mind. I assumed my brother and his family would come crawling up to my front door after going without, though, I will tell you that. My brother, he thought it was a waste of money to build that house. I don't know where he is now, but I bet you he's wishing he would have listened to me."

"I think a lot of people wish they would have listened to doomsday preppers."

They'd walked a little deeper into the mine when Nash spotted a crude steel door. He reached out to try and open it.

"What's that?" Ennis asked, standing beside him.

Nash shook his head, staring at it. "I don't know. I don't remember seeing this before. I must have walked right past it, or maybe it was covered up somehow so we wouldn't notice it."

"What do you think is in there?"

Nash stared for another moment before turning away. Curiosity was eating at him, but they had other priorities to deal with first. "I have no idea. We don't have time to try and get past that lock right now. The leftover cables aren't too much farther. We'll grab them and start walking back," he said.

He found the coiled cable lying on the rocky ground, right where he remembered. Picking up one of the thick coils of cable, he realized it weighed a lot more than he had initially expected. And when he looked at Ennis, he realized the man was probably not going to be able to carry one of the coils.

True to expectation, Ennis reached down and struggled to lift the cable. "These are heavier than they look."

Nash nodded. "Grab that spool of wire. I think this will be enough cable. We only need it to run the small pulley near the bottom of the turbine. The rest of it seemed to be in good shape."

Ennis grabbed the wire before reaching down and picking up a roll of duct tape. "You can never have too much duct tape," he said with a smile.

Nash chuckled as he started walking, the cable weighing him down. It was going to be a long hike back to the house, and over rough terrain. He'd taken easier terrain while traveling before, conserving his supplies, which was another reason he'd taken so long to get from the mine to Ennis' house, but it only made sense to go straight there now. His arms, shoulders, and back were going to be aching by the time they got back.

"How long have you lived up here?" Nash asked, trying to

make conversation and keep his mind off the pain in his shoulder.

"I only started living up here full time about a year ago. Before that, I had an apartment in the city. I still went into Denver on occasion to work, but most of it I could do from here. I wonder, with all that's happened... Does this mean I'm retired?" he mused aloud.

Nash laughed. "I think we're all retired for the time being."

Ennis nodded beside him, and caught his eye as they walked, his expression going more serious. "I'm glad you came along. I know I could have lived in the house for a long time, but I was really going stir crazy in there," Ennis said.

"I'm happy I could help, and I'm happy I came along, as well. I wasn't sure what I was going to do."

"I guess what they say about needing a community to survive the apocalypse is true," Ennis said quietly.

"We'll all have to work together—even Wendell," he added pointedly.

He was hoping Wendell would move on soon, though. Nash got the idea Wendell wasn't at all who he said he was, even if Ennis had known him for twenty years. For now, Nash would keep his guard up around the guy.

After several hours of walking with short breaks along the way, the house came into view just as the sun began setting.

Nash left the cable sitting outside on the front stoop and dropped to his knees to crawl under the door first. He was hoping to have enough cable to take care of the door. For now, though, all he could think about was drinking, eating, and resting his aching body.

"You're back!" Wendell greeted them from his place sprawled out on the couch with a book in his hands. He was wearing a pair of sweats borrowed from Ennis and a t-shirt. Nash had to fight back the urge to scream at the man for being so lazy. Still, he kept his frustration in check and headed for the kitchen to fill a glass with water, drinking heartily before refilling it and downing the second glass.

He could hear Ennis and Wendell talking in the other room, but ignored them and focused on replenishing his body. Tomorrow, he would get to work on fixing the broken cable on the turbine and restoring full power to the home. That would be his immediate contribution to their little tribe. He was still waiting to see what Wendell brought to the table.

31

Austin rode ahead of Amanda, driven on by the latest news they'd gotten of the Loveridge group. They'd come across a small family living in a tiny cabin off the grid. It had taken some convincing, but the family had admitted to seeing the band of revivalists a short time ago. They'd confirmed Savannah was with them, and it had buoyed Austin to know she was alive and well, and within reach—kind of.

"Austin, slow down!" Amanda called out.

"We're close," he shouted back.

"Yes, we are, which means we're going to be on them soon, but they could be anywhere. The family said they were sticking to the trees," she argued. "We need to watch for them. They're going to be hiding."

Austin ignored her, riding on and knowing he was close. He

couldn't stop now. He couldn't wait to wrap his arms around his little girl and hold her tight. More and more, he was furious with himself for ever leaving her in the first place. He should never have met Callum. He should have been at the trailer and waiting for her that night.

Even as he heard Amanda call out again behind him, he saw a young woman up ahead. She was bent over, picking something up from the ground.

"Hey!" he called out.

She shot upright, stared at him for a moment, and then took off running into the trees. The reaction wasn't exactly what he'd been hoping for.

"Now you scared her!" Amanda scolded him, riding up alongside side him.

"I didn't mean to."

"I told you to slow down. You know they're skittish," she lectured. "That family said they were keeping a low profile, which is good and you know it. It's not like they'll recognize you on sight."

Austin shot her a glare. "I get it."

"You look scary with all that facial hair and that wild look in your eye," she continued.

"Alright, alright, I get it. I'll slow down, but we do need to hurry so we can catch up with her. She has to be part of the revivalist group," he insisted.

Amanda looked after her as if to question the conclusion but didn't end up disagreeing. "We don't know that for sure, Austin. We'll ride up to the tree line, but then we'll have to walk the horses through," she advised.

He nodded, heading for the area where the girl had disappeared into the trees. He slid off Raven as soon as he got there, pulling the reins over the horse's head to use them as a lead even as he stepped into the trees, only to be met with a gun in his face. He put up both hands, eying the kid with long black hair. He recognized him—he thought. He was a lot thinner and his eyes were hollow, but it had to be the kid Savannah had been crushing on.

"Malachi?" Austin asked.

The kid blinked at him, and then pressed the gun forward another inch toward him. "Who are you?" the kid asked, his eyes wild as he looked behind Austin.

"I'm Savannah's father. This is my friend, Amanda," he said slowly.

"How do I know that?" the kid asked, the gun shaking in his hand.

"I'm Austin Merryman. Savannah left me a note in our trailer indicating that she was traveling with your family to my brother's place," he said evenly, fighting to remain calm when he knew his daughter was so close.

Malachi stared at him another moment before lowering the gun. "I'm so sorry!" he burst out, tears suddenly streaming down his pale cheeks.

Several people emerged from the trees behind him before Austin could think of how to respond, including a frail woman who went to Malachi and wrapped an arm around his shoulders.

"You're sorry?" Austin repeated, his mouth suddenly very dry as he looked at the woman with dark hair the color of Malachi's.

The woman turned to look over her shoulder. "Gretchen, get the note for Savannah's father," she whispered.

Austin looked from her to the boy. "Where's Savannah?" he asked, his voice low.

Already, he knew something was horribly wrong. If Savannah had been with them, she would have showed herself already. His stomach churned, and he literally felt weak in the knees.

"The man took her!" he wailed.

He could hear the sound of his own blood rushing in his ears as the world tilted a little. Amanda's hand on his arm helped ground him, and he swallowed the lump in his throat and dragged in a breath.

"The man took her? What man? When? Where?" he asked, needing answers and wanting them right then.

The woman, Gretchen, rushed forward, handing Austin a piece of paper.

If you want to see your daughter alive again, bring IT to the David Tower in Denver. You know what I'm talking about. Don't wait too long.

Austin read the note several times. "When did this happen?" he asked through gritted teeth, cursing Callum for dragging him into a seriously dangerous situation and inadvertently putting his daughter's life at risk.

"Last night," Malachi answered. "I woke up. I heard her scream, and I tried to follow, but he was on horseback. By the time I got our horse to chase them, they were already gone. I searched everywhere."

Austin closed his eyes, knowing he couldn't blame the boy. It was his own fault that his daughter was in danger. It had been his actions that had led to this.

"Austin, can I talk to you for a second?" Amanda asked, tugging on his arm.

He turned to face her. She used her head to gesture away from the small crowd of about ten people. He followed, already having a pretty good idea what she wanted to talk to him about.

"What?" he snapped, going on the defensive.

"What is this *it* the man is referring to?" she asked, her eyes staring into his.

He took a deep breath, knowing he owed her a real explanation. She'd been patient with him long enough, and never pressed him about how he'd come to be in the water. It was time to confess.

"That night you found me, I was meeting someone. He handed me a USB drive, and a second later, a man on an ATV opened fire on us. He was killed. I dove over the side of the bridge to escape being shot, and the next thing I knew, you were pulling me out of the water," he explained. "I wanted to tell you before, Amanda, but... well, I wasn't sure it made sense. By the time I trusted you, I didn't want to inadvertently put your life in danger."

She crossed her arms over her chest. "Do you still have this USB drive?"

He slowly nodded. "I do."

"What's on it, Austin, and why did a man kidnap your daughter?"

He shrugged, staring her directly in the eyes. "I don't know. I haven't exactly had access to a computer. You're going to have to trust me on this. Callum wanted me to look into it and make the information public—we knew each other in college, and he knew I was a journalist who, at one time, had a reputation for exposing cover-ups and whistle-blower territory. I had no idea that I or my daughter would be in danger when I went to meet him."

She held his eye for another second, but then her expression softened, which he took for her giving him at least a modicum of trust. "Where is it?" she asked.

He patted the front pocket of his jeans. "Here."

She eyed it, and then asked pointedly, "How do you know it even survived the water?"

"I don't. It was sealed inside a plastic case. When I checked it at your house, it was dry as a bone."

"This friend of yours, who was he exactly?"

Austin took a deep breath and glanced back to Malachi and his group. "Look, I know you have a lot of questions, and I do, too, but I don't have the time to stand around here playing twenty questions. I need to get to Denver and get my daughter back."

"You can't go into war with a single sidearm!" she protested with a raised voice.

He turned back to look at the group then, knowing they'd have overheard her; sure enough, all of them were watching them intently. He met Malachi's eyes and saw the real grief there before turning back to face Amanda. "I can't leave her there."

"You said your brother's house was close. Let's go there first. We'll gather some guns and see if we can get him to come along. We need all the help we can get," she said.

He swallowed, not wanting to tell her what he'd already decided. "You can't come," he stated.

"I'm not letting you go alone," she shot back.

"Amanda, I don't know what's on this drive, but if the man is willing to kidnap my daughter after trying to kill me once already, and succeeding in killing my friend, I can't let you go with me. It's too dangerous."

"And I'm not letting you do this alone. You'll die. I did not save you and travel halfway across the country to let you go and die and leave me alone in the middle of nowhere!" she hissed.

He stared at her another moment, and then turned to mount Raven. "I need to get to my brother's," he growled.

"Austin, wait! You can't leave me, and what about them?" Amanda practically shouted.

"I don't have time to wait around. I'm going now!"

She stood there staring at him in that way that told him she wasn't going to back down, her hand on Raven's harness to hold her still. The woman was stubborn and obstinate.

He looked back toward the road, struggling with his own

instincts. He was fond of Amanda, and he wanted her along. He just didn't want her hurt. At the same time, he owed her his life, and couldn't abandon her with the revivalists. He owed her the promised land, or in this case, Ennis' house.

"Fine," he snapped.

She smiled. "And them?"

He dismounted and stalked back towards Malachi. "Did Savannah tell you where her uncle's house is?"

"She didn't really have an exact address. She said she would know when she saw it."

Austin groaned—he should have known and doubted she ever would have found it, despite what she'd told the boy. "Do you have a pen, paper, pencil, anything?" he asked, not hiding his frustration.

The woman who'd been standing next to Malachi nodded at Gretchen, and the woman ran back in the direction she'd gone before the woman in front of him extended her hand to Austin. "I'm Tonya Loveridge, Malachi's mother."

"It's nice to meet you. Thank you for taking care of my daughter this past month," he said, finally remembering his manners. For better or worse, these people had been there for his daughter when he'd been unable to take care of her. And the danger she was in now was his fault, not theirs.

"Of course," she said with a wan smile.

The same woman who had brought the note returned with a notebook and a pencil. There were only a few clean pages left in the spiral notebook, and he could see someone had been using it as a journal of sorts. He quickly sketched out a map that would lead them to Ennis' house, promising them they could at least take a rest there and have a meal; he'd help them however he could, he assured them, after all they'd done for Savannah. He had a feeling his brother was going to kill him when he found out there was a whole group of people on their way, but he'd cross that bridge when he came to it.

"This is the way to the house. If you leave now, you should be there by late this afternoon if you don't stop. I'm sorry, but I can't wait—I need to get there," he said, hoping they understood.

"Of course, please go and save her. She's been a blessing to have along on this journey," Tonya said quietly. "We'll be praying for you."

He looked at Malachi. "Thank you for keeping her safe," he said.

Malachi nodded, not saying a word. He could see the fear and heartache in the kid's eyes, and knew the boy had feelings for his daughter. He'd deal with all that later, though, when he had her back, safe and sound. Then, he would ground her for life and forbid all contact with boys until she was at least thirty.

"Let's go," Austin said, turning back to Amanda and the horses.

"It was nice to meet you all," Amanda said with a wave before heading away from the crowd.

Back on the road, Austin gestured to Amanda to hurry. "We're not far," Austin said, kicking Raven into a trot.

"Are you sure you want to travel on the road?" Amanda called out behind him, and then she was beside him, keeping pace on Charlie.

"I'll shoot anyone who gets in my way," he replied.

His brother's house was way out of the way, but close. They'd stick to the roads, however. Austin needed them to help refamiliarize him with the area. The last thing he wanted was to find himself lost in the mountains while his daughter was locked up by a dangerous man. He knew the roads were treacherous, but he didn't have the luxury of going through the forest, not when there was a chance he could get turned around. He'd been serious when he'd said he would shoot anyone who got in his way.

32

W endell didn't like the kid, and it was really that simple. He stood outside, leaned up against the side of the house watching Nash and Ennis work to get the wind turbine running. The kid was cocky, and thought he was smarter than everyone else. He wasn't. He knew a little bit about physics and whatnot, sure, but who really cared about any of that in this day and age? The jerk had invited himself to stay with his old friend even though he didn't know Ennis like Wendell did. He had no right to crash at the house and eat Ennis' food and sleep in one of the beds.

Not to mention the fact that he was buddying up to him, which was all the more clear as Wendell watched Ennis and Nash talk. He couldn't hear what they were saying, but he didn't like how chummy young Nash was getting with Ennis. The two men were doing something, though, pointing and gesturing when Nash finally fist-bumped him.

"It worked!" he exclaimed.

Ennis slapped Nash on the back before throwing his arms around him and giving him a big hug. Wendell glared, his lip curling with disgust as he watched the exchange.

Ennis turned to look at Wendell then, finally. "It worked! We'll have power tonight!" he shouted, jumping up and down.

Wendell forced a smile. "Great!"

The two of them came down the hillside, both of them laughing and chatting as they moved. Then they froze, looking up at Wendell just as he heard what they did. There was a loud commotion coming from the front of the house. Wendell moved away from the wall to see what it was even as they hurried forward.

"What is it?" Ennis called out, now jogging down the hillside.

Wendell held up two fingers. "Two people on horseback!" he called out.

Nash was down the hill first, standing next to Wendell as they watched the people ride up the driveway. Ennis came up behind them, breathing hard.

"Austin?" he called out, disbelief in his voice as he passed around the two of them.

Wendell turned back to look at the bearded man and realized that, yeah, it was Austin. He smiled, thrilled to be with the Merryman brothers at the end of the world. He'd always known it would be like this one day. The three of them, riding out the storm.

"Ennis!" Austin shouted his brother's name, pulling the horse to a stop and sliding off.

The two brothers embraced, and the woman who'd been riding alongside Austin dismounted and stood a few feet behind the brothers. Wendell couldn't hide his excitement as he stepped forward, ready to greet Austin with his own exuberant hug.

When the two brothers separated, Wendell stepped up. "Austin! It's so good to see you!"

And Austin looked at him with zero recognition before turning to look back at his brother, completely dismissing him. Wendell felt like he'd been slapped.

"This is Wendell, from high school," Ennis said, making the introductions. "Remember him? That's Nash back there," he said, gesturing for the kid to join them.

Austin looked at him and nodded, but clearly, he didn't remember him at all. Talk about a jerk.

"This is Amanda," Austin replied, his eyes back on his brother. "Look, I know we have a lot to catch up on, but I'm here because I need help."

"What's wrong?" Ennis asked.

"Savannah's been kidnapped. I need guns," Austin said flatly.

"What the hell? Kidnapped? By who?" Ennis asked.

"It's a long story, and I need—" He stopped talking and looked directly at Wendell and then Nash. "Can I have a minute?" he asked in a lower voice.

"Of course. Come in, and we'll get you guys some water. Are you hungry?" Ennis asked, already moving to the front door.

"We're fine, I need to talk to you, now," Austin insisted.

Wendell stared at him, trying to figure out why the man would be ready to exclude an old friend. Nash, he could understand, but him? There was nothing to say about it, though, not when so much urgency was in the air and Ennis was already ushering him toward the door.

"Okay, okay, sorry about the door, but you need to get on your hands and knees and crawl in. Be careful you don't hit the jack. That's a long story, as well," he muttered.

The group filed into the house one by one before the brothers headed into Ennis' room. Nash acted like he was king of the castle and got a glass of water for Amanda before offering her something to eat. Wendell stood against the wall, trying to hear what was happening in the other room. The bedroom door was partially closed and he could hear the harsh voices talking back and forth, but he couldn't make out the words.

Austin and Ennis came back into the main living area something like five minutes later. Wendell fetched himself his own glass of water, doing his best to appear cool and casual, as if he regularly hung out with the Merryman brothers.

"What's going on, guys?" Wendell asked.

Austin and Ennis exchanged a look.

"I need to go to Denver to get my daughter. Ennis is letting me use a few of his rifles," Austin said.

"Rifles? You have weapons?" Wendell asked with surprise.

He'd searched the house when Ennis and Nash had gone up to the mine. He'd only found a single handgun in a drawer in a nightstand.

Austin was looking at him now, though, suspicion in his eyes. "He does."

"What's in Denver?" Nash asked.

"My daughter and the man who has her. I'm supposed to show up at David Tower to get her back," Austin said, a grim look on his face.

"You're going to walk in there and ask for her back? Is that wise?" Wendell asked.

Austin shot him another glare. "It's my daughter. Do you think I'm going to leave her there?"

"No, no, I only meant you're not going to go alone are you?" Wendell corrected himself, recovering quickly. The fact was, he didn't think any daughter was quite worth a trip into the city to confront what he guessed to be armed men.

"I'm going with him," Amanda chimed in.

Austin turned to look at her and gave her a small smile. Wendell cringed. Clearly, there was something going on there. Leave it to the jock to hook up with a woman in the middle of an apocalypse.

"I'm from that area. I'll go with you," Nash added immediately.

"I can't ask you to do that," Austin said. "You don't even know me…"

"I'm up for it. If you give me a shooting lesson, I'm sure I can be a huge help. I know the area really well."

"Thank you," Austin said, reaching out and shaking the kid's hand before slapping his other hand over it.

"You know I'm not letting you take my AR anywhere without me," Ennis said with a laugh.

"Thank you. You know how much I appreciate it. Your niece will be very happy to see you," Austin said, his eyes drifting to Wendell.

Wendell thought fast. He was not the kind of guy who marched off to battle.

"I guess that means I have to stay here and watch the house," he said, as if upset by that decision.

"That's a good idea. Do you know how to shoot?" he asked.

"He won't be alone," Austin chimed in before Wendell had a chance to answer.

"What?" Ennis asked.

Austin cleared his throat. "Uh, I need to give you a quick version of what else has been happening. I was hurt and unable to get to Savannah. Amanda saved my life. While she was nursing me back to health, Savannah was taken in by a group of people—preachers, revivalists, whatever. Anyway, Savannah was bringing them here, to wait for me, and she almost made it. They're not far behind us. There's probably ten of them. They took care of her," he said, looking at his brother and apparently communicating without words.

Wendell watched them, more and more jealous of their close bond. He had always wanted to be a part of their group, but always found himself on the outside looking in. Now, all of those old feelings were rushing back. So much for being glad that Austin had turned up.

Ennis nodded. "We'll help them out."

"Thank you," Austin said.

Nash looked at Wendell. "Now you won't have to be alone."

Wendell pursed his lips, biting back the scathing reply he wanted to make. "Good."

"My family has a small summer cabin on the South Platte River. It's isolated and shouldn't have been looted—not much there beyond recreational stuff anyway. The point is, we have kayaks stored there. We can go in by water. The tower isn't too far away from one of the small shoots off the river," Nash said.

Austin's eyes lit up. "Really? You know the city well enough to navigate it at night, on the river with no lights?"

"I do. I have a photographic memory. I can picture the tower in my head along with the buildings around it. I've been there before. We can come in on the kayaks and we should be able to get to the building without him noticing. If he's alone, that is. Do you know anything more about this guy?"

"I don't, but I'm going to assume he's working with a group, possibly even an army, and I know they're armed with semi-automatic rifles if the man I met is anything to judge by."

Nash nodded, and Wendell could practically see the kid thinking. It made him sick. He hated people who thought they were smarter than everyone else.

"I'm going to step outside and see if our guests are close," Wendell said. He waited for a moment then, for someone to acknowledge he was leaving, but they were all talking about their strategy for going into the city. He wasn't wanted or needed.

He crawled under the door and went into the trees, his anger bubbling to the surface after being held in for too long. He punched a tree, immediately sending pain through his hand. He felt his skin tear and looked down to see little droplets of blood running down his fingers. More annoyed than ever, he punched the tree again, another violent burst of pain exploding through his hand and up his arm in reaction.

"I hope they all die," he hissed.

It would serve them right. They were acting like some hotshot cowboys when he knew they were on a suicide mission. While they were up there trying to get killed, he'd do what he could to get rid of the Bible thumpers and live in the house all alone. Maybe he'd find a lady to keep him company. There were sure to be a few of them wandering around, lonely and in need of protection. He could provide that. With the house and the supplies, his status would be elevated. The pretty ladies would come crawling to him, begging. He'd get to be choosy. He'd get to be the one doing the rejecting. He had to believe this was Karma finally working in his favor.

Even as he thought of what type of woman he'd really like, he heard voices and knew their guests were close. He wiped his hand on his shirt and schooled his features before emerging from the trees. He stood in the middle of the driveway, wanting everyone to know who was going to be in charge.

"Seriously?" he groaned under his breath. There was no way he could turn them away now, when those damned horses were tied to a nearby tree and the group clearly recognized them. Not when Austin and his brother were right inside.

Making things even more aggravating, a teen boy started up the hill toward him, leading the group. A pretty woman was right behind him, followed by a variety of young and old. It wasn't exactly an army, but the kid in front was carrying a gun. Wendell hoped he knew how to use it. He certainly didn't want to have to play hero, should they actually be attacked while Ennis and his brother were gone. He preferred to stick to the shadows where it was safe. It had kept him alive this long. He wasn't stupid enough to go towards danger. Only idiots and dead men did that.

33

Savannah had never been so afraid in her life. The man had said very little to her since those first conversations, if they could even be called that.

Since then, they had shown up at a huge tower after a break-neck ride on horseback. It had felt surreal to navigate the city streets on a horse, weaving around stalled cars and more dead bodies than she'd cared to count. The stench had been disgusting, and made her vomit twice.

Then, when they'd finally reached their destination, she'd been made to climb six flights of stairs with the man essentially dragging her most of the way up before she'd been tossed in a tiny maintenance closet with no windows. He'd later brought her a candy bar and a bottle of water, and led her to a bathroom that stunk to high heaven. At the moment, she had no idea how long it had been since he'd let her out of the closet. It felt like hours, but it could have been only an hour for all she knew.

Footsteps coming closer alerted her to company, and she steeled herself for what was to come. He'd made it clear that if her father didn't show up with what he demanded, she would be killed. She didn't know if there was a time limit involved, but it had sure sounded like it.

The door opened and sunlight flooded the closet, blinding her. "Hello?" she asked, her hand over her eyes to guard against the sudden light.

"Get up," her captor demanded, his voice now familiar.

She scrambled to her feet, blinking several times to let her eyes adjust to the light. He reached for her without waiting, grabbing her arm and leading her down a hallway. They were in an office building, she knew, with desks in the center and smaller offices along one side of the hall. It seemed like a strange place for a kidnapper to hole up, but there was no way she'd question him about it.

"Where are we going?" she asked, trying to hide the fear in her voice.

She wanted to be brave, to make her father proud, but the man terrified her.

"It's dinnertime," he grumbled.

"Oh," she whispered, worried it was a last supper situation.

He pushed open another door, to what looked like a break-room of sorts. There was an assortment of vending machine food offerings scattered on the circular table in the room.

"Eat," he grumbled, shoving her into a chair.

She reached for a Snickers bar, tearing the package and taking a greedy bite.

"Why am I here?" she asked, hoping to get a more complete answer than she'd yet been given.

"You're here because your dad has something we need."

"We?" she asked.

He sat down across from her, his steely gray eyes intimidating and almost lifeless, like he was a man without a soul.

"We are the New World Order. We are the people who will be running the world. Your dad has the last piece we need to implement our domination."

She raised an eyebrow at him when he stopped there, apparently serious. The man was crazy—like, certifiably psycho. He belonged in a hospital. How had she been so lucky to grab his attention? He was one of those guys they made movies about, and she certainly didn't want to be a part of his story.

She swallowed another bite of the candy bar. "The New World Order? What is that?" she asked, hoping to get him talking.

He smirked. "It's a group of people who want to make this

world a better place. We're saviors of sorts, I guess you could say.

"Saviors?" she repeated, choking back the hysterical laugh that had just threatened to escape her lips.

He stared her down, unbothered by her obvious disbelief. "You were traveling with a group of religious people, right?"

"Yes."

"Then you've probably heard about the cleansing of the earth," he said, as if it was something obvious.

She slowly shook her head. "No, I haven't."

He didn't look like he believed her. "We have to cleanse the earth and start over. The governments around the world are useless. They're only out for themselves. There is so much scandal and cheating as the politicians scramble to get rich off the backs of the people. We're here to wipe the slate clean."

"How are you going to wipe the slate clean?" she asked quietly, unsure if she even wanted to know the answer.

He glared back at her, looking at her as if she something to be squashed just for asking a question. "It's already started. We're cleansing the cities, starting with this one. We're not a big enough group to eliminate those who wish to rebel against us or don't want to buy into our new way of living, so we've had to resort to other methods," he said with a disgusting smile.

"The lynch mobs," she whispered as realization dawned.

He grinned. "Smart girl. People love to hate and blame others for their problems. We're strategically helping them decide who they should hate. They're eliminating the problem for us."

"You mean they're killing each other, like the people who killed the man I was traveling with!"

He reached for a bag of chips and tore it open. "Yes," he replied, no hint of remorse in his voice.

"Jim was a good man! He never hurt anyone. They tried to kill us because Jim was a preacher!" she exclaimed.

"Like I said, people need someone to hate. We provided them with a target. Only the strong will survive. Those are the people we want in the new world we're building. We can't have weak people who think they know better. We need people who will accept our rule and help us become the strongest nation in the world. No, scratch that—there will only be one nation that will rule over the entire world, and that starts right here," he said, jabbing his finger into the table.

"What do you mean, it starts here?" she asked, trying to decide if he was really a mad man with a very active imagination, or if he was truly working with a group of people.

He smiled. "This city will be our home base. You are sitting in the future headquarters of the New World Order. You are getting a front row seat in the making of history."

"I don't understand why I'm here. Why me and my dad? Why us out of all the people in the world?" she demanded.

He chuckled. "You're no one special, so understand that right now, and neither is your father, really. But he was given something that involved you. You're here because your father has that something I want, and that's it. When he gives me what I want, I don't care what happens to you."

She flinched at the cold tone. He wasn't exaggerating. She could see it in his eyes—he truly didn't care one way or another if she died.

"What does he have? He's a writer. We don't have a lot of money. He's no one special, either," she said, hoping to dissuade the man of whatever crazy idea he had about who her father was. "What people give him are words, to tell their stories. That's it."

The man looked at her, sneering with disgust. "He has far more than words, but what it is isn't your concern. That's between me and your daddy. He knows, and I know, and you don't need to worry your pretty little head about it."

"If it's really that important, he's not going to give it to you," she said defiantly.

"Are you saying you're not important to him? I know that's a lie. He's traveled across the country, injured, to get to you. He'll bring it," he said with that fake smile again.

"Injured?" she echoed, freezing in the motion of picking up another candy bar. "What do you mean?"

The man shrugged before crumpling up his empty bag of chips and tossing it into the trashcan. "He was in the wrong place at the wrong time, and he took a bullet, or two."

Savannah felt physically ill. "Shot? You shot him?" she whispered.

"I didn't, but I believe my colleague did."

She shook her head, imagining what her father had gone through. She'd known there was no way he'd have left her alone. He'd been shot! Her mind reeled with what that could mean, but she assured herself he had to be okay if he was on his way to her. That was a good sign. Her eyes met the man staring her down, and she fought to keep from flinching. There was a dead quality to them, and he was an evil man, but they'd somehow come out on top. She knew her dad, and knew he would do whatever it took to save her. This man would get what he wanted, and they'd be okay. Somehow.

Savannah was about to tell him exactly how she felt about him when he stood up abruptly, his chair flying backwards.

"What's wrong?" she asked.

"It's time to move," he announced. "Move. We've wasted enough time here."

She knew that if she didn't move under her own steam, he would drag her. She quickly followed him out of the room before he pushed her in front of him, pointing her back the way they'd come. This time, though, he took her past the closet where she'd been stashed before. As they moved down the hall, she heard voices, and then they moved into a more open area that looked to have been cleared of furniture.

There were men and women everywhere, all of them wearing plain black jumpsuits, milling around the area. Some were talking and laughing while others looked to be hard at work, sitting at desks on the outskirts of the room and hunched over drawings. Her eyes scanned the area as her captor forced her past them and into what was a huge corner office suite.

"Have a seat. This is where you wait for your daddy," he sneered, pushing her down onto a leather couch.

There was a large desk positioned in front of a bank of windows that overlooked the city below. Artwork covered the walls, and weird sculptures were positioned on shelves built into a wall.

"Where are we?" she asked.

He looked around the room, his lip curled with disdain. "This is the heart of corporate greed. All the crap in here probably cost millions of dollars. Money stolen from hardworking citizens."

Savannah looked down at the rug between the couch and matching leather chairs and saw a dark stain. Her stomach turned, knowing it was blood.

"Why?" she whispered, staring down at it.

"He was part of the problem. He owned this building because he was a cheater and a liar. Men like him were some of the first eliminated. This is our building now, and I will be using this office for the time being," he said, plopping down in the massive chair behind the desk and putting his legs up on the corner of the wooden desk.

She shook her head, not understanding what he had planned. "Now what?"

"We wait," he said with a smile.

34

The city was burning, and Austin couldn't believe his eyes as they looked at the orange glow filling the night sky. His daughter was in there somewhere. He only prayed she was uninjured. He would kill anyone who hurt her.

"You're sure you know where we're going?" Austin asked Nash again as they each climbed into their own kayak.

"I do. I'll lead. We need to stick to the shadows along the edges of the water."

Austin folded his big body into a kayak, praying he didn't tip the thing over. He'd gone kayaking exactly once in his life, and that felt like a hundred years ago. Each of them had slid an AR-15 into their kayak, and they were each carrying a handgun and extra magazines for each of their weapons. They were prepared for a gun battle, no question. The only thing they were missing was Kevlar. He could have really used some Kevlar in this moment.

With nothing more to be said in preparation, they began their slow ride down the river, the paddles barely making a sound. Water lapped against the sides of the kayaks, each person looking left and right as they surveyed the massive destruction beyond the river's banks. At first, there was nothing to see but abandoned homes, but then came worse—bodies, destruction, and fire. A lot of fire.

The trip felt like it took forever at first, approaching the inner city as silently and calmly as they were, but Austin soon got the hang of kayaking again and began to see the beauty of this approach. Nobody would be expecting gun-toting outsiders to come in via kayak of all things, and their movement was all but silent. Before long, the city loomed up around them, rising from the banks of the river in a way that felt more surreal than anything as they rowed closer to the heart of the city.

"Freeze," Nash hissed.

Austin struggled to bring his vessel to a stop, sliding close to the bank of the river.

They could hear shouting, and suddenly, shadowy figures emerged from one of the buildings. It was a large group of people, with men, women, and children all huddled together as they moved into the street. It was then Austin saw two men, both of them wearing all black, escorting the crowd out. They had semi-automatic rifles aimed at the huddled group as smoke billowed from the windows in the five-story building. Clearly, it had been lit on fire.

"We told you, leave. Leave or you die," one of the men in black said.

"We have nowhere to go," a woman's voice pleaded.

"You can't stay here. We warned you," the man replied.

Austin's hands tightened on the paddle. Could he stand by and watch these men kill women and children? He turned back to look at his brother in the shadows cast from the orange glow of the fires blazing on either side of the river.

"We can't," he whispered.

"I can't watch this. I have to do something," he hissed.

"Austin, they'll kill us," Amanda said gently from behind him.

"Not if we kill them first," he replied, pulling his AR-15 from beside him, resting it in his lap as he steered the kayak forward and into the shore.

He could hear the groans of frustration from the others as they all followed suit—from everyone but the kid, Nash, anyway. The river was several feet below the roadway above, giving them a slight advantage. They spread out, all of them flat on their bellies as they slid like alligators up the embankment.

"Please, we'll leave in the morning," a man begged.

"We warned you, leave or be killed. This is our city," one of the men replied, the first flames licking up the side of the building from where the group had just emerged.

Austin watched in horror as the man in a plain black uniform, which looked identical to those of the men in the wrecked Humvee, raised his gun, aiming it at the man begging for his life.

He popped up, not able to watch a man be shot at point-blank range in front of his wife and children. He aimed his weapon and fired, somewhat surprised at himself for the steadiness he felt, and the lack of hesitation. His aim was true, hitting the man in the center of his chest and dropping him like a rock. From his left, he heard the loud crack of a gun. He glanced over and saw Amanda with her Beretta in hand before he looked back at the other man in black where he lay on the ground, his face now missing.

It was then he heard children screaming, and the crowd of people they'd been attempting to save moved away from them. Hysteria and panic made them loud, which was sure to draw unwanted attention.

Austin held up his free hand, his weapon hanging limp and pointing at the ground. "It's okay, we're not going to hurt you," he called out.

Murmurs erupted, some of the children quieting down into sobs, and then a figure stepped forward. "Thank you. You saved my life," the man who'd been targeted said, stepping up to shake Austin's hand.

"No problem. What's going on here?" he asked.

"They came into the city a couple weeks back. They've been systematically clearing everyone out. They warned us we would be killed if we stayed, but my little one, she's been sick. We have nowhere to go," the man explained.

Austin nodded in understanding. "I think it's best you try and leave now."

"We will. We knew we couldn't stay forever. But why are you here? Are you with the government? Are you here to kill them?" he asked hopefully.

"No. Someone has my daughter. I'm here to get her back."

The man grimaced. "These are not good people. I hope your daughter is okay," he said.

"Do you know anything about David Tower?" Nash asked, moving up to stand beside Austin.

The man's face visibly paled, the orange glow of the fire burning in the building behind them making him look ghostly.

"That's their building," he stated.

"Their? Their who?" Amanda questioned.

The man shook his head, suddenly looking as if he wanted to

run. "I don't know. They call themselves the N.W.O., the New World Order. That tower is their headquarters. They come and go out of there all day long. At night, they do their sweeps," he explained.

"Sweeps?" Ennis asked.

"Anyone trying to hide in the city is killed or run off. They go through every building. They're well organized."

Austin felt his heart sinking. "How many of them are there?"

"I don't know. I would guess a hundred or so, maybe more. They've been handing out flyers, trying to get people to turn on each other. I think they want us to kill each other so they don't have to waste their bullets. My family and I, we've been lying low with one of our neighbors. We hoped to ride this out. I don't know what's happening, but it's bad, real bad," he said, looking towards his family.

"We need to go," Austin said, feeling an ever-growing sense of urgency to get his daughter as far from the New World Order as possible.

"If you don't mind, we're going to take their weapons. We need the protection, and seeing as how you're already armed, I'm guessing you won't mind?" the family man asked, if in a way that said he wasn't asking at all.

"Go for it," Ennis replied.

"Good luck," the man called out, and with that he headed off to snatch the rifles before rejoining his family.

"Do we take the kayaks, or should we try and walk?" Ennis asked.

"Water. There's still a good three miles between us and the tower. I think we need to avoid the sweeps," Nash advised.

"I agree," Amanda said.

"Then let's go," Austin said, already moving back to the water.

Once again, the group of four moved silently through the water, each of them lost in their own thoughts as they moved deeper into the city and saw the incredible amount of destruction. There were large piles of smoldering rubble where buildings had once stood proudly, and bodies lying limp on the ground near dead vehicles and burned buildings. Whoever the New World Order was, they obviously didn't care about retaining the existing structures or respecting life. It seemed almost as if they were aiming to wipe out any signs of civilization.

"Here," Nash whispered from his spot at the front of the line.

They all moved to the side, banking their kayaks under a four-lane bridge that connected the new downtown with the older part of the city. Nash led the way once they disembarked, running across a major thoroughfare dotted with stalled cars.

"Where?" Austin whispered.

"Two blocks south," Nash replied, pointing in the general direction of the tower.

Austin nodded, looking for another place to shield them from view. Once he made his decision, he raced across the road, the others following behind them.

"Hey! Who's out there!" a male voice shouted, cutting through the darkness.

"Down," Ennis hissed, dropping to a low squat.

"We'll shoot first and ask questions later!" a female voice yelled.

Austin couldn't help being surprised to hear a woman. He'd come to the silly conclusion that only men would be a part of this movement to destroy the country one city at a time.

"I'll shoot first and ask questions later," Amanda snapped back in a whisper, clearly not happy.

"We'll wait until they come into view, and then we shoot," Austin instructed them.

"You sure you want to kill them?" Nash asked. "We could wait for them to pass by."

"No. No survivors. We need to take out as many as we can. We can't have them reporting back that we're here. All we have on our side is the element of surprise," Austin hissed.

"You don't think the gunfire will alert them to our presence?" Ennis asked.

Austin thought about it for a second. "No. They're shooting people already. We'll check the bodies for comms, though, and this time, I want us to take their weapons."

"Good idea," Ennis agreed. "Let's do this."

"Spread out. If you see one, shoot. Don't ask questions. Be prepared to get shot at. Stay low," Austin ordered.

Austin stayed with Amanda while Ennis and Nash moved to hug the side of a building about forty feet away. They could hear voices coming closer, and now Austin realized it was more than two. He was suddenly very nervous about his plan.

Amanda quietly raised her weapon, the butt of the AR resting against her right shoulder as she prepared to take her shot. Austin followed suit, praying he would get lucky a second time and hit his mark.

The glow of a cigarette gave him a place to aim, and he lined the shot up and pulled the trigger. The crack of the rifle made his ears ring, muffling the sound of Amanda's rapid-fire shooting as the bullets began to fly in their direction. It was a solid twenty seconds of firing as both sides shot blindly in the dark.

Amanda eventually put her hand on his arm, quietly telling his to stop shooting. He did, still holding the rifle up at the ready.

"Did we get them?" he asked, hoping he was whispering but sure he was probably speaking way too loudly.

"I'll check!" Nash hollered.

"I'll cover you," Amanda said, stepping closer to the road where the cigarette butt still glowed red on the ground.

Austin stayed next to the building, prepared to shoot. Then he heard a single shot from a small caliber gun.

"Clear!" Amanda's voice rang out.

Austin shook his head with amazement. Amanda presented herself as a beautiful, well-mannered woman, but she could be ruthless and deadly. He was glad she was on his side. The four of them quickly searched the six bodies that lay dead in the street, and Austin was surprised to realize there had been so many of them. It had been pure luck that none of their own group had been shot. It buoyed him, helping him believe in the surprise factor.

"These'll come in handy. Full-automatics," Ennis said, holding up one of the rifles he'd taken off the men and single woman of the group before beginning to dig for extra magazines along with the rest of them.

"Are they military?" Nash asked, studying the gun he had grabbed.

"Altered," Amanda said firmly.

"Altered?" Nash questioned.

"Bump stocks," Ennis clarified. "Make sure to check every pocket, guys—we need the extra magazines.

"Whatever works. Take them and let's go," Austin said, anxious to get to Savannah.

They were all weighed down with their proffered weapons now, each of them carrying a semi-auto handgun, their original ARs, and now the soldiers' modified AR-15s, as well. Austin finally felt confident they had a fighting chance.

They walked through the city streets, sticking to the back alleys and shadows. More burning buildings and fresh dead bodies littered the streets, so that Austin wished he could kill the group that had been responsible for these deaths all over again. People lay everywhere in the streets, some of them killed execution-style with their hands still bound behind them, their bodies half-kneeling and slumped against one another, blood covering the ground.

"This is awful," Amanda gasped as they passed a family of five who'd been killed in the street in front of an apartment building.

"We need to get Savannah and get the hell out of here."

"That's the tower," Nash announced, pointing to the tall building in front of them. It was easy to pick out, too. It was the only building with lights glowing in the windows.

Austin turned to look at Ennis, Nash, and Amanda. "This is where I go alone. Thank you for all your help. If I don't see you again, I want you all to know I appreciate all you have done. If Savannah makes it out and I don't, take care of her," he said to his brother.

Ennis slapped him on the shoulder. "We'll see you soon. Hurry up now, so we can get back home before Wendell finds the rest of my stash."

That earned a smile from Austin as he gave a nod and set out on his own.

35

Austin approached the front entrance of the tower from the shadows, seeing eight armed guards standing in front of the four sets of double-doors that opened into a lobby. Each of them had another modified AR-15 slung over their shoulder. Knowing there was no way he could kill all of them without being killed, and also understanding that he was expected—if not now than later—he moved out into the open so that they all had a clear view of him, and began walking slowly up toward the doors.

"Stop!" one of the guards said, stepping forward. "State your business or leave before we shoot."

The other guards all aimed their weapons at him. It was intimidating, but he'd have walked through fire to get to his daughter.

"I'm here to see Zander," he said. "He left me a note to come here, for my daughter."

The guard stepped closer, looking him up and down. "You are?"

"Austin Merryman."

The guard looked over his shoulder, back to where another man stood near the wall, apparently guarding a door. The tall Hispanic man gave a curt nod. At that, the guard who'd been speaking to him walked forward and met him just beyond the doorway.

"We'll relieve you of your weapons. This one looks like one of ours," the guard said, pulling the strap of the rifle down Austin's left arm before removing the second. Then it was the gun holstered on his thigh before he was given a quick pat-down.

"I'll take him up," the Hispanic man called from behind them.

Austin stepped forward, anxious to get it all over with. He highly doubted he was going to be able to walk out with his daughter. There would be some kind of showdown, and he was honestly prepared to die if it even gave her a shot at survival. All he could do was hope Savannah made it out alive and got to Ennis.

"Where are we going?" Austin asked, his eyes scanning the dark lobby.

It appeared that lights were only being used on the upper floors. Everything here lay in shadows. Small glows emanated from what looked to be glow-in-the-dark strips along the halls, but that was about it.

"Stairs, ahead and to the left," the man answered.

Austin pulled open the door marked with a picture of stairs and entered into a stairwell that was nearly pitch black. He stuck his foot out, feeling for the first stair and began the climb.

They moved upward at a faster pace than he was comfortable with, but he let the guard lead. Soon, his bad leg especially was burning, but he could feel strain in both his legs' muscles—he hadn't been getting as much exercise as these guards, clearly. He wasn't sure how high they'd gone, but despite his muscles aching, he wouldn't let himself ask for a break.

"How much farther?" he grunted.

The man chuckled. "A couple more flights."

Austin wasn't sure why Zander couldn't have met him on a lower floor. He realized that putting his home base on an upper floor added a measure of safety, but this high up seemed unnecessary. Of course, maybe it had been calculated, designed this way to slow any visitor or interloper down. He hadn't even come face to face with his daughter's kidnapper, and Austin was already spent, his legs on fire, and near on to gasping for breath. He wouldn't be hard to take down in his current condition.

"Here," the man ahead of him huffed out, clearly not unaffected by the climb up what Austin had estimated to be twenty short flights.

Austin reached for the door and pulled it open and was met with a gun aimed directly at his head. He held up his hands.

"I'm here for Zander," he said, trying to hide just how out of breath he was.

His escort shoved him hard between the shoulder blades. "Move," he ordered.

Austin blinked several times to adjust his eyes to the lit hallway. He could hear a humming noise, and realized it was the sound of computers and electricity in general. After living without the sound for so long, it felt foreign. He was pushed to the end of the hall and directed through a pair of wide wood double doors. And beyond the doors, there on a couch, he saw his daughter for the first time in more than a month, her eyes wide with fear.

"Savannah!"

Her face brightened and she jumped up, only to be shoved hard back onto the couch by the tall man who'd been standing next to her. Austin would have run to her himself, but his escort was still with him, holding him from behind by his upper arm. Smarter to stay here anyway, he told himself. If the man shot him, she wouldn't be caught in the crossfire.

Still, he looked her over. She looked unharmed, but she'd lost weight and there were dark circles under her eyes. He hated that she'd suffered, and he hadn't been there to help or take care of her.

"Dad, I was so worried!" she choked out. Austin thought she might jump up again, but she stayed still.

"Quiet, girl. Your daddy and I have business to discuss," the man beside her snarled.

Austin tensed, but swallowed down curses and told himself to stay calm. "Zander?" he asked, staring at this man who'd dared kidnap his daughter.

"In the flesh. You're looking hale and hearty. I guess you didn't take a bullet after all," he said, looking Austin up and down.

"I'm here."

Zander smiled. "Then you give me what I want, and you get what you want."

Austin slowly shook his head. "I somehow doubt that. Here's the deal. You let me and my daughter walk out of here, and your precious USB doesn't fall into the wrong hands; I'll even destroy it if you want me to. In case something happens to me or her, however, I've left it in the hands of someone who has the means to look at everything on the drive."

The look on Zander's face showed a combination of irritation and disbelief. "Liar. You wouldn't risk your daughter's life."

Austin shrugged, willing his face to remain flat. "I would be happy to work out an arrangement once we are out of here."

In a move so fast that Austin couldn't have anticipated it, Zander reached down and yanked Savannah from the couch by her hair. She screamed in pain, struggling to stand. Zander wrapped his arm around her neck in a terrifying chokehold before pressing the barrel of a Glock 19 against her head. Austin made an instinctive step forward, but the soldier behind him tightened his grip on his arm, yanking him a step back toward the door.

"Now, give me the USB or I will shoot her. You don't want to play with me. I was sent to do one job, and I will complete my mission. I'm not one of those men who has a rule about shooting kids. I shoot anyone who is in my way," Zander growled. And Austin believed him.

His heart pounding, Austin realized he should have anticipated this move. He'd already known the guy was ruthless, kidnapping a defenseless girl to get her dad's attention. He looked back at Savannah, tears running down her face as the man held her tight. Her face was turning red as she struggled to breathe.

"Okay, okay, let her go. I'll give you the drive," Austin said, reaching for his front pocket.

The man who'd led him upstairs tightened his arm on his arm, but Zander nodded and Austin yanked it out of his grip, shooting him a glare before using his fingers to reach into the pocket and pull out the USB he'd stored there, still in its plastic case. He held it up, watching Zander's eyes light up.

"I knew you'd bring it," Zander said with a grin, not releasing Savannah.

"Let her go or I will smash this thing right here," Austin warned him.

Zander hesitated. Austin used his finger and thumb to pop open the case, ready to follow through with his threat. Finally, Zander lowered the gun from Savannah's head and loosened the chokehold grip he had around her neck.

Savannah took advantage of the small respite and clamped her teeth down on the flesh of his forearm. Zander shouted, and shoved Savannah hard, sending her directly into Austin's arms as he raised the gun at father and daughter. Austin pushed her to the side as she reached him and lunged forward, more than prepared to take a bullet if it would keep her out of the line of fire.

Austin outweighed the smaller man and tackled him to the ground, the USB getting knocked out of his hands and sliding under the sofa where Savannah had been sitting. There were shouts all around them as the man who'd been guarding Austin came forward to break up the wrestling match on the floor, and other men entered behind him to help pull Austin off Zander. They were slow to appear, though, and the rage coursing through Austin gave him superhuman strength; he punched Zander hard in the face for a third time, blood spurting from his nose.

He cocked his arm back, ready to hit the man again when he was yanked backwards. Savannah screamed behind him, and Austin looked up to find two men pointing their AR-15s directly at him. Zander climbed to his feet in front of him and picked up the Glock that had fallen from his hand when Austin had tackled him. He used the back of his hand to wipe the blood from his nose, staring at the red on his hand before looking at Austin, who was on his knees in front of him.

"Stupid move," Zander sneered, blood staining his teeth an ugly red.

"No! Don't!" Savannah screamed.

Austin wanted to comfort her, to tell her everything would be alright, but that would have been a lie. He'd screwed up. He'd made a move, and it had been the wrong one.

"Let her go. You have me, you have the USB, so let her go," Austin said in a quiet voice, staring into the eyes of the man who he now knew for sure would be killing him.

"You seem to think you have bargaining power. You have

nothing. I've won," Zander said, aiming the Glock directly at Austin's head.

"Actually, I've won!" Amanda's voice cut through the room.

Austin froze, shocked, and then he fell to the right and back when the men who'd been surrounding him turned; he lunged forward for Savannah's legs and toppled her to the ground at the same time weapons began firing. Savannah was screaming as Austin moved his body over hers, covering her the best he could.

Then the gunfire stopped for a brief, precious second. Austin's ears were ringing as he lifted his head to see his little brother motioning for him to get up and out of the room. Austin sprang to his feet, pulling Savannah up with him and out of the room before racing behind Amanda as she ran for what he assumed to be the opposite stairwell from the one they'd used coming up. There were bodies scattered in the hall, their throats cut. Austin didn't take the time to think about who had done it. His brother, Amanda, and Nash had done what was necessary to save him and his daughter, and he'd never hold the gruesome murders against them.

There was shouts behind them as they ran, and Austin glanced over his shoulder to see Ennis pause briefly to turn and open fire at the men in the black uniforms racing after them. Austin pushed Savannah in front of him, placing her between himself and Nash with Amanda leading the charge. Amanda smashed out a window at the end of the hall and practically dove through, surprising Austin. Nash and Savannah followed suit. He jumped onto the fire escape and looked back to make sure Ennis was still behind him.

His hearing was shot. All he could hear was a loud ringing sound. Seeing Ennis coming, he raced down the stairs. The fire escape was sturdy, and though the height and open air had caught his breath for a moment, navigating the iron escape downward was almost a relief since it meant they were in open air, that much closer to the ground as they made their way down one flight after another. The trip down took half as long as the climb to the top as they slipped and slid downward, preferring to fall over being shot or caught.

"Everyone okay?" Amanda asked breathlessly once they were all on the ground.

Austin looked at Savannah first, and saw no obvious signs of injury.

"All good!" Ennis shouted, clearly suffering the same temporary deafness.

"We need to go! Now!" Nash yelled, pointing behind them before lifting his gun.

Everyone moved behind Nash and Amanda while she and the kid mowed down the men in black pouring around the corner of the building like ants out of a dirt mound.

"Run!" Austin shouted, pulling his daughter behind him as

they raced back towards the river. Behind him, he heard Amanda and Nash stop shooting and join his family, signaling that the soldiers must have been stopped, however temporarily.

"Not that way! The kayaks are too slow. We'll be easy targets," Nash called out.

Just then, an explosion rocked the ground they were standing on. Austin turned to his left and saw a building explode with another huge boom before fire filled the night sky.

"Run!" Ennis screamed.

Austin couldn't believe what he was seeing. A rocket launcher? They were trying to kill them with a rocket launcher? He was glad someone was a really bad aim. Another loud boom rang out and the building a few feet to their right burst into flames, sending shards of glass and cement flying into the air. He automatically tried to cover his head to protect it from falling debris.

Ahead of him, Savannah was racing up the street behind Nash, terror giving her unhuman speed. Austin's leg pinched as he chased his daughter, running faster than he'd ever run in his life. The heat coming from the fires was overwhelming, especially combined with the acrid smell of burning insulation and what he had to assume was flesh. His stomach turned as they continued to run. Every few seconds, Ennis would stop to spray a round of bullets at their pursuers.

After running until their bodies simply wouldn't allow them to run another foot, they slowed down to a fast walk, each of them breathing hard as they sucked in smoky air.

"Dad, are you okay?" Savannah gasped.

"I'm fine, keep moving," he ordered.

"You gave him the USB thing?" she asked.

"You did?" Amanda asked, turning to look at him with horror on her face.

Austin grinned. "I gave him *a* USB. Not *the* USB."

Amanda smiled. "Good job. Now, can we please get out of here before this entire city goes up in flames?"

They picked up their pace after the brief reprieve, but all was quiet behind them. They hurried out of the city, heading for the mountains and what Austin hoped was a safe place to stay for the foreseeable future. He wasn't naïve enough to believe they'd taken out the entire team of men in black, but they had done some serious damage. Zander was dead. He only wished he could have been the one to shoot him.

Once they reached the woods outside the city that would lead to Ennis' house, Savannah stopped walking and threw her arms around Austin. "I'm so glad you're alive," she suddenly sobbed.

Austin hugged her back, feeling her emotions bubbling to the surface. She'd held it together this long, just as he had, but having her back in his arms meant everything. "I'm here. You're safe. We're going back to your uncle's house. We'll have plenty of time to catch up then," he promised her. "We're okay now. I love you, baby."

She nodded, muttering 'I love you, Dad' back, and finally wiping her eyes before she released him and started moving again.

Austin walked behind the others, staring at their backs. He would be forever grateful and indebted to the people in front of him. Nash was a complete stranger, and he had put his life on the line to save Savannah. The idea of that would have been unfathomable for him just a month before. He couldn't have been happier to face the end of the world with Nash, Amanda, Ennis, and his daughter.

36

N ash hefted the crowbar he held, confident it was what they needed to get into the door in the mine.

"Are you sure this is worth our time and energy?" Austin asked as they stood in front of the mine, one of the glowsticks they'd taken from Ennis' stash of survival gear illuminating the area.

"I guess we're about to find out," Nash said with a grin. With that said, he put the crowbar into place and got to work. Soon, with him and Austin pulling, they managed to break the lock on the door and then pry it open.

"Holy—" Austin muttered, holding up the light stick and moving it around the room.

"Why? Why would this be in here?" Nash asked. He hadn't known what to hope for or expect, but the mystery of this door had been too much to pass up. He'd maybe expected a generator, or extra gear related to the mine, or even safety equipment or stored water bottles, but this...

It was a room of about twelve by twelve, filled with electronic equipment and machinery, including several laptops, flashlights, and satellite phones. This wasn't anything related to mining—it was storage of laptops and gear related to survival.

Recovering from their shock, Austin and Nash traded looks and then began gathering a sampling of items, placing it back outside of the door and then doing what they could to disguise the break-in. They'd carry away what they could, planning to come back again if needed.

"What do you think?" Austin asked as they emerged from the mine.

"About?"

"Who put all that in there? Doesn't it seem like someone purposely hid that equipment in the earth to protect it from the EMP blast, like they knew it was coming?" Austin asked.

Nash looked at him. "I don't know who, but I wouldn't be surprised if it was the people who've taken over Denver."

"You think they know about the house?" Austin asked.

The question had been weighing on Nash's mind since they'd found the stash. "I don't know, but I think we have to be prepared for anything."

Austin stared straight ahead. "It's off the beaten path. We're miles away from the mine. Someone would have to go out of their way to find it."

"I found it," Nash reminded him, "if only by accident."

"Yeah, I know," Austin acknowledged. "We'll need to set up some security. There's enough of us at the house that we can set up watches. Four people watching, one in each direction. We'll need to train some of those religious folks in how to use guns," Austin said, thinking aloud.

Nash hesitated as he listened, not sure how to say what was on his mind, but he figured he may as well get it off his chest. "What do you think about Wendell?" he asked.

Austin shrugged, glancing at Nash and smiling. "You don't like him," he stated.

Nash's gut told him that it wasn't a matter of liking him, but of being able to trust him for even a moment, but he couldn't say that without more reason than a gut feeling. "I don't know. There's something about him that rubs me the wrong way."

"I don't remember him, no matter how much he tries to tell me we were buddies in high school. I don't remember him at all. He was younger than I was, and I was more into athletics than the band," Austin commented. "I haven't been around him enough to get a feel for him one way or another."

Nash nodded. Austin was an attractive, athletic guy, and

wouldn't likely have been hanging around the likes of Wendell. Nash himself was a bit of a nerd with his high IQ, but he wasn't whiny like Wendell, and he'd always been committed enough to geology that he'd stayed in shape. That along with his natural athleticism had barely elevated him above the rest of the nerd crowd, but it had.

"I don't think he likes me, either, so maybe it's partly that," Nash said, pushing a tree branch out of the way. If nobody else had the feeling he had, maybe it was mostly that, Nash told himself. It was hard to like someone who didn't like you, right?

"Why do you say that?" Austin asked.

"He's always staring at me when he thinks I'm not looking. Like… aw, heck, the look I see, it's like he wants to kill me while I'm sleeping—that kind of stare."

Austin chuckled. "I think you can handle Wendell. Don't let him bother you. If you see him doing something shady, though, tell me. With close to twenty people living in that house, we all need to be able to trust each other."

"How long do you think those revivalists will stick around?" Nash asked. He knew he didn't have any more of a right to be there than they did, but the house felt crowded now.

"I don't know. I have a feeling Tonya and Malachi Loveridge will probably stick with us for a while. She's not doing so well. I don't know if she's ill or grieving, but I think it's better if she rests and regains her strength," Austin said quietly. "They were originally planning on dropping off Savannah and heading on to their home in Utah, but I just don't think she's up to it now, after losing her husband like she did."

Nash agreed with Austin. The woman had lost her father and husband in a month's time. She was dealing with a lot more than the rest of them. Nash wasn't sure about his own family but had to believe his brothers were taking care of their mom. The family home was in the country outside Nashville. His brothers all lived around the area and would have rushed to her when things got bad. The way things were now, he felt he had to trust them to take care of her—setting off on his own to cross the territory between him and them might not be suicide, but with the way things were at the moment, it would be a far cry short of smart, too.

The men continued to walk on in silence, focusing more and more on the effort required to haul what they'd found back to the house as the terrain got rougher. There was plenty to think about, too. It had been two days since they'd barely escaped with their lives from the city. They'd spent the day before taking stock of supplies and organizing the household a little.

They'd traveled another mile or so when Nash's thoughts finally turned to the laptop he'd taken from the mine and put in his pack. It took his mind back to the USB that had gotten Austin and Savannah into trouble in the beginning, and now that the strange door in the mine had been opened, it was the most immediate mystery at hand.

"What do you think we'll find on that USB?" Nash asked.

"I have no idea. The guy who gave it to me was a bit of a wingnut. The kind of guy who sees a conspiracy at every corner. We were drinking buddies in college, but I hadn't seen him since then. Obviously, this time, he was onto something. It cost him his life, and Zander went to great lengths to try and get it back."

"What are you going to do with it once you figure it out?" Nash couldn't help asking.

Austin laughed. "I think you might be needed for the figuring out part of it. I'm not a techy. I can plug it in and pull up files, but if there's a bunch of technical stuff, I'm going to refer it to you."

Nash remained quiet for a minute. "I think it's best if we keep this stuff to ourselves for now, if you know what I mean."

Austin turned to look at him. "Wendell?"

Nash nodded, glad Austin had understood what he meant without bringing the guy back up again. "Something isn't right with that guy. I'd like to think I'm imagining it, but I've learned to trust my instincts. There's something off, there."

"We'll keep it to ourselves," Austin agreed.

37

Austin, Nash, Ennis, and Amanda huddled in Ennis' bedroom. The door was closed and locked. The hum of voices from beyond the door filled the room that was otherwise quiet enough for them to hear a pin drop as Austin turned on the laptop. It had long since been agreed that no one else needed to know they had a working computer or anything else about the USB.

Savannah had had a good idea about what her father was doing when he'd left that morning, but Austin had kept their discovery vague. He didn't want to risk her knowing too much and being in danger once again. He also didn't know Malachi or any of the stragglers the revivalist group had picked up. Trusting Nash was maybe something of a risk, but his gut told him the kid was okay. Plus, Austin didn't know enough about computers to do much more than plug the drive in.

"Wait," Amanda said when he turned on the laptop.

"Wait for what?" Austin asked.

"Do we really want to know what's on that thing?" she asked. Beside her, Nash's eyes went wide, as if the idea of not finding out hadn't even occurred to him, and Austin had to hide a grin in reaction—mysteries ate at the kid just like they ate at him.

Austin met Amanda's eyes, and his voice was firm when he answered, "Yes."

She sighed. "Alright, but once we know, we know. You said your friend wanted you to get that to someone in the government. What if having it incriminates you and all of us?"

He shrugged. "We'll destroy it if it looks like it could be something that gets us in trouble."

"It could be a bargaining chip for the future," Nash commented.

"I want nothing to do with that group," Austin said.

"Maybe not, but that ship has sailed. We picked a fight with them. They didn't seem the type to go away with their tails between their legs," Nash replied quietly.

"Who cares about that?" Ennis demanded. "Let's see what it is and then we'll figure out what to do with it!"

Austin agreed with Ennis. He plugged the USB into the port and waited.

A few seconds later, the screen lit up, and his eyes glued themselves to the screen. Gasps from over his shoulder drowned out the hum of voices in the living room. Austin could only stare, his mouth hanging open as he took it all in.

END OF SURVIVE THE CHAOS

SMALL TOWN EMP BOOK ONE

Survive the Chaos, 11 July 2019

Survive the Aftermath, 8 August 2019

Survive the Conflict, 12 September 2019

PS: Do you love prepper fiction? Then keep reading for exclusive extracts from **Survive the Aftermath** and **Suriving the Swamp.**

THANK YOU

Thank you for purchasing *Survive the Chaos* (Small Town EMP Book One)

Get prepared and sign-up to Grace's mailing list and be notified of her next release: www.gracehamiltonbooks.com/mailing-list

If you enjoyed this book:

Share it with a friend, www.GraceHamiltonBooks.com/books

Leave a review at:

ABOUT GRACE HAMILSON

Grace Hamilton is the prepper pen-name for a bad-ass, survivalist momma-bear of four kids, and wife to a wonderful husband. After being stuck in a mountain cabin for six days following a flash flood, she decided she never wanted to feel so powerless or have to send her kids to bed hungry again. Now she lives the prepper lifestyle and knows that if SHTF or TEOTWAWKI happens, she'll be ready to help protect and provide for her family.

Combine this survivalist mentality with a vivid imagination (as well as a slightly unhealthy day dreaming habit) and you get a prepper fiction author. Grace spends her days thinking about the worst possible survival situations that a person could be thrown into, then throwing her characters into these night-mares while trying to figure out "What SHOULD you do in this situation?"

You will find Grace on:

BLURB

The New World Order is at hand.

Civilization has crumbled since the EMP thrust humanity back into the Stone Age, and dangerous factions now scavenge for scarce resources in this terrifying new world.

Austin Merryman wonders what the future holds for his

teenaged daughter, and if the madness surrounding them is even worth surviving. For now, the group is safe in his brother's prepper house nestled in the Rockies. But the calm can't last forever. With sixteen people crammed together in the tiny mountain home, tensions are bound to erupt. It doesn't help that his brother's lazy friend gets twisted pleasure from stirring up animosity, pitting brother against brother and daughter against father as battle lines are drawn.

But decisions about who stays and who goes are ripped from their hands as information on the USB drive lays bare pieces of the NWO's plans. Austin realizes the horrifying truth of why he's in their sights, as well as the danger he's brought down on those he loves most. When tragedy again strikes the small group, it will be up to Austin to make the hard choices necessary to ensure their survival.

Until a dying man utters the single word that changes everything…

Get your copy of *Survive the Aftermath*
Available July 11, 2019
www.GraceHamiltonBooks.com

EXCERPT

Austin Merryman walked outside his brother's luxury home,

which had been built with the apocalypse in mind. The place was a treasure, given all that had happened, but that didn't stop it from being cramped. Breathing in the fresh air of the outdoors, he took a minute to look around and take stock of who was where. It was tough keeping up with sixteen people. He could hear male voices coming from the right, mingled with the repetitive *thwack* of an ax hitting wood.

Down the driveway, he saw a couple of the women from the revivalist crew. They were carrying plastic grocery bags filled with what looked like weeds. Well, scratch that—they actually were weeds, technically, but the women were using them for some project or another. He couldn't remember what it was.

Thinking he just needed space, he started walking into the trees to find a little peace and quiet. Ever since they'd gotten into the USB the day before and scanned through the litany of files on the thing, his mind had been in overdrive. He'd barely slept at all, thinking about everything he'd seen and trying to make sense of it.

"Hey, is everything okay?" Amanda Patterson asked, her voice coming from behind him.

He turned to look at the woman who'd saved his life and become what he had to think of as one of his best friends. She was stubborn, opinionated, intelligent, a heck of a shot... and very easy on the eyes.

"Everything's fine," he acknowledged, and when she didn't

look like she believed him, he moved to sit on a large rock surrounded by tall pine trees, out of sight of the house.

"I wanted a minute to think without being asked what to do next," he explained quietly. She smiled back at him, and he could tell just from her expression that she understood his feelings.

"There's a lot of people who are lost and confused... needing some direction. I guess you're the guy to give it," she said, sitting down beside him and nudging his arm.

"Lucky me," he grumbled.

His eyes moved around the area. It was pretty. A place he would have loved to park his fifth-wheel and hang out for a couple weeks. His brother's property was high up in the mountains north of Denver, Colorado, completely off the grid and off the beaten path—way off. There wasn't a single road that would lead directly to the house. You had to take a series of dirt roads and know the way if you wanted to find it without getting turned around, which made it an ideal hideout in a world gone bad.

It was a safe haven, without a doubt, and he was grateful for the roof over his head, but he didn't know if it was the right choice for a long-term living situation. With all that had happened, though, how could he know what the right choice was? He needed a few minutes to himself, away from the busy household filled with relative strangers. It had been nearly a week since they'd all begun cohabitating, and he'd barely said more than a few words to most of them. He didn't know them and wasn't sure he could blindly trust anyone. They were living in different times that required him to be a lot more careful than he'd once been.

But Amanda was something else. Outside of his brother and his daughter, she was the one among them he felt sure he could trust. After all they'd been through together, he had to trust her.

Beside him, she picked some dry moss from the base of the rock. "Good tinder," she muttered.

He looked down at the moss in her hand. "I suppose."

She frowned back to him. "Come on, Austin, what's the deal? We walked how many miles to get here? We've barely caught our breath! And now that we're here, you're thinking about leaving, aren't you?" she asked.

He couldn't stop the slow grin from spreading over his face. "You think you know me so well."

"I think I know you well enough to see you're feeling a little stir-crazy."

"Do you ever get that feeling that the other shoe's about to drop? I keep looking over my shoulder. All that stuff on that drive…" He stopped talking, shaking his head at the thought of what they'd been caught up in.

"I get it, I do. But let's celebrate our win. You're here, Savannah is here, and the house is solid," she said.

Austin nodded, knowing she had a point. He was happy to be reunited with Savannah, and grateful to the revivalists for keeping her alive and getting her to the house, but he wasn't sure where they went from here. There'd also been no talk of the others moving on since they'd arrived, and that only served to complicate things. He didn't want to be ungrateful, but how long could the house support all of them?

"We have to figure out what happens next," he said. They'd been putting off the conversation, but it had to happen.

"Austin, everyone is recovering from the long journey here. Let's give everybody a minute to figure stuff out."

"If they don't leave in the next couple months, winter will set in and traveling on foot will be impossible. The Loveridge family has a home in Salt Lake City—that was their original destination. Is it still? How do I ask them if they plan on staying or going without sounding like a total jerk?" he asked.

She shrugged, her eyes ranging over the forest around them. "Like I said, give it a few days. Tonya Loveridge is still grieving and recovering from the trip. I don't know if she can make it on her own."

"She has Malachi and the others," Austin pointed out.

"You know what I mean. None of them are ready for that."

He nodded, knowing she was right. "That may be true, but sixteen people in that house all summer is going to be rough."

Summer promised to be hot and miserable in a world without AC. Fortunately, the house was surrounded by trees and lots of shade, but that only went so far, and it was one of the few things they had going for them. The metal walls and roof were great for keeping out unwanted guests, but they promoted the feeling of living inside a steel box. The only opening was the front door, which they'd taken to leaving open all day to allow fresh air into the house.

"It is getting a little stuffy in there," she commented, her eyes moving around the area before she spotted more hanging moss and moved to climb up on another rock to pluck it down. She added it to her little pile of tinder and then crouched to rub some more moss from the rock where they'd been sitting.

He looked down at her, watching her gathering supplies even as they chatted. Looking for supplies had become second nature. Today, her dark hair was pulled back in a ponytail, showcasing her pretty eyes, and she was so easy to look at— watching her had become second nature for him. "Yeah, stuffy is one way to put it. I wish Ennis would have stockpiled deodorant," he muttered.

Amanda chuckled. "I know you're not telling me I stink," she said, nudging his knee.

He smiled. "No, you know what I mean. We need to get better ventilation in there."

"It's only going to get hotter," she replied with a grimace on her face, finally looking back up to meet his eyes.

Austin nodded, staring off into the trees and thinking about the many issues they had to deal with. He felt like they were treading water, barely getting by and not making any real plans for the future.

"It'd be nice to have more blankets or sleeping cots, too."

"Who needs a blanket when it's eighty degrees in the house?" she quipped.

"Sleeping on the hard floor is getting old. It's like we have everything except for comfort. It's better than sleeping outside on the cold, rocky ground, sure, but I think it would be a morale booster if we could all sleep better. Let's face it, almost none of us are spring chicks anymore," he said.

Amanda laughed. "Speak for yourself, buddy. I'm young and spry."

He chuckled in return as she gave up on the moss and sat back down beside him. "I've seen Gretchen weaving pine needles," he told her. "Maybe she can make sleeping mats. She could use grass, maybe, which might be softer if we could find enough. Anything would be better than sleeping directly on the floor. If only we had yarn. I heard one of the other women say she loved to knit."

"I know how to knit," Amanda said casually.

Austin turned to look at her. "Really?"

"Yep. I'm pretty good at it, too."

"I don't think there's anything you're not good at," he offered, making her blush a little.

"What else is running through your mind? Besides knitting, I mean," she joked.

He shrugged. "I don't know. A lot. I'm thinking long-term, just in case we have to stay here. You say the Loveridges aren't ready to travel, and that's fine, but I think we need to know what everyone is planning, and when, or we're going to be caught unprepared. Right now, we're burning through resources pretty fast. We need to be thinking about how to make it all last."

"Like what?"

"The propane, the food, the water—everything," he murmured.

She nodded, looking unsurprised. "The propane is definitely going to be an issue. We can't keep using the stove to heat water. It's wasteful. We should be cooking our meals outside."

"The ladies did build a fire the other day to heat the water," he commented.

"Yes, but we need a stove. It wouldn't be hard to make, what with all the rocks around here. If we're here in the winter, we'll be able to use it then, too, if we build a cover over it," she added.

"Good idea.

Amanda looked off into the trees, lost in thought as she continued and he listened. "We can use foil to make a solar oven and save on using the propane stove, as well. We won't have to worry about building a fire. We can make bread, stews, or even casseroles in it," she said. "And we can use it to boil water."

"You sound very excited about aluminum foil," he teased her, but a smile had come to his own face also—maybe he just needed something to focus on, he thought, to feel like they were doing something instead of treading water.

She all but giggled, knocking her shoulder into his as she replied. "Foil's better than gold in this off-the-grid situation. There are so many ways to use it! If those windows were exposed, we could cover them with foil to block the sun or use it in the winter to keep the heat trapped inside. It's a great way to clean dirty pots and pans, too. Trust me, foil is a big deal," she said.

"All right, I'm going to take your word for it," he told her, and then he caught her hand in his and gave it a squeeze. He didn't need to tell her that part of what she'd offered him that day was simple companionship—a like mind to share the worry. That meant as much as any idea, no matter how valuable.

"I think your idea of weaving a grass mat is good, too, Austin. It will give Gretchen and the others something to focus on that could really help. I feel like they're always waiting for something, for us to tell them to do something," she added a moment later.

Austin raised an eyebrow. "We've been here a week. Didn't you just tell me to give it some time?"

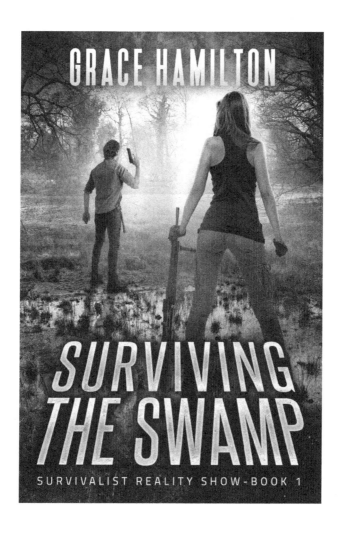

BLURB

Skin of Your Teeth Survival is a reality show made famous for pairing part-time survivalists with a real-life survival situation. Always carefully planned out by world-famous Prepper and Survivalist Wolf Henderson, season ten promises to be different This time none of the contestants are survivalists. They've all been picked to fail.

But when an EMP hits, the cast scatters and Wolf is left to care for a husband and wife team, a quietly scrappy chick, and a bumbling scientist. At the spur of the moment, Wolf offers them safety at his island bug-out location and takes off with his ragtag team to move through the wild and dangerous swampland of Florida.

The loner of the group, Regan, isn't sure what to do. She can't survive on her own, but she also doesn't work well in a group. She believes she has a better shot in one of the major cities on the coast than in the swamp, so she joins the team with every intent of striking out on her own once the opportunity arises. But with the world around them growing more dangerous every day, she has to figure out whether she's better off with the group or alone in the post-EMP world.

And whether Regan or Wolf realize it, the dangerous journey through swampland will soon become a literal fight for survival once they reach the chaos of 'civilized' South Florida.

Get your copy of *Surviving the Swamp (Survivalist Reality Show book One) from*
www.GraceHamiltonBooks.com

EXCERPT

Regan Goodfellow wasn't a quitter. This last week had tested her strength and her will to survive, but she'd taken on every challenge willingly. More than anything, she wanted to prove to herself how tough she really was. Facing off against a dangerous swamp with deadly animals was a great way to do that. Maybe not the most practical or conventional method, but exciting, nonetheless. If only it wasn't so damn wet. Of course it was wet; it was a *swamp*, complete with endlessly boggy ground, damp hand-holds, and humidity like she'd never imagined.

Moving through it was brutal, and easily the hardest thing she'd ever done in her life. She stopped yet again, to drag in several deep breaths, her lungs sorely lacking oxygen after the breakneck pace she'd set for herself through the dense foliage that kept slapping her face. Thankfully, she had worn a light-weight, long-sleeved shirt. It was certainly coming in handy now, even if it was snagged and torn in places.

With her feet sinking into the muck that counted as ground in this area, three inches below water and settling into mud, her legs felt like they had a million pins pricking her flesh, tingling as they did from overexertion. She was so close to making it to dry ground. Or, drier ground. There was no way she was going to stop now. She had to get her feet out of the water.

Most people would have been terrified to be alone in the Ever-glades, and she knew that might be the rational mindset, but it wasn't hers. She had something to prove to herself and all the people who had tried to keep her down over the years. No Florida swamp was going to beat her. People thought that because she was a bit on the small side, and didn't look like one of those badass chicks from any of the movies, she would fail. They were wrong.

"Keep moving," she whispered to herself, willing her legs to carry her through the swampy bog.

She had once thought running on sand was tough, but this marsh was a completely different challenge. Every step was a battle. Her hiking boots sank into the mud, making a sucking sound as she pulled each boot out and took another step. So much of the land was muddy ground, much of it covered by at least a few inches of water—and every bit of it fought her forward momentum. Thankfully, it wasn't overly hot. Although, the humidity made it uncomfortable even in the shade. Florida humidity had turned her skin into a sticky glue that bugs and debris clung to. It was gross, and the first thing she was going to do when she got out of this swamp was take a long, hot shower. Maybe the weather wasn't bad when you could lay out on beaches and then jump in the ocean, but this journey she was on was a long way from any beachside vacation.

"Focus," she reminded herself when her mind started to acknowledge her physical discomfort yet again.

Shifting her weight, she took in another deep breath and grimaced as the sucking sound of the mud beneath her feet responded to her renewed attempts to move forward. She had to get to dry land. She'd never make it through another week if she had to stay in the thick swamp with its millions of mosquitoes and other bugs feasting on her body. Every sting reminded her that she had used the last of her bug repellant earlier that morning when things had gone from bad to worse.

The worst of it all was, her feet were wet, something she knew was bad. Wolf Henderson would lecture her for days when he found out she had lost her spare socks somewhere along the way. When they'd first set out on this little adventure, he had warned them all about foot rot. Human skin was not meant to be wet; he'd told them more than once. And now she knew why. Running was rubbing her toes and heels raw despite the fancy socks she had on. If she ever managed to find him and the others, she was fully prepared to be called out. He could complain and lecture all he wanted so long as he had some dry socks for her.

A small clearing ahead greeted her when she glanced up from the boggy ground to take new stock of her surroundings, and she pushed her body more upon seeing it. The clearing would provide options. At the very least, she wouldn't be smacked in the head with the branches that came from every direction, creating the dense canopy of the swamp. The shade was great —the bugs that came with it, not so much.

"Stop it!" she scolded herself aloud. "I can do this. And someone will come looking for me if I don't check in. Right?"

Her sinister laughter in the quiet swamp sounded funny to her ears. Everything about this situation was so wrong. Why had she ever thought a reality survival show would be a good time? It wasn't supposed to be like this. She'd been ditched by her partner earlier, and now she was alone. And yeah, of course, that's what she'd *said* she wanted, but now….

Reaching the sandy ground of the clearing, Regan gave herself a moment to enjoy the solid footing and take in her surroundings, weighing her options and calculating what path made the most sense. There was a wide pond in front of her, and going through it would be the quickest, shortest route to where she was trying to get to. Heading left would lead her deeper into the swamp, and she was not going back the way she'd come. Her eyes drifted to her right, where a steep hill of a rock stood ominously above her, stretching a good twenty feet into the sky. Going that route would take her a little out of her way, but she could circle back and get to her rendezvous point. It didn't look insurmountable, but it was steep. Especially considering her soggy footwear.

She let out a long sigh. None of her options promised she would make it to safety. The pond covered with floating green algae actually looked like the easiest choice, but Regan knew simplest was not best, especially in her case. Who knew what was under that algae, creature-wise? The tree that stretched out over part of the pond, keeping it in the shade, was also a problem. There was a wasp nest hanging over the area. That was a major deterrent. Even being in the vicinity of the nest was freaking her out. One sting and she would go into anaphylactic shock, and she couldn't exactly pull out an EpiPen while swimming. Her allergy was no joke. That had been a hard lesson learned when she'd been a little girl, and the single EpiPen she carried wouldn't be enough to save her if she was stung by more than a few of those horrible wasps.

Standing around and debating what to do could get her killed, too. She had to keep moving. She looked at the murky water, knowing it would likely be a safer option in some ways, but there was always a chance there'd be a deadly snake waiting to clamp down on her leg. Snakes were one of her least favorite animals on earth. The swamplands of Florida were rife with snakes; a fact she should have thought more about before signing up to do this stupid survival show. Sure, only a fifth or so of Florida snakes were venomous, but in her mind, snakes were snakes.

She stared at the water, shaking her head and cursing the rain they had been dealing with all week. It had made the swamp extra treacherous, which was never a good thing when survival was the goal. Staying upright had been her main goal as she'd traversed slippery rocks made deadly by the layers of moss and slime covering them, and remaining on her feet hadn't even been easy on what counted for solid ground around here, given the mud and the water.

"Relax, Regan. You've been in worse situations," she said aloud, trying to calm herself down.

She had to stay calm and think rationally. It was how she had stayed alive as long as she had. She couldn't lose her head now at the thought of a snake brushing by her.

Finding herself staring up at the slippery hill of rock that could lead to safety, she groaned. It was her best option. She knew it. The risk of being stung was too great. She had to avoid the wasps at all costs. Could she climb the rock wall alone? Having a partner would have made this path an easier prospect, but it was too late for that.

Besides, depending on other people always ended badly. Another hard life lesson she had learned over her twenty-seven years. People sucked. They were unreliable, and they always promised to help and be there for support, and then when you actually needed them, they screwed you over. Regan was done with all that. Being on her own had been a lot easier. She never had to worry about people letting her down or inserting their drama into her life, like her first partner on the show had done. Little Miss Sunny had been a nightmare. Regan had wanted to kill the producers for pairing her up with the school teacher. Thankfully, Sunny had been booted off, leaving Regan with a new partner. And while anyone was better than Sunny, her so-called partner was now nowhere to be found. *Typical.*

"You can do this. You don't need anybody. This is all you. Get your butt up that slope!"

The rock-covered hill was a slippery mess and her boots were coated with mud, making it even more difficult for her to get a strong foothold. Having clambered five feet above the base, she closed her eyes and focused on the goal. Getting to the top. It wasn't all that high. A couple stories, if she'd been trying to scale a building. Not something she had actually done, but she easily imagined jumping out of a second-story window and the height involved there—*that*, she had done.

With renewed strength, she stretched an arm up, felt around, and found the smallest hint of a ledge. It would have to do. With all the power she could muster in her five-foot, five-inch frame, she used her leg muscles to propel herself up the hill several inches. When she got a good foothold, she breathed a sigh of relief.

"You can do this," she repeated to herself.

Then Regan made the mistake of looking up. She had barely made it half way up, and there was nothing to hold onto.

"Come on!"

She was only a few yards off the ground, which wasn't a big deal, but if she did jump off the hill, she risked twisting an ankle or falling into the nasty, bug-infested pond. There was also the chance that she would hit her head on the way down, given the slick slope involved. It wasn't like she could run to the hospital to get patched up or take a couple Advil to relieve the pain of a head or ankle injury. The swamp wasn't exactly the best place to take risks.

"Well, this sucks," she muttered, holding onto the side of the hill and not knowing whether to keep trying to climb up or admit defeat and jump down.

Get your copy of *Surviving the Swamp (Survivalist Reality Show book One) from* **www.GraceHamiltonBooks.com**

WANT MORE?

WWW.GRACEHAMILTONBOOKS.COM

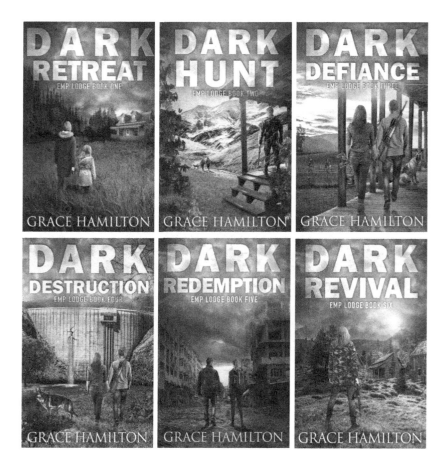

Made in the USA
Columbia, SC
01 May 2020